Carpool

CARPOOL

Mary Cahill

RANDOM HOUSE NEW YORK

Library of Congress Cataloging-in-Publication Data

Cahill, Mary.
Carpool / by Mary Cahill.
p. cm.
ISBN 0-679-40477-5
I. Title.
PS3553.A36C37 1991
813'.54—dc20   91-9686

Manufactured in the United States of America
2 4 6 8 9 7 5 3
First Edition

To Bill Bowden, with love

I have seen perfectly healthy, young, upright women climb into a car in September. By spring, they walked like Groucho Marx.

—Erma Bombeck, *The Grass Is Always Greener over the Septic Tank*

Acknowledgments

I hesitate to try to list everyone who helped with this book—there isn't enough ink and paper. All my friends and all my family have made contributions that are invaluable, and I truly thank them. I have also been fortunate to have a tireless crew of technical advisers, among them Marie Forbes, Jennifer Ash, Tony Hulse, Dolly Merritt, John Newnan, Don Thomas, Janet Zinzeleta, Craig Hindman, David Brown, Phil Platt, Tim Herbert, Molly and Heather Cahill, Bill Launder, Carol Carew, Jean Byrd, and the staff at Miller Branch Library. Thank God for all the really terrific people that have come into my life and helped me to "keep on playing."

Carpool

Chapter One

At fifty-five hundred feet there's nothing between me and the sun rise but a few wisps of clouds over Chesapeake Bay. I have enough fuel to clear the flat, monotonous fields of the Eastern Shore, dip down and check out the grey-green waves of the Atlantic off Fenwick Island, and maybe spot some dolphins before heading back to the gentle hills west of Baltimore. The engine hums as I think about trying a roll or two, alone in the autumn sky.

"You went through a yellow light," said a small, nasal voice like fingernails on chalkboard.

It was only the fourth week of school, and already I was wondering if Pterion Acres, the local psychiatric facility, had a drive-in window. The dog and I had been having some really great conversations in the car, and there were times when I actually felt like I was back in my Piper Cherokee, flying way, way up—above it all.

I drove across Route 40 and shook my head.

"The light wasn't yellow, Matty dear," I said as sweetly as I could, shifting the Honda into fourth with a vicious little snap.

I'm thirty-five years old—I began reciting the litany to myself—
I have a college degree; I've been co-owner of an air delivery
service, and designed a safety device that is being used in all single-
engine aircraft. And now, with three children in three different
schools, I seem to be spending all of my time in a silver hatchback.
If Henry Ford were alive I would strangle him.

"Matty touched me with his elbow," whined another voice from
the back seat. Linnea, my youngest.

"Let's keep our elbows to ourselves," I said.

"Maahhhhhhm! He's still touching me! Make him stop!"

"See, you just did it again, Mrs. Meade. You went through
another yellow light."

"For your information, Matty dear, the light was green." Could
a kid hear homicidal thoughts lurking in an adult's voice?

I pulled up in front of St. Obturator's Parish Day School. The
two four-year-olds squeezed past the front seat without pushing
it forward and got out of the car. Linnea threw me a kiss; Matt,
who wouldn't kiss his own mother, let alone Linnea's, paused only
long enough to jut out his sticky little chin. "Yellow," he said,
and disappeared into the Gothic shadows of the school building.

I looked at the schedule I'd clipped to the sun visor with a
wooden clothespin:

A.M.	5:30	Phil/swim practice (M,W,Th,Sat)
	7:00	Home for breakfast/get everyone up
	7:15	Phil lvs for bus
	8:00	P.U. Crista Galli
	8:10	Take Patsy & Crista to school
	8:35	P.U. Matty Kohlrausch
	8:45	Take Linnea & Matty to St. O's
	11:45	P.U. Linnea & Matty

Beside this, a large rusty paper clamp held another schedule:

P.M.	2:10	P.U. Patsy, Crista & Pontine Kohler
	5:00	P.U. Phil/track prac.
	5:10	P.U. Linnea

A red, three-by-five-inch plastic paper clip with the word TODAY written on it in Magic Marker clung tenuously to the end of the visor. I read the scrap of paper it held and then headed off for one more day of my life on the road.

A drizzly rain has begun to fall.

"Friendship Flight Service Station reports all clear at five thousand feet. We'll level off on top at sixty-five hundred feet and get to Atlanta by noon."

The familiar farmland around Friendship blurs and then disappears in the mist as the Cherokee rises higher and higher. As we level off in brilliant sunshine, I look over at my father studying a chart with his characteristic scowl.

"We'll have to watch out for those pines at the end of Greeley's runway fourteen," he grumbles. "Jason says they still can't get permission to cut 'em down."

"Don't worry, Dad. We won't feed any plane-eating trees." I reach over to pat his knee.

"Wooo! Jenny, where'd you get such cold hands? I know—from your mother. I swear, the two of you could work at the morgue, reviving the dead."

"Well, you know what they say—cold hands . . ."

". . . Hot gazungas."

"Mom!" My daughter Patsy flung open the car door and leaped inside. The circular drive in front of Elk Glen Country School was lined with station wagons waiting to pick up sweaty children.

"Mom!" the breathless ten-year-old repeated, reaching over the front seat to grab my shoulder. "Earth to Mom . . ." Her young voice switched to its NASA-control tone. "Come in, Mom . . . prepare for landing."

I turned to face her.

"What? What is it?" How had the kid gotten past me that morning wearing camo pants and one of her father's awful T-shirts?

"You won't believe this—see that tree over there?" She pointed a grimy forefinger at an enormous oak beside the antebellum mansion that had been converted into the day school.

"Yes. It's really something, isn't it?"

"But that's just it! Mom, they're going to cut it down! See that red ribbon around it? That means they're going to cut it down to make way for the new high school building!" Patsy finally paused to catch her breath. Little beads of sweat glistened above her upper lip. Such a pretty girl, although she'd never believe it in a million years. And *smart*—smarter than both her parents put together. She hadn't done well in the "open space" classrooms at the public school, but now that she was in private school, in classrooms with real walls and doors that could shut out the noise of nearby classes, maybe her grades . . . I shrugged my shoulders just as Jane Fonda did on our VCR every morning, and rolled my head in a circular motion, trying to get the kinks out of my neck.

"Who needs a new high school, anyway?" Patsy threw her book bag over the back seat, into the trunk of the hatchback. When she was upset, she looked a great deal like her grandfather. I drew a deep breath.

"Where are Crista and Pontine?" I scanned the faces coming out of the Old Hall.

"Pontine's out sick. Crista's coming. She's bringing the petition."

"*Petition?*" This had to be Patsy's doing.

"The Save the Tree petition," Patsy sniffed. "They can't take down that tree just to put up some stupid high school. We won't let them."

I wished it were that simple.

"That's an *important* tree," Patsy continued. "An *ancient* tree. Why, it's even older than you are, Mom."

"Thanks."

"I bet Indian kids used to play under that tree." She leaned over the front seat and rolled down the window for a better view of it. "With little Indian Barbies."

I tried to picture Barbie dolls with long black braids and buckskin-covered tits. Barbahontas and Chief Ken.

When Crista Galli finally got in the car, the girls immediately dissolved into a frenzy of whispering. It sounded like Alka-Seltzer. I threaded the trim silver Honda through the wallowing station-wagon fleet, down the long private road through the woods, and out onto Benson Mill Road. At the corner of Benson Mill and Hilltop, I turned left and drove towards the Flower Lady's place. During the growing season, she would set out Mason jars full of fresh-cut flowers—old-timey bouquets of zinnias, marigolds, coxcomb, and flowers whose names I didn't even know—on an old wooden table beneath a shady tree.

"Stop, Mom," Patsy pleaded. "She's got some out today. Get a bouquet. . . . Puleeez? For Linnea?" Linnea was the other plant-lover in the family: If it grew from the ground, it was wonderful to her.

I pulled into the Flower Lady's driveway and got out. Looking across the road at the Jensen place, I reminded myself to stop there tomorrow for eggs.

Even in the rain, it was still dry beneath the Flower Lady's tree. Peaceful green fields stretched beyond it to a limestone farmhouse in the distance. I took out four dollars and crammed them into a Mason jar already full of money. Then I pulled a bouquet from its container and wrapped it in wax paper from a roll on the table.

"The Flower Lady really cleaned up today," I said, handing the flowers through the open window to Patsy. We always referred to her as the Flower Lady, even though the name on the rusty mailbox said "Stott." None of us had ever seen her. I liked to imagine her cutting armloads of flowers early in the morning, arranging them in the jars, and then sitting down on the old-fashioned porch to have a lemonade and let the dew dry on her wet shoes and apron.

"How come nobody takes the money?" Crista asked, twisting her long black braid.

"This is the country, Crista. People are different out here. They trust one another." In the rearview mirror I could see Crista chewing meditatively on the end of her braid.

Thursday, Sept. 25

Even with the air conditioning running full blast, the atmosphere in the car was hot and funky. It was one of those days when everybody wants to talk and nobody wants to listen—except the dog.

Of course, a lot of people do talk to their dogs. But how many of them have dogs who answer back? That's when I first knew I was in trouble. What really got me about the dog, though, was that she was a much better conversationalist than most of the people I had to be around. With the four-year-olds—my daughter Linnea and her schoolmates—I'd get things like:

"Mommy, Matty's staring at me!"

"I am not!"

"He is, too! And he's breathing wet air on me."

With Phillip, my fourteen-year-old, and his friends, I wasn't allowed to participate in the conversation at all, but was forced to listen to long discussions about why seventy-dollar sneakers are better than thirty-dollar sneakers, and why the Ninja Way would see you through any difficulty you might encounter in life. Often, the dialogue would turn to some of the finer points of physiology:

"Who farted?"

"Not me."

"Not me."

I would, of course, be eyed with undeserved suspicion.

When Patsy and her ten-year-old buddies were in the car, the question of my participating in the conversation was less than moot: I actually didn't exist. I'm not sure how they thought the car got from Elk Glen Country School to home, but as far as they were concerned, *I* certainly wasn't there. A favorite topic was the Fairness of Life, something they seemed to believe in, in spite of copious evidence to the contrary:

"Donald Grootman showed his weenie to Allison Klemper on the way to music appreciation, and when she told Miss Jackson, *she* got in trouble for being a tattletale."

"That's OK. Donald Grootman will get his."

"He will? How?"

"The next time he pulls it out, a blackbird will peck it off."

From what I knew about the Fairness of Life, I figured Donald Grootman would wait a few years and then wind up getting paid to wave his weenie on MTV, or something like that. But nobody was asking for my opinion.

With the dog, it was different:

"Did you see that, Bacall?" I'd say.

Bacall looked around, ready for action.

"That idiot in the green Lincoln cut in front of me like he was the King of Siam."

Bacall snorted, her tail shooting up to full alert.

"Look at him," I continued, "and what did it get him, anyway? He's waiting at the same red light we are. The jerk!"

On my ear I felt a lick of affirmation, followed by a nuzzle of approval.

"You know, Bacall, you are *so* mature. It doesn't *kill* you to agree with me. Unlike *some* people I know."

This sort of thing does have its appeal. And I guess it might have been OK, if it were the *only* thing. But about the same time the dog and I became the Siskel and Ebert of suburban driving, I began to take to the air, so to speak, without actually leaving the car. I'd be driving along, and the next thing I knew, I'd be pulling up through the clouds, heading for the wild blue yonder. The Red Baron had Snoopy's doghouse; I had a '79 Honda Accord.

Friday, Sept. 26

A.M.   Shoe repair/cleaners/exchange
                   Patsy's backpack–Macy's
P.M.   12:30   Phil/orthodon.
       1:00   Lunch/McD.

I was too early to pick up Linnea and Matty, so I drove behind the nursery school to the parking lot of St. Obturator's Episcopal Church. The beautiful old building had always made me feel as if I'd fallen into the nineteenth century: Under the stern protection of towering oaks, it looked like the setting for a Thomas Hardy novel. Just beneath the frivolous play of morning light along the hoary limestone, smooth slate, and glimmering stained glass was the unmistakable promise of infinite darkness. Then again, maybe I'd read too many novels while waiting to pick up kids from school.

A mild breeze made the leaves in the church graveyard dance. What a relief to be around trees that didn't slip sideways along my peripheral vision or grow smaller in the rearview mirror. I have to admit, the magnificent trees drew me to the place as much as the stories told by the marble gravestones. And the absence of human voices was heaven itself. It was a good place to be.

"You stay here, Bacall." She gave me a dirty look and mumbled under her breath.

"Same to you, lady," I sniffed.

I got out of the car and walked down the path to the graveyard. In one row lay three nineteenth-century graves, their confines marked with four-by-four beams of once-white marble. Within each outline lay an engraved marble slab. Heavy slabs, maybe three hundred pounds apiece—heavy enough, I couldn't help thinking, to hold most anything down.

I rambled uphill to a grove of dogwoods. Their limbs were bright with red berries—it would be a good winter for the cardinals.

Rising up in the center of the grove, like a terrible Druid surrounded by innocent little children, stood the oldest oak on the hill. Its lowest branch stretched out as if beckoning the dead.

A monster acorn landed at my feet. I picked it up, rolled it in my hand, and then let it fall. With the toe of my running shoe I pushed it into the soft ground.

"Good luck." It was a silly ritual I'd picked up from Linnea. Funny how children get enmeshed in the fabric of your life: One minute they've never existed, and the next—*pow!*—you're all so intertwined that you're not sure whether it's your eyes you're seeing things with, or theirs.

I dropped off Linnea and Matty at his house and drove over to Mt. Pisgah Senior High. HOME OF THE BENGALS, the sign out front proclaimed; "Home of the Pissers" sounded more appropriate to me.

Phillip was waiting on the curb of the circular drive. He'd been short for most of his fourteen years, but finally he'd begun to grow with a vengeance.

"Hi, Shorty," he said, his favorite greeting for me. He hit his head as he climbed into the car.

"Don't slam the door." I was too late. I leaned over and gave my oldest child a peck on his still-smooth cheek.

He wiped off the kiss. "Maaa-um."

"No one's looking." I guided the car back down St. Obturator's Lane.

"Stop, Mom, stop!" Phillip was pointing to the edge of a field between two houses. "Over there." He hopped out of the car and dashed into the tall weeds.

Phillip was the family pack rat. His room and the basement and the garage were all cluttered with the "treasures" he had picked up along the road. Target arrows and Frisbees, old bottles, a size-eighteen tennis shoe ("It had to belong to Kareem Abdul-Jabbar, Mom")—they would all eventually fit a purpose in Phillip's life.

"Isn't this *excellent*?" He held up a piece of ancient hemp rope so frazzled with use that it looked like a mohair neck-warmer for a python.

"Oh, yeah." As he buckled up, I pulled back onto the road.

"Hamden's a butthole," he said, scowling.

"Phillip!"

"He is, Mom. You know what he did? He said the test was going to be Tuesday, and then he gave it today! Everybody flunked it." He slumped down in the bucket seat and slammed his palm against the dashboard. "Jeez."

"Everybody, huh?"

"Probably everybody."

"Had you studied?"

"Jeez, Mom. I was going to study tonight."

"Maybe you ought to give up swim team."

The thought of driving him to swim practice four times a week at five-thirty in the morning made me gag.

"Oh no, Mom. I can do better. Anyway, it's Hamden's fault. He should've given the test when he said, the butthole."

"Don't say that!" I would have stomped my foot, but it was on the accelerator.

Dr. Masseter's office was Teen City. The walls bore posters of rock stars, bicycles from France, and surfers catching the perfect wave. There was a bilious orange beanbag chair that preteeny-boppers fought their younger siblings for. But nobody fought over the other seats that ringed the waiting room: chrome-and-leather deck chairs that made a farting noise when you sat down on them.

The magazines in the wall rack—except for *Ranger Rick* and *People*—were fiercely upscale, implying that the parents of Dr. Masseter's patients could actually afford his orthodontic services. I leafed through *Gourmet, Baltimore*, and *Washingtonian* before rejecting them. Who cared what the top ten tofu restaurants were? Empty-handed, I sat back down. The chair farted.

"Could you step back here a moment, Mrs. Meade?" The orthodontist beckoned from the operatory room.

"Dr. Masseter, is that you?" I couldn't help it, it just came out.

Four months ago he had been a fat, middle-aged man with glasses that continually slid down his nose. But the man who was poking around in Phillip's wiry mouth was trim, tanned, and had a Kenny Rogers beard that may or may not have known Grecian Formula.

"Ahh-uh," Phillip whined, trying for a *Maaa-um*, but not daring to close his mouth with one of Dr. Masseter's fingers in there.

Dr. Masseter smiled and patted his abdomen. "Lost fifty pounds."

"And your glasses. Where are your glasses?" I ignored Phillip, who was squirming in the examining chair—apparently trying to say "Maaa-um" with his feet.

"Contacts," said Dr. Masseter. "I feel so free now. I feel like a new man!" It seemed to me that his eyes were a heck of a lot bluer now than they'd been four months ago. I stared at the odd color. Ty-D-Bol blue.

You've got three strikes against you, Dr. Masseter, I thought as I let Phil out at Mt. Pisgah and headed for the dry cleaner's: A man your age who loses weight might be trying to improve his health on the inside; a man your age who loses weight and gets contacts might be trying to improve the way he looks on the outside; but a man your age who loses weight, gets contacts, and grows a beard is probably hoping to improve his chances of getting more than a little something on the side. Odds are, Doc, you're having an affair.

"I think Dr. Masseter is having an affair," Fran Kublik hooted over the din of preschoolers buzzing with sugar highs. "McNoise," she called it.

I had to laugh. "I was just thinking the same thing. Who do you think it is?"

"Jif thinks it's his secretary."

"Georgina? Naah," I said. "Too old. Has to be someone at least ten years younger than him."

Elena winced and reached for a cigarette. She had grown terribly thin since last Christmas, when she had come home early from the Cub Scout Tree Pageant and had found her husband cavorting with his new, twenty-year-old secretary. In Elena's own bed.

I wished I had said something else. "Maybe it's the mother of one of his patients," I said quickly. "One of those preppy types you see sitting there reading *Southern Living*, not a hair out of place."

"A vision in lime green and watermelon pink," Fran added, stuffing another french fry into her cute, pudgy mouth.

"With rope-soled wedgies. And *nylons*, even when it's ninety degrees!" We gazed down at the four pairs of running shoes under the table and grinned.

"Thank God the Y started up the Mothers' Day Out program again," Fran said. If it hadn't been for the YMCA's willingness to take on three-, four-, and five-year-olds for a few hours each week, we'd never have had the chance to have lunch together. (Some called it lunch, I called it suburban psychotherapy.)

I looked at the four of us reflected in the booth's mirrored wall:

Jif Ludloff: short, freckled, with a runner's trim body and a voice that could be heard across a school cafeteria at high noon. "She taketh no crap," as Fran had once described Jif's direct, no-holds-barred manner. Even her hair, blond and kinky, was feisty.

Elena Popliteal: The change in her since Christmas broke my

heart. Her clothes hung shapelessly from a body that used to make men suck in their guts and haul up their chests when Elena passed them on the street. Tobacco-stained fingers drummed continuously as she puffed on Camels and glanced nervously about the room. Her beautiful olive skin and straight black hair seemed almost colorless in the harsh McDonald's light. But, I was glad to notice, the corners of her mouth still managed to twitch up as a toddler waddled by, both fists full of napkins, a box of McDonald Land cookies tucked under his chin.

Fran Kublik: Having her last kid at forty-one hadn't been such a great idea. She'd kept on working at the phone company when the first child, Vince, had been born fourteen years ago. But after Kelly, she just didn't seem to have the energy. The twenty extra pounds she'd gained over the past five years hadn't helped either. At forty-five, Fran had ten years on Elena and me; fourteen on Jif. At the moment, she was definitely between diets.

We are as different, I thought, as four people could be. But we were bound by ties stronger than any alumni affiliation or Old Boy network in the world: Our children were all in the same grades, and we had never been together when we hadn't laughed. We were the Old Mom Network.

"Is Berlie back from Pittsburgh yet?" Fran asked me.

"Yep. Back and gone again."

"How can you stand him being away so much?" Elena's voice was barely audible.

I shrugged. "It's a trade-off: He had a chance to go to Columbus—there was a big slot in the home office—but he decided it was more important, after fourteen moves, for us to stay in one place, put down roots. So he's staying on at Buckeye Trucking as Eastern sales manager. It's a lot of time on the road for him, but we get to stay put."

I sighed, and everyone looked up as if it were a signal. It was.

"I know that marriage has its ups and downs," I said. "But ours seems to be stuck on the Piedmont Plateau."

Fran nodded. "You're not going anywhere? Not up to the good times . . ."

I thought about the early years Berlie and I had had together, when I'd plan my flying schedule to coincide with his homecomings after long weeks on the road. I thought of the births of our children, and the day we found our house—the one we were still living in after five whole years.

". . . and you're not sinking down to the bad times?" Elena's hollow brown eyes gave silent testimony to what the bad times could bring.

I shook my head. "Not up and not down. Just coasting."

"It'll pass." Jif leaned back against the booth and folded her arms across her taut midriff. "You know it will."

I tried one of those weak little smiles you give when you don't want anyone to worry too much, but you still want lots of sympathy.

"I know. But I don't wait well."

Fran laughed. "We know."

"Waiting makes me crazy." I wasn't sure if I should tell them just *how* crazy.

"We know." They all smiled.

"But I'm serious." I took a deep breath. "Last week the dog told me to lock Matty Kohlrausch in the trunk until he stopped singing 'And Bingo Was His Name-Oh.' "

Fran patted my hand. "But you didn't do it, did you?"

"No."

"Well, then," she said, as if that settled the whole thing.

"But, Frannie"—I could feel my ears getting red—"the dog has been talking to me!"

They just smiled. I could see they didn't believe me. So I told them about the "flying" episodes. Same thing. "Ha-ha. Jenny's just trying to make us laugh."

Oh well, I thought. At least they'd come visit me in The Home. Might as well change the subject.

"What's that you're making?" I pointed to the yarn sticking out of Fran's tote bag.

"A scarf—muffler, I guess—for Kelly." She held up a knitting needle with about five inches of pink and mauve garter stitch on it. "I work on it while I'm waiting to pick up the kids."

"It could be twenty feet long by Friday." Jif finished off her chocolate shake with a loud gurgling sound. "Same time next week?" She put everyone's trash on her tray and stood up.

"God willing," said Elena.

"If the Renault makes it," said Fran.

"As long as nobody's sick," I began, "or has an appointment or has to be—"

"Oh, shut up," said Jif.

Monday, Sept. 29

A.M.		Groc./bank/lib.
	10:40	Patsy to Dr. Masseter's (11:00)
P.M.	1:00	Lunch/Wendy's
	3:00	Lin/art lesson
	3:30	Patsy/clarinet lesson
	7:30	PTA/Elk Glen

Somehow I slept through the alarm that morning and was spending the whole day trying to catch up. That's why I surprised myself when I actually remembered to stop for eggs on the way to the bank.

Holly Jensen and her husband, John, lived on Hilltop Road, across from the Flower Lady's place, out near Patsy's school. In their mid-twenties, John was a Clark County farmer, born and bred, and his wife out-farmwifed them all: She kept chickens, she made quilts and apple butter, and she probably got up and had a hot breakfast ready for her husband before he left for a long day in the fields. On their hundred-acre farm they grew wheat and corn, a little hay, and the inevitable soybeans that made up the bulk of the local crop yields. We'd been buying eggs from Holly and cordwood from John since before Linnea was born.

The Honda splatted through the puddles made by a predawn rain, making a calico cat look up from her ablutions on the Jensens' rough-planked front porch. Holly came out of the cedar-shingled house, drying her hands on her apron. She wore her hair in a single long braid down her back, and there was something about the way she carried herself that suggested the strong influence of a private girls' school rather than early years spent in 4-H.

"No eggs today, Jenny," she said, stepping down one of the porch steps. "Skunk got in the henhouse and got every last one of 'em." She scrunched up her sweet young face into a knot of disgust.

"Think you'll have any by next week?" I hoped I could remember to stop at the Super Saver on the way home.

"Oh, sure. John'll get the stinker before he knows what hit him."

I could just picture John Jensen staked out somewhere behind the henhouse with a shotgun, his curly brown hair hanging three or four inches farther below his cap than did the hair of most farmers, his high-laced boots firmly planted in chicken muck—a red-bearded, time-traveling French trapper accidentally transported to rural Maryland. I had no doubt he'd hit his mark.

"Oh, well," I said. "I'll be back."

She turned to go back into the house but stopped at the screen door. "Hey, you know it's almost time to start getting in your firewood," she said. "How much you want me to tell John to deliver?"

I'd forgotten about cordwood; it was still too warm. "Oh, whatever he gave us last year—it came out just right. Only two or three logs left."

"That's John." She smiled. "He always seems to know how much to lay up. Kinda spooky." She waved good-bye, and the screen door closed behind her with a gentle slap. I drove on down the Trail of Errands.

A gigantic bus roared past as Patsy and I were waiting to pull out of Elk Glen's drive. The monster was going so fast its draft shook the Honda as it thundered by.

"Those damned Zephyr buses! They think they own the road." Worse yet, the little Honda had to follow the diesel-stinking hulk all the way to where we turned off for the orthodontist's office.

"Ooooh, look at that." Patsy went over to a red Porsche parked outside Dr. Masseter's building and ran her hand over the fender.

Don't touch that, I wanted to say, you don't know where it's been. We went into the office and sat down carefully.

"Like, whose Porsche?" Patsy asked the receptionist.

"Don't say *like*," I reminded her.

"It's mine," Dr. Masseter's voice answered from somewhere farther down the hall. "Isn't it a beauty?"

"It's, like, awesome," Patsy yelled back. It reminded me of the conversations at home: People didn't speak to each other face to face; they yelled from room to room or—worse yet—from floor to floor.

"A red Porsche!" she yelled again. "Awesome."

Aha, I thought. Wait until Fran hears this.

"That clinches it," Fran crowed. "A red Porsche. That man's on his way to hell in a breadbasket."

"*Handbasket*," Jif said on her way back to the Wendy's salad bar. "To hell in a *handbasket*."

"I always thought it was *hat basket*." Elena picked at her salad.

"To hell in a red Porsche." I finished the matter.

"If we keep having lunch at this rate, I'll weigh four hundred pounds." Fran poked her baked potato for emphasis.

"Oh, Fran," Elena said, "I can't make it next Friday. You don't mind, do you—really?"

"Of course not. I can go out to lunch anytime, anyplace. I'm glad you're taking the kids to see your mother. It'll be good for all of you."

"Yes." Elena lit up a cigarette. Her right hand was shaking—a tremor so small that no one but me seemed to notice. "I didn't think the school would let me take them out for so long, but both of them were ahead in their work, so it was OK."

"Elena," I said, "are you still trying to quit smoking?"

Jif gave me a "watch your step" look.

Elena turned and looked out the window. "Well . . ."

"Did you see in the paper about that woman who noticed a truck following her on Cumberland Road one night last week?"

Jif said, lining up the salt and pepper shakers with the "Have a Frostie" placard on the table.

"What?" I asked.

"I saw that." Fran gulped down a slug of diet soda and then continued. "It was Jamie Dolan's mother. She was on her way home from the Super Saver, and this truck started following her real close. So she turned left, and he turned left. She turned right, he turned right. So she really stepped on it and made a dash for home. When she pulled into her driveway, the truck pulled right in behind her. Blocked her way. So she made a run for the door, but the guy in the truck jumped out and caught up with her, and he was waving his arms all around and pointing to her car. She was about to scream, when he whispered, 'Lady, go inside and call the police—there's a man hunkered down in the back seat of your car.'"

"No," I said. The story made goose bumps rise on my arms. "What happened?"

"Right about then her car door opens and this scuzzy man leaps out and starts running across all the yards. She goes and calls the police, but by the time they get there, the truck driver has the guy up against someone's BMW, and the owner's out there screaming, 'Get that slime bag off my car!' " Fran was laughing so hard that tears ran down her cheeks. "Can you beat that?"

"What would you do," I said, "if someone started following you way out there on Benson Mill Road or somewhere like that?" I didn't feel like laughing.

"Well"—Fran wiped the tears on her cheek—"if I were in Bob's car, I'd use his phone to call for help."

"But what if you were in the Renault?"

"I guess I'd floor it and head for the nearest gas station."

"And maybe flash the headlights on and off the whole way," Elena added.

"I'll tell you one thing." Jif wadded up her trash so tight she could have used it for duckpin bowling. "If I see one of you guys charging down the road with your headlights going on and off, I'll stop and call a shrink for you. Too much carpooling."

I must have looked pretty exasperated: She added, "Then I'd come after you, catch the bastard, and rip out his liver."

"Get his nuts, too." Elena smiled a sweet, ghostly smile.

The Elk Glen PTA meeting provided a rousing evening of debate on whether to admit girls with crew cuts or boys with earrings to class; what to do about the Save the Tree petition—some enterprising child had gotten signatures from Senators Ted Kennedy and John Glenn (this was Patsy's doing, I was sure—I sank way down in my seat); and whether to allow field trips to Washington museums and government buildings now that bomb searches were routine at all the entrances. If all that weren't bad enough, a thick fog had rolled in during the meeting. I could barely find my car. In this soup, I comforted myself on the lonely road home, no one could even see me, let alone follow me. I hoped no animals were on the road.

When I got to the house, I made sure everyone was asleep, turned out about a thousand lights, and climbed into my empty bed.

In the morning the fog was still clamped down tight. I couldn't see the Bromptons' house across the street. The end of the driveway was just a guess. The Honda crept over to Matty's and then on to St. O's. After I dropped off the kids, I drove around to the church and stopped to check my schedule:

Tuesday, Sept. 30

A.M. 9:15 P.U. Phil/wart (9:30 Dr. Robard)
Grocery store

A slow day. Phil had to get a wart removed from his elbow. (It had been a case of peaceful coexistence, he and his wart, until one of the girls on the track team said something, and now it *had* to come off.) And I figured the grocery store ought to be fairly empty even late into the morning because of the fog—unlike the mere suggestion of snow, which could fill the Super Saver with consumers faster than a Karo spill in an ant farm.

So I had fifteen minutes to kill. Even with the fog, I decided, I'd rather mark time at St. O's than over at the high school. I got out of the car and headed down the path to the graveyard. When I looked over my shoulder at the old church, it seemed to be floating on milky air. Three more steps down the path and it had vanished.

It was so quiet here. No one fussing. No one asking to go to the mall. Even the leaves beneath my feet failed to rustle in the visible dampness. I stopped to sniff the delicious silence.

Although I knew I was surrounded by some of the oldest families in the place—the Carvers (1783), the Renschlers (1779), and the Finks (1790)—I could only see the four markers right in front of me. I turned left at the Gordons (1888) and carefully climbed the hill toward the grove of dogwoods.

I paused in the clearing to catch my breath, but the thick air was not much comfort. All around me, acorns dropped like an artillery barrage. One of them, almost as big as a grenade, bombed my foot. I bent over to pick it up, but it rolled forward. Pouncing like a cat, I grabbed it before it rolled out of sight into the fog. But as I straightened up, something hard and wet conked me in the back of the head.

"What!" I staggered forward, crunched into a dogwood, and froze in my tracks. Nothing. I could see nothing, hear nothing. I turned and took two steps forward. Still nothing.

With the third step I ran smack into a brick wall. Only it wasn't a wall: It gave a little. I reached out cautiously and felt—a hand. A hand that was even colder than my own.

Chapter Two

I RAISED MY EYES and saw a rope disappearing up into the oak tree. The near end was firmly cinched around a man's neck. I stared stupidly at him. Bulging brown eyes stared back. He had on a lumberjack coat and jeans, and something was dripping from his work boots.

"Holy shit!" I whispered. I started to run, but a thought made me stop and turn back. Carefully, like a dog crossing a room full of mousetraps, I inched towards the man and gingerly touched his wrist. No pulse.

I took off into the dense fog. The most direct route back to the school was straight down the hill. Tripping over foot markers and grazing headstones, I ricocheted down the hill and jerked open the back door of the school building. I hoped that by the time I got to the front office I'd have composed myself enough not to scare any of the children.

. . .

It wasn't hard to honor the desk sergeant's request that I keep the nursery-school staff away from "the scene." That is, except for Mrs. Dowdle, a teacher of three-year-olds and a Margaret Rutherford look-alike, who was determined to march up the hill herself, police or no police, unless I answered all of her questions.

"Were his eyes all bugged out?" she asked, licking her lips and rubbing her hands together. "Was there blood running out of his ears? Was his tongue black and bulging?"

I wondered what this woman dreamed about at night—what kind of stories she read to the children. The only thing that finally kept her away from the body was my realization of what had been dripping from the man's boots: "All his sphincters have relaxed, Mrs. Dowdle. Believe me, you don't want to go near there."

So I waited alone at the top of the hill. What on earth was there in my life that had landed me here, sitting in the fog, next to a dead man, waiting for the police to come? I had enough things going on without this. Or did I? When my number was up, what kind of life would I have had?

I thought back over yesterday. If it had been the last day of my life, would it have meant anything to anyone? There had been some good moments with friends and the kids—was that the best I could hope for?

An acorn thunked me on the shoulder and brought my thoughts about Monday back to Tuesday's damp reality. I looked up at the body. It was hard to tell, given the odd color of his face, but the poor man seemed to be young—thirty at the most. His hat, with the word *DeKalb* above the sun visor, had fallen off and rolled up against the old Druid oak. I looked at the tree's furrowed bark, at the gnarled branch that held fast the rope with the horrible knot at the other end. An overturned milk crate, like the ones stacked up behind the nursery school, lay on its side beyond his feet.

The man's hair was curly and brown, like Phillip's, but he had a beard. Where his jacket hung open, I could see that his shirt had been freshly ironed. Somebody's going to miss you, I thought.

A little bit of pink paper peeped out from his shirt pocket. A suicide note? I looked around. Nothing but fog. I stood on my tiptoes and eased out the paper. The air was so still. Nothing in the whole world was making a sound. I unfolded the note, written in a precise, old-fashioned hand:

Please forgive me. I love you Holly.

Holly! I looked at the horribly distorted face once more and prayed it wouldn't look anything like John Jensen's. It didn't. But the hair and the beard—and I guess even his high-laced boots finally convinced me it was him.

"Playing detective, are we?" A deep voice growled behind me, making me jump a mile.

"Aaaah!" I was almost afraid to look.

A tall man in jeans and a fisherman knit sweater stepped around me and checked the hanging man's—John Jensen's—pulse.

"Dead." Beyond him I could see a dozen police and rescue squad personnel swarming up the hill like blue bees heading for the hive. The fog was lifting.

"You scared me!"

"Detective Sergeant Perry, Clark County Police Department." He flashed his ID and reached for the note I was holding.

I looked down at the paper and then at the narrow, long-fingered hand he held out to me, and I gave the note to him, feeling like a child caught with a five o'clock cookie. By now the medics had cut the body down and had laid it on a stretcher.

"You the one who found him?" Sergeant Perry glanced at the note and stuffed it in his pocket.

I nodded.

So quickly that I wasn't sure his hazel eyes had moved at all, he looked me up and down. "Why don't you tell me what happened."

There wasn't much to tell, but it was noon before I got home, laden with groceries and guilt about breaking Phil's nine-thirty appointment.

"Nap?!" Linnea and Matty wailed in unison.

"Why do we have to take a nap?" Matty persisted.

"Because," I answered, trying to imagine how Don Corleone

would phrase it, "from the things that would happen to you if you chose to stay awake, I could not protect you."

Matty was about to speak, but my daughter took him by the arm and led him towards the door. Together they curled up on Linnea's four-poster bed, under a comforter appliquéd with Peter Rabbits.

I sank down into the depths of Berlie's old blue easy chair and stared at the ashes in the fireplace. Holly Jensen got some terrible news this morning, I thought. Maybe she was ironing shirts when the phone rang.

"What about my wart?" Phillip demanded when I picked him up from practice at five. He threw his track gear on the back seat. "I waited thirty minutes for you"—he pointed out the window, his finger loaded with righteous indignation—"*right there.*"

"Something happened." I turned onto St. Obturator's Lane.

"What? You had to hit a sale at Macy's?"

I held the steering wheel so tight my knuckles grew white, a little trick I relied on to keep from smacking him. "I said"—I made myself speak very slowly—"something happened."

"What could be more important than—"

"For God's sake, Phillip. Stop it."

"You don't care about me." He was really warming to the subject. "You don't care about my wart. You just—"

"PHILLIP!" I pulled onto the shoulder and slammed on the brakes. He stared at me as if I were an extraterrestrial.

"This morning I ran into a dead man." I let all of my breath out in one long, heart-emptying sigh.

"You did?" He was all attention now. This was better than warts. "Wow, did you dent the car?"

Wednesday, Oct. 1

A.M.   P.U. pumpkins for Lin's class (& big one for us)
Shoes and radios to thrift shop
10:40   Phil to Dr. Robard's (11:00)

Had I slept well Tuesday night? No. Was I going to let finding John Jensen in the graveyard throw me? Of course not. After all, the feelings I had about the matter were a mere stubbed toe compared to the wave that must have crashed down on Holly Jensen.

A circus parade of plump cumulus clouds lined up across the blue October sky. When I looked at something like that, driving west on Cumberland Road, I couldn't help but calm down. The beauty of the countryside almost always soothed my nerves, and luckily, no matter where a person lived in Clark County back then, it wasn't more than a two-minute drive to farmland. I turned down a road lined, on one side, with trees promising a brilliant autumn, and with munching Holsteins on the other.

Ten years ago I had been unable to drive through the rolling hills, past the fields and barns, the cattle and the horses, without picturing what they would look like from the air. When I saw horses running across a pasture, they became another herd from long ago, galloping before the sound of my plane's engines, the muscles of their strong backs working in unison across the stubble of a winter corn field, their hooves kicking up towering clouds of fine snow into the crisp air. But now, after being earthbound so many years, I could finally enjoy looking horses in the eye as they came to the fence to beg carrots. I could treasure gazing up at the sky through cathedral arches of ice-glazed tree branches glittering in the sun. At least, that's the way it had worked until lately.

I turned right at the end of a rail-fenced pasture. Horses raised their heads momentarily to glance at me. A chestnut mare seemed to be nodding in commiseration. Did horses have tight schedules too?

Beyond the pasture lay a field full of pumpkins, some as big as dishwashers, others more like microwaves, Mr. Coffees, and on down to kitchen timers and Tupperware pudding cups. The four-year-olds at St. O's needed the Mr. Coffee size, although why they needed them so long before Hallowe'en was beyond me. Maybe October was Pumpkin Month.

"Guess you saw the sign," John Ballow said as he helped me load fifteen carefully selected little pumpkins into the trunk.

I kicked at the mud clods on my shoes. "What sign?"

He raised a massive hand and pointed to the field beyond the pumpkins. "Harry Simms's place. Sold it to Randall Homes."

"No!" Randall Homes had filled too many once-beautiful meadows in Clark County with four-bedroom colonials and gulag-looking cluster homes, paving over brooks and bulldozing orchards, all in the name of economic progress (was there any other kind?).

An orange cardboard sign flapped in the breeze.

"Yep. That damned sign is for the zoning hearing. They want to get a variance to break Simms's farm up into half-acre lots." We both looked at the field, lush with winter wheat, basking in the mellow autumn sun. In my mind I saw it crowded with frame prefabs and concrete driveways, with regiments of cheap shrubs trimmed in geometric shapes guarding the perimeters of the houses. Ballow probably saw convoys of Volvos and Nissans roaring up and down streets, barely missing teenagers with blaring radios balanced on their scrawny shoulders.

"That's awful."

Together we lifted a seventy-five-pound pumpkin into the trunk.

"Yep." His tanned face was full of lines, a farmer's fifty-year allotment—much greater than a stockbroker's or an attorney's. " 'Least I don't have to worry about them raising my taxes on account of it. Or complaining about the size of my manure pile."

"How come?" It *was* a remarkable manure pile. I could sense it ripening against the day when Ballow would load it up and spread it across his famous pumpkin field.

"Farmland Protection Program. Got my place registered in the district. In two or three years I'll sell the county an easement—that means I promise to keep my acreage as farmland, and they'll pay me the difference between what it would sell for as a farm and what it would sell for as a housing development."

"But then it's not yours."

"Yeah, it is. I can build my boys' houses on it. I can even sell it—but only if it'll be used as a farm." He pried a clod of dirt off the big pumpkin and threw it back into the field.

I opened the car door. "I wish everyone out here would sign up."

"Don't count on it."

The light in his blue eyes flickered for a moment and then softened. "You knew John Jensen, didn't you?"

His question jolted me. The verbs were all in the past tense.

"Yes." No need to tell him about me being the one who found John. I needed a little distance from it right then.

"Terrible thing. Just terrible." He kicked at a clod of dirt with his heavy shoe. "You going to the funeral tomorrow?"

"Yes."

"See you there, then."

He stood in the drive and waved as I turned the car around and drove off, easing my heavy orange cargo over the worst of the bumps. Before I got to St. O's, I had to brake hard four times to avoid hitting rabbits and squirrels darting out into the road. It reminded me of the scene in *Bambi* where all the animals stampede blindly before the forest fire's towering wall of flame. Only it wasn't fire these animals were running from—it was the phalanx of bulldozers rolling inexorably forward over dens and burrows; it was the hot breath of developers that was flushing them out into the paths of oncoming cars.

Chapter Three

The body of a local resident was found hanging from a tree in an Endicott Mills cemetery Tuesday morning. Initial findings indicate that the man died shortly before dawn, but county police speculate that heavy fog prevented earlier discovery of the body, found on a hill behind St. Obturator's Parish Day School. The death has been ruled a suicide.

—*Clark County Courier*

Thomas Black Cloud, I told myself, let it ride. I turned to the weekend section of the local paper and picked up a forkful of breakfast: fettuccine Alfredo. The thing about fettuccine for breakfast is, it's quiet. Man, you eat Rice Krispies—or even toast or bacon—you've got the *1812 Overture* in your mouth, right up there next to your ears. Besides, everybody and his brother eats that stuff for breakfast. And making the pasta and tossing it with the cream and butter and cheese, it wakes you up. Nice. Quiet. And it smells good. My mother, she used to cook cabbage first thing in the morning. Imagine starting the day with that smell. Maybe that's why she died young.

You are tired, a voice in my mind whispered. You are tired.

I *was* tired, from trucking three huge beeches—windfall from the state park—to my back yard the day before and I was irritable from another round of sleepless nights.

"Suicide!" I snarled, rattling the paper and swallowing the delicate pasta, longing for some wine to follow it up with. I had to remind myself it was only eight o'clock in the morning.

I like things to be in balance. Tab A into Slot A. But suicide, that throws everything off center. Nothing ever fits again.

Well, it really pissed me off. *Suicide.* Even after two years of medical leave from the D.C. police force department of detectives, I found that the word still sent my mind trudging down methodical paths of speculation. Before I had left the precinct, the speculation had been both automatic and professional: Could a retired Army general who was agile enough to keep up with his new twenty-three-year-old bride also be acrobatic enough to shoot himself, as the widow claimed, in the back of the head while cleaning his deer rifle? Would a woman who was planning to snuff her own candle by sniffing carbon monoxide in a two-Audi garage bother to make out a bank deposit slip and stuff it in her purse? Would she even take her purse? Such questions were part of my daily routine.

But then I began to visualize ways to improve the methods of true suicide victims, and that's when I knew I was on shaky ground: *I* wouldn't have stood in a pan of water and stuck my finger in the light-bulb socket; I would have jumped into the bathtub and pulled the answering machine in after me—eliminating two bad ideas at the same time. I wouldn't have launched myself from the Pepco Building, accidentally pulverizing a bag lady on the pavement below; I would have leaped, arms flapping like the Angel of Death, from the roof of any of the apartments in Clifton Terrace and taken out at least five or six drug dealers with my omega flight.

Even now, two years later, I could still hear my partner Dreyfus's voice urging me to cop a medical and move out of the city—to set up the workshop, keep my mind on wood and off the human refuse I'd been dealing with. It had worked, pretty much. Now, I thought, if I could only work my way up to four or five hours of sleep a night, I'd count myself in pretty good shape.

I looked at the newspaper, folded to display an article about a local apple festival. Without really thinking about it, I riffled back through the pages until I came to page five.

The body of a local resident . . .

I picked up the phone and dialed.

"Clark County Police, front desk." It was the voice of a young kid. Twenty, I'd say, at the most.

"Give me Grimes, in the lab." The phone clicked ominously for several moments, and then the voice of Harry Grimes, sounding to me like old times—good times—came on the line.

"Harry," I said, "what can you tell me about the stiff in the graveyard?"

"Black Cloud, is that you? Is this a joke or something? A little Indian humor?"

"I'm talking about the guy they found in the graveyard Tuesday. What can you tell me about him?"

"I thought you quit Metropolitan."

"I did. This is occupational therapy. You want to meet me for lunch?"

I looked at the name Grimes had given me. Jenny Meade. The woman who had found the body. What would she have been doing in a foggy graveyard at eight-forty-five in the morning? Maybe I'd just keep my eye on her—just a little—just to see if I still had the touch.

At 7 A.M. Ms. Meade, in a silver Honda Accord, had already been out somewhere and was heading back to her house. I parked my old Cutlass on the main street in view of the house and pretended to poke around under the hood. Wasn't two or three minutes before a gangly boy, fourteen or fifteen, exploded out the door and charged up the steep court to the street above. A moment later a school bus picked him up.

At eight the garage door opened and the Honda, like a bat out of hell, flew up the hill. Inside were Ms. Meade and two little girls. I got back into my car.

By the end of the day, I had a pretty good idea how Jenny Meade spent her time: She transported children—her own and assorted others—to various schools and activities all day long. Back in the second precinct, if I'd been tailing someone who spent every waking minute of their life driving around in a car, I'd have written them off as a dealer. But in Clark County, a person like that was probably just someone's mother: Head 'em up; move 'em out.

I tried to imagine what that would be like—tried to imagine Thomas Black Cloud with a carload of kids, how I'd get them to be quiet, what it would smell like in there, what I'd do if one of them got sick. Then I tried to stop thinking about it.

In the lunchroom of the Clark County police station, I looked out the window and saw a fox trotting into the woods bordering a field.

"You sure you're not getting too wrapped up in this Meade family, B.C.?"

"Christ, Harry. I tailed 'em only one day." I looked at the clock on the wall, thinking about going back to my house and workshop. I needed to be working this out on my own.

"And what were you planning to do tomorrow?" Harry looked me straight in the eye. I never had him pegged as a mind reader.

"I'm just trying to get back in practice, Harry—I've been thinking about maybe going back to work."

"But you *do* work. I've been to your studio. You've got real talent." He took out his key ring and jangled it until the tiny figure of a brown bear worked itself to the front. He ran his fingers over the smooth, dark wood. "You have a gift."

"I'm good at tracking, too." I stood up to leave. "You can take the Indian out of the reservation, but you can't take the Indian out of the Indian."

Some people would get uncomfortable with a remark like that. Harry just laughed.

"I've got to run," he said. "I've got a report that has to be ready by three. I'll give you a call next week; I know Betty'll want to see you, now that you're . . . uh . . . back in circulation." He picked up his empty lunch bag and hurried off.

From the parking lot I could see the fox poking his sharp nose out of some elderberry scrub. I wondered if I could pick up Jenny Meade's trail cold, in midday.

Chapter Four

I RATTED AROUND in my dusty studio for half an hour before I quit looking for the right size box to ship the bear cub in. I'd carved it from Osage orange, and I wanted to send it to my Aunt Wiyanna, in Montana. Well, I thought, no single act was ever really a single act. One thing connects to the next. Sometimes it makes you want to give it up, not do anything.

I sat down on the front porch with the bear between my feet, and after a while I realized I was stroking its smooth back and rounded ears. I'd have to build a crate. I could picture my aunt's face when she opened it and found a life-sized cub.

"Hinu!" she would say. "I will call him *Wazaza*, the little Osage who returns." That would be a hint, a cosmic prayer sent out to her nephew, telling him to return to the Blackfoot Indian reservation in Browning, something I had no intention of ever doing, except for an occasional visit to see the old woman and to tell her amazing stories of life in the East.

What would I have told her about my life if I had been sitting next to her right then? That it was simpler since I quit the force. That I was beginning to see more than evil in the world around me. That people were becoming interesting to me in a way I did and did not understand.

Jenny Meade, for instance. She was interesting because she had found a body hanging in a graveyard—she figured in a case that aroused my professional curiosity. That much I could understand. But I found myself wondering about her in ways that had nothing to do with the hanging at all. It wasn't sex—at least I didn't think so. I propped my feet up on the bear cub and pushed back in the rocker and gave the problem some more thought.

After two days of informal observation, I knew this much about Jenny Meade: She was somewhere in her mid-thirties, about five foot three. She had short, curly brown hair and a rosy complexion; she was round in the right places, but trim. I hadn't seen any husband, although the place had a certain feel about it that made me think a man called it home. She had three kids: a girl about ten, a boy around fourteen, and a little girl three or four years old. The children all went to different schools, participated in most of the extracurricular activities known to man, and were driving her crazy. Well, not necessarily crazy, but she did talk to her dog.

How did I know this? Last Thursday afternoon I happened to pull up to a red light on Route 40, and Bingo! there was her car next to mine. It was a warm day and everybody had their windows rolled down, and I distinctly heard her say, "Bacall, did you see that guy in the green Lincoln?"

I checked out the front and back seats of her car, but there wasn't anyone else in there but a yellow Labrador in the hatchback. She seemed to be looking at the dog in the rearview mirror whenever she spoke.

"Of course, he cut me off—and look where it got him—waiting at the same red light as we are. The jerk!"

The guy in the Lincoln, in the far lane—the offender, I figured—seemed oblivious to the attack. The dog, on the other hand, was wagging its tail and bobbing its head up and down.

Lots of people talk to their pets, I had to remind myself. It wasn't all that strange.

"Bacall," Ms. Meade exclaimed, "watch your language!"

Uh-oh. I'd always known Pterion Acres, the local psychiatric facility, wasn't big enough to hold all the loonies around here. But it's still surprising when you see so many of them on the loose. Take me, for example: Sure, I was in a lot better shape now than I had been even a year ago. But I wasn't the old Cloud. Even *I* knew better than to believe that.

For one thing, I was thinking too much. The old Cloud used to think only about the case at hand: Why would someone bother to trash an apartment and then only steal the TV? How would someone set up an ambush in the lobby of a hotel so they could blend into an innocent gathering of guests in the ballroom?

Maybe Harry was right, I thought. Maybe I ought to hire on with the department in Clark County. It had to be quieter than working the second precinct in D.C. Up until Tuesday's hanging in the cemetery, the worst crimes recently reported in the local paper had been a rash of mailbox bashings and a disgusting protest demonstration against the new pooper-scooper law.

On the other hand, maybe I'd gone soft. Peggy had started the process, getting me to think along lines—domestic lines—I hadn't thought along in years. With Peggy there might have been someone who cared whether I came home; there might have been kids of my own, something to connect me to the universe—all this had almost been a reality. And then she was gone.

I marched back into the workshop and picked up the phone.

"Harry?" I could hear Vivaldi flooding the crime lab with culture. "Who do I talk to there about a job?"

It wasn't as tough as I'd thought it was going to be to convince Chief Goldstein that a part-time detective would be a good deal for the force. Cimonetti, down at the second precinct, was glad to recommend me. Of course, it solved his problem of what to do with me when I finally came off extended leave.

"Just one case at first," I'd said to Clark County's chief of police, "to get my feet wet." I brought up the subject of the man in the graveyard, but Goldstein had nixed it. Suicide, he'd said. Case closed.

But there had been a series of thefts from construction sites, he said. There might be a pattern; there might not. He didn't have the personnel to handle it right now. Maybe I could work on that.

And I intended to—while I looked into the hanging incident a little more. "Unofficial inquiry" was my specialty. I'd start by interviewing Jenny Meade.

"Interesting approach," Harry said. I knew he wanted to know why I wasn't starting by talking to the widow, but he'd never ask.

The dead man's funeral was tomorrow, and I figured I'd go. But I wasn't going to pursue a conventional line of investigation. I planned to start with Ms. Meade and find out why she had been in the cemetery. I wanted to know more about—

"Watch your step, B.C." That was all Harry said, but I knew what he meant. He didn't have to worry. I wasn't looking for a replacement for Peggy. She was gone, and no one could replace her.

Still, there was something about Jenny Meade that had already seeped into an unprotected region of my mind; something that had gotten me thinking about the kind of life she was leading, and somehow that had led to a compelling vision of what Peggy and I would have been doing if things had worked out differently.

It hurt to do this, of course. But in the same way a kid wiggles a loose tooth with his tongue, it was something I'd probably keep on doing to remind myself that everything was still in place.

I wasn't sure if the busy Ms. Meade would be at the funeral. Perry, the detective at the scene, said she claimed to know the deceased, but not well. I was betting she'd be there.

Chapter Five

"Don't seem like a funeral at all without the coffin bein' open."
An old woman with a cloud of frizzy grey hair spoke in a stage
whisper to no one in particular. I could hear her all the way back
in the last row. Someone beside her leaned over and answered,
"Holly said that's the way John wanted it. Said he didn't want
nobody gaping at him when he's dead. I ask you—what kinda
conversation is that for a husban' an' wife?"

I thought about my conversations with Berlie lately. The Jensens'
discussion didn't seem all that bad. I went back to watching the
crowd.

Fifty-five people sat on rows of wooden folding chairs in the
cramped chapel of Dawler's Funeral Home, on Cumberland Road.
They watched the glossy walnut coffin as if it were a TV set. Even
when they spoke, they merely leaned towards the listener, keeping
their eyes on the box. Did they think Death might reach out and
try to pull one of them inside when they weren't looking?

"If he didn't want nobody lookin' at him, how come he went

and hung hisself for the whole world to see?" A red-faced man in his fifties settled back in his chair in the row in front of me, crossed his arms above a pork-fed belly, and watched the comments ripple forward until they hit the front wall.

"Twenty-eight years old . . ."

"Good thing him and Holly hadn't started a family yet."

"Maybe she's—"

"Nah. Said they were waitin' for just one good year."

"John hadn't had a good year since he started out six years ago."

"Heard he borrowed heavy just to get the harvest in."

"Well, shit, who didn't? Didn't you? No, that's right—you sold out to that damn builder Randall."

"Heard he was after John to sell."

"John'd never sell out. Said he'd rather die than leave that farm."

"Well, now he's gone and done both."

"Heard Arvis Dutton's going to do the eulogy."

"Who asked him? Ever since he took over the Farm Association, he's had a bee up his butt."

"His farm backs up to the Jensens'."

"I don't care. He rubs me the wrong way."

"Hush, Gardner." The whispers ceased as Holly, wearing a denim jumper and a starched white blouse, was led to a seat in the front row. She sat down, took a quick glance at the coffin, and then stared steadily at her hands.

Arvis Dutton, a small bald-headed man in a corduroy suit, walked across the front of the room, the *wheat-wheat-wheat* sound of the fabric simultaneously announcing his arrival and what he raised for a living. When he reached the podium, he looked around at the flocked wallpaper, the stuccoed ceiling, and the worn green carpet. He cleared his throat.

"John Jensen was a good man. He was a good farmer and the best neighbor I ever could have had." He paused and drew a deep breath. "I knew John ever since he was a little kid—used to hunt rabbits on my place. Got the holes in the barn to prove it."

A few people laughed, that low mumbley sort of laugh you hear only at funerals.

"And I watched him grow up, take over his daddy's farm, and work hard to make it even better. Watched him get married to a fine girl. Seen the two of 'em workin' on that house, paintin' it, fixin' it up."

He looked over at Holly, but she kept on staring down at her hands. The recessed lighting, intended to illuminate the coffin, transformed his bald head into a beacon. He pursed his lips and sighed.

"But it could be John Jensen was born into the wrong time. John Jensen was an old-time farmer. He wasn't down at Wood's Diner seein' how much more land he could hustle up to rent. He wasn't playin' footsie with Giordano and Randall and that bunch so's he could jack up the price on his property and then sell out."

He sought out several faces in the room and then continued. "No. He was too old-fashioned for that. I say *old-fashioned* because he cared about only a few things: He cared about his family, he cared about his farm, and he cared about his neighbors. And that, friends, was somethin' don't seem to be in keeping with the times around here anymore. When John Ballow stove in his leg, who helped him cultivate for three weeks? Any of you? No. It was John Jensen.

"When my henhouse burned down and our whole family came down with the flu, who come over in twenty-degree weather with ten jars of his wife's soup and went out and rigged me up a shelter for those birds? John Jensen, that's who.

"But John wasn't living in the past. I think he could see the future—could see it a whole lot better'n most of the farmers in Clark County. I think he could see what happens when every man just looks out for himself. Could see what it would be like when little farms get swallowed up by bigger farms. And what Clark County will be like when all those farms get sold off—farms that have been in county families for four, five generations—sold off for thirty pieces of silver. I think he could see what most of you evidently don't: that when the farms of Clark County are gone, ain't nothin' gonna bring 'em back. Ever.

"When you consider the sort of values he lived by, it might look as though maybe John Jensen was born a little late in time. But it might be"—his eyes scanned the entire group—"it might be that what he saw of the future—our future—made him choose to leave us a little early."

He walked back across the room to the door, accompanied only by the sound of creaking chairs and the *wheat-wheat-wheat* of corduroy.

With my pockets stuffed with soggy Kleenex, I began inching my way across the row filled with strangers. But just as I reached the end, a hand tugged on my sleeve. I looked around to see a man with dark, steady eyes. He rose and followed me out the side door.

He was just a little taller than me, but powerfully built. I sneaked a quick look around the parking lot: Nobody had come out yet. Oh well, I thought, what would a mugger be doing at a funeral?

"Jenny Meade?" he said.

I nodded. His eyes were black, like onyx, and his blue-black hair, straight and thick, could have used a trim. He shifted on his feet like an outdoor man who'd been indoors too long.

"Thomas Black Cloud, detective, Clark County Police." He flashed his ID. "I understand you and Sergeant Perry met last Tuesday at St. Obturator's."

He made it sound like a tryst or something. I gave him a second look. His broad, tawny face seemed to be made for smiling, but the smiles, if there had ever been any, were long gone.

"I've taken over the investigation of Mr. Jensen's death," he said. "Tell me"—he shoved his hair back out of his eyes—"how did you happen to be in the cemetery last Tuesday morning?"

I looked at my watch and then back at him. I wasn't sure what the protocol was for parking-lot police interrogations, but I was going to be late if I didn't leave right away.

"Is there some other time we can talk about this? I've got to pick up a kid at St. O's in ten minutes."

I got into the Honda, hoping he didn't think carpooling was a form of evasion. Then it hit me, what he had just said. I rolled down the window halfway. "What investigation? Detective Perry said the medical examiner ruled it a suicide."

"That's correct." His face might as well have been granite. He placed a calloused hand along the top of the window glass.

"You think it was something else?" I looked up at him from the car. I knew I'd seen him somewhere—I just couldn't think where. Probably the bank or the Super Saver. Where else?

"You better get going, if you're going to get to St. Obturator's in ten minutes. Wouldn't want you to speed." He made a little *tsk tsk* sound, and for a second, as I shifted the car into first, I thought I saw the granite ease into the beginnings of a smile. "But tomorrow I'd like to ask you a few questions."

"Tomorrow?" I wasn't sure, but I thought Friday's schedule was crammed pretty full. "How about Saturday at ten A.M.—at McDonald's?"

I saw him nod as I let out the clutch and pulled out onto Cumberland Road.

"Thanks for coming with me," Elena said. "I just couldn't handle the funeral, but I wanted Holly to know I cared." The car was floating in the aroma of Elena's apple strudel.

"I wasn't going to go to the house," I said. "I didn't want to be a reminder of how he . . . you know. But maybe it'll be OK." I hoped so, anyway. "How long have you known Holly?"

Elena ran her fingers through her long black hair. "I guess we've been coming out here for eggs eight or nine years."

"I wonder why Fran and Jif never get their eggs from her."

"Oh, you know those two." Elena smiled. "If it doesn't come from the Super Saver, it isn't food."

She was right. We lapsed into silence the rest of the way.

It was a beautiful day, I thought. Too beautiful for a funeral. It should have been raining. A skunk ran along the edge of the field beside the car for a moment before disappearing into a ditch. Halfway across a distant field, three men were bringing in the last of the hay for the winter.

I could see the Flower Lady's house as I drove down the hill. No flowers, no signs of life, but across the road, the Jensens' long drive and much of the side yard were filled with cars. As we got nearer, I could see a little bald-headed man getting out of a blue pickup. Arvis Dutton—I could just make out his corduroy pants.

Even from such a distance, I could see throngs of people milling about inside the house. Several had come outside—probably to escape the crush—and were sitting on the porch. I pulled into the drive.

Fran was a terrific friend to watch all the kids so Elena and I could come to the house. Except for John Ballow, we didn't really know anybody there but Holly. I hadn't known her very well before, but there was something about her that made me think that we were on the same wavelength. Maybe it was the way she had always spoken about her husband. Maybe it was the way she touched inanimate objects as if they were alive. I don't know. It was just a feeling I had.

Elena and I went inside, handed the strudel to someone in an apron, and found a corner to stand in, hoping we wouldn't look too out of place. As it turned out, it wasn't all country people, after all. I assumed everyone here had been at the funeral. But from the back row, I guess I hadn't had such a great view. Here and there were some older couples with Washington's Connecticut Avenue look about them—women with mink stoles and manicured nails, men with silk school ties and snowy shirts that had never known the strain that a button-popping belly could produce.

"It was a nice service, Holly, dear," said the plump old lady with the fright-wig hair. "But I still don't see why you had the coffin closed. Why, when my Albert died we had him up there afore God and ever—"

"Mrs. Reynolds, isn't it? I'm so bad with names." A slim blond woman in a black shantung suit smiled sweetly as she took the old lady by the arm and firmly propelled her towards the dining room. "You really must try the ham salad. My husband made it."

"The cavalry to the rescue," Elena whispered in my ear. "Listen, I've got to find the bathroom. I'll be back in a minute." She crossed the room and headed down the hallway. I turned my attention to the people standing at the table.

"Frazier," the blond woman said to a tall, lean man with close-cropped, greying hair. He was probably in his fifties. "I just know Mrs. Reynolds would enjoy some of your ham salad." The man picked up a small blue-speckled plate and began to pile food onto it. "Mrs. Reynolds, this is my husband, Frazier Claiborne. I'm Kay, Holly's sister."

Holly's sister. I'd never thought of Holly having a sister. Especially one who seemed so different from her. Trail boots had never touched those feet; it was Perry Ellis all the way.

"But—" Mrs. Reynolds looked helplessly at Kay as the mound on the plate grew higher and higher. She cupped her hand towards Kay's ear. "What sort of man makes ham salad?" she said in a whisper that caused people clear across the room to look up. "Why, in my day . . ."

Kay smiled sweetly, leaving her standing there with an overloaded plate, and went back into the front room. "You OK, Holly?"

Holly had moved to the window. Her rough hand held back the white muslin curtain, and she stared out across the fields. She gave no reply.

"Holly." Kay reached out and touched her arm. "Are you all right?"

Holly slowly turned around to face her. "No. I'm not all right. How can I be?" She sat down on the pine "packing crate" sofa and drew an afghan around her shoulders. "Thanks for rescuing me, Kay." She smiled briefly.

I felt like a voyeur, but I couldn't help listening. Where was Elena? I wondered.

"What are big sisters for?" Kay sat down close beside Holly and pulled half of the cream-colored afghan around her own shoulders, too. They have a very close relationship, I thought, even though Kay looked at least ten years older than her sister. They didn't even notice me as I stepped backwards into the room to avoid a swell of late arrivals bearing cakes and fried chicken and steaming casseroles.

"Why did he do it, Kay? What did he mean?" Holly said.

"Mean?" Kay turned to face her sister.

"The note—'Please forgive me.' What did he mean?" The words rushed out in a stream. "He'd never done anything in his life I'd have to forgive him for. Never. So what did he mean?"

I'd wondered the same thing.

"I don't know." Kay stroked her sister's dark brown hair. "Try not to think about it." Through the archway I could see her husband, Frazier, standing behind the pine trestle table. He was handing overflowing plates to two new arrivals. I drifted into the dining room.

"I'm Rebecca Stott," the newcomer said to Frazier, trying to balance the plate and silverware with one hand and shake his hand with the other. "We live across the way. This is my husband, Barton."

It was the Flower Lady—I'd finally seen the Flower Lady. She was even better than I'd imagined her to be. She was still tan from a summer spent in the fields, and there was something about her bearing that suggested subtle strength. She was a fine silver cable in a room full of hawsers and barbed wire. But her husband—he wasn't just barbed wire—he looked as if he'd give you tetanus if you tangled with him. Someone like that didn't easily fit into my fantasies of the Flower Lady and her bucolic life.

"Jenny." Elena's whisper exploded in my ear. "Ready to go?"

We weren't doing Holly any good standing around like bumps, and I was feeling a tiny bit guilty about eavesdropping. We mumbled a few inadequate words of condolence and left.

Kay's husband extended his hand to Rebecca. "I'm Frazier Claiborne. I'm—" He stopped and then began again. "I was John's brother-in-law." He was startled by her eyes. They were green, the green of the ocean off Cocoa Beach. He thought she might be about the same age as Kay, but she made him think of carriages and candlelight and high-buttoned shoes. Her dress, though of a fine, grey silky material, looked as if she had found it in a trunk in some attic.

She rubbed her bare arms as though she might be cold, and glanced around the room.

"Where's Holly?" she said.

"She's in the living room." Frazier Claiborne watched as she set her plate on the sideboard and moved off into the front room.

There was something about her walk that reminded him of a wheat field sweetly rolling beneath the push of the wind. Her long black-and-silver hair was drawn back into a bun at the nape of her neck. He wondered what it would look like if someone were to take the hairpins out, one by one.

Her weasely little husband turned to Claiborne, claiming his attention. "You're not from around here, are you?"

"About ten minutes from here."

"Not *Ulyssia*?" Stott said the name as if it were pig shit.

"Yes, I live in Ulyssia." Claiborne's posture, which had been unusually correct to begin with, became even more so. The two men looked as if they were sizing each other up.

"You like farming?" he asked Stott. He handed a plate of ham salad to the bald-headed man who had spoken at the service. As the man noisily made his way over to a group of people in the hallway, Claiborne started filling another plate.

"It's a living," Stott said. "I got part interest in the dehydrator. Keeps me busy."

"What's a dehydrator?" Claiborne asked him. Stott reminded him of a ferret.

"The Elk Glen dehydrator? Big processing plant—kinda like a big oven with lots of silos—dries out seed and grain so it don't rot and makes fodder into feed pellets."

"I see. You must be pretty busy about now."

Stott grunted.

"Is it around here? I'd like to see it sometime."

"The dehydrator?" Stott said. "It's down the road—you know where that private school is—Elk Glen Country School?" His voice dumped another load of dung.

"Yes."

"It's right next to that. Back in the woods."

"In the woods," Claiborne repeated thoughtfully. He nodded towards the field across the road. "Nice place you've got. You ever think about selling it?"

"Sell it?" Stott looked around. "Actually"—he raised his voice just a notch—"I'm thinking about signing on with the Farmland Protection Program."

Claiborne saw the bald-headed man in the hallway turn ever so slightly in their direction.

"Seems like the right thing to do, you know?" Stott moved a step closer to Claiborne and lowered his voice. " 'Course, I like to keep an open mind about these things, y'know what I mean?"

"An open mind. I'm for that." Claiborne dropped his hand to his side and tapped his fingers against his thumb, as if knocking the ash off an invisible cigarette. "Maybe we could talk sometime."

A wave of hungry mourners suddenly washed around the table. He dished out ham salad with rapid precision—thirty plates in just over a minute. When he looked up, Stott had sidled over to the men in the hall and every once in a while one of them would look in Claiborne's direction.

Claiborne smiled as he went to the kitchen and brought out a 7UP cake in one hand and an apple strudel in the other. Watching the people in the living room, he hoped his sister-in-law might make some move to bring the afternoon to a close. But she was looking rather strange.

Slowly, like a hollow tree that could withstand the wind no longer, Holly leaned sideways, farther and farther to the right, until, just before her head hit the end table, Kay rushed to her side and pulled her forward. They both landed on the floor.

Claiborne watched his wife pull her sister to her feet and, with the help of Rebecca Stott, guide her past the gaping people, down the back hall to her bedroom. As they passed the table, he could see his wife's lovely thigh where the kick pleat in her skirt had given way. Rebecca's arm curved firmly around Holly's waist, and her black-and-silver hair, shining in the candlelight from the table, had started to come unpinned.

Chapter Six

I DROPPED ELENA OFF at her house and had just enough time to swing back out to Elk Glen and pick up Patsy, Crista, and Pontine. I was thinking about what Detective Cloud had said—or not said—about John Jensen's death. I was thinking about Holly and her interpretation of the note John had written, the one I had found sticking out of his shirt pocket.

"Mom!" Patsy's voice broke into my thoughts. "Aren't you going to take Pontine home?"

I had passed Pontine's driveway. I went to the end of the street and turned around.

"Sorry. I was thinking about something."

"You'd better straighten up and fly right." Any other child would have sounded impudent saying that. But Patsy, once again, had managed to sound just like her grandfather. It gave me a weird feeling.

The traffic on Route 40 was heavy by the time we let Crista out at the house beside her father's Fur and Fin taxidermy shop. In the plate-glass window a brown bear and a raccoon were frozen in attitudes of eternal confrontation.

"Poor raccoon," Patsy said. "Poor bear." This was the child who used to sleep on the floor because her stuffed animals took up all the room in her bed.

"I think about those two a lot," I said, trying to get John Jensen off my mind. "I think they represent Clark County." This was a theory I'd developed after hundreds of trips to Crista's house—and thousands of carpool hours all over our rapidly changing countryside.

"Maaa-um." Patsy's father and I could embarrass her even when nobody else was around to hear. She was going to be a marvelous adolescent.

"No, really," I barged ahead. "See, the bear is all of Clark County that isn't part of Ulyssia—it's the trees and the fields and the streams and the wildlife."

"Maaa-um!"

"No, listen. And the raccoon is Ulyssia, the little upstart city animal that spreads garbage all over the place and turns nasty on you when you try to shoo it away."

Ulyssia was a "planned" city in Clark County, a city that sprang from the loins, as it were, of a Baltimore developer with the unlikely name of James Joyce. He had a broad investment base and a smooth line about open spaces and bike paths.

Twenty years ago Clark County had been nothing but farmland, with a large reservoir to the south, a state park to the north, and a small carbuncle-like industrial area to the east. But mostly it had been beautiful rolling farms, with one high school and the fourth-lowest pay scale for teachers in the entire state.

But soon the original five thousand acres purchased by the visionary developer could no longer contain the rampant growth of the city. Ulyssia had metastasized across pastures, fields, and woodlands, drowning out the voice of the turtle with the blare of speaker cars leased by candidates for the increasingly powerful county council.

"The way things are going," I sighed, "I think the raccoon might win."

"Oh, Mom."

So much for symbolism.

As I turned the Honda onto Tragus Court, the postman was just beginning to stuff the Meade mailbox. I tapped the garage-door opener and stopped to pick up the mail.

"Daddy's home!" Patsy jumped out of the car and ran up the driveway. Berlie's new company car, a burgundy Chevy Caprice with OH KARST on the license plate, was parked in the garage. He'd already put a new bat decal on the rear window and slapped on his favorite bumper stickers, which proclaimed MUD POWER and FREE FLOYD COLLINS.

Patsy wasn't the only one who could get embarrassed. Berlie is a caver—a guy who spends his spare time in caves. I wish I had a nickel for every time I've had to explain about karst—an expanse of limestone that tends to produce caves—and about Floyd Collins—a colorful (to be polite about it) old guy who spent his final days trapped in a cavern. Still, with or without the bumper stickers, I was glad to see Berlie home again.

I pulled the mail out of the box. On top of the pile was the October issue of *Flying*. You'd think it was a copy of *Dicks and Balls* magazine, the way I had to look over my shoulder and slide it under the floor mat of the car. I'd been sneaking flying magazines into the house for years. Just one of the things I used to do to avoid confrontations.

I tossed the rest of the mail onto the seat and pulled into the garage, beside the Chevy.

Patsy was standing in the middle of the kitchen, her sweet face looking like rain. Two hundred feet of sheathed-nylon climbing rope, hanging from pegs in the rafters, was dripping water onto the floor.

"Where's your dad?" I asked.

Bacall pranced around the doorway with her legs crossed.

"You want to go out, Bacall?" Not waiting for an answer, I held open the door.

"I don't know where Daddy is," Patsy muttered. "I can't find him."

But we knew he was around somewhere. On the counter lay a

Baggie half full of trail mix, a high-impact helmet, and a handful of aluminum D rings.

"Did you try the basement?"

"He's not anywhere." There were going to be tears.

"Oh, come on. If you can't find your father . . ." I began.

"I know. 'Keep checking farther down.' "

I hated to hear that kind of resignation in a ten-year-old. But she and I both knew him too well.

Berlie is a man in love with holes. If we drive past a construction site, he'll pull over and go look through the peephole in the fence to see how deep they've dug. If a snake or a chipmunk makes a home in the garden, Berlie gets a flashlight and shines the beam down the little tunnel as far as it will go. The happiest day of his life was when he awoke to discover a sinkhole in his own back yard.

Patsy and I gave each other a look and tromped down the basement steps.

"See? Not here," Patsy declared. She ground her toe into the family room carpet.

I opened the patio curtains. At the lower end of the terraced garden a man, digging steadily into the hillside, stood up to his knees in a hole.

"Daddy!" Patsy paused for the slightest of moments, hands on her newly rounded little hips, before running out to get a muddy embrace. Berlie winked at me over her shoulder.

"Daddy, what are you doing?"

His lopsided grin made him look seventeen—almost. "I'm making us a root cellar—you know, for our potatoes and carrots and stuff."

"He's making his own cave," I said, only half teasing.

Berlie cocked his head as if considering the idea. "Yes"—his grey eyes flashed a familiar message to me—"and as soon as it's done, I'm going to lure you down into my lair and ply you with rutabagas and acorn squash."

Patsy laughed. "Kinky, Dad."

I had to laugh too. "Berlie, I'm glad you're home. When did you get back?" I stayed on the patio, under the eaves.

"I got in about noon." He resumed his digging.

I could see his back muscles moving beneath his khaki T-shirt. His body was as strong and almost as trim as when I'd first met him, the new boy next door, eighteen years ago. But now that he was thirty-nine, I could definitely see the beginnings of a beer belly—the result of too many evenings sitting around with his weird old caving buddies, reminiscing about the time they rescued some kid from an abandoned well, or "did the pit" at the Golondrinas.

"You've been caving?" I knew the answer. Just going through the formalities.

"It was right on the way home—just a couple of hours." There was always something very irritating about these conversations about Berlie's caving. He sounded like a teenager trying to explain why he'd come in late. And I always felt like his mother. I didn't like it, but I couldn't seem to keep from getting sucked into it every time.

"When do you have to go back to Pittsburgh?" I said to change the subject.

"I'm leaving tomorrow night."

Patsy's shoulders, inside one of her dad's raggedy old sweat-shirts, drooped. And so did mine. I'd hoped for more time to talk about John Jensen. I'd told Berlie about it on the phone, of course. But it wasn't the same as sitting next to him on the sofa, talking it over, with his arms around me—a chance to try to make some sense out of it.

I wondered if talking it out would make the dream go away, the one where I was wandering around in the fog, trying not to bump into the men—fifty, maybe sixty of them—hanging from every tree in the cemetery. The real scene had been ugly enough, but it shouldn't have bothered me this much. Still, I'd bet that Detective Cloud didn't think it was suicide. And, now that I'd had a little time to reflect, John Jensen was about the last person I could think of who would voluntarily quit living. . . .

A little sigh escaped—I couldn't help it. I hate sighing. But no-body noticed anyway. Maybe there'd still be time to talk to Berlie tonight. I could drop the kids off at the movies.

"Where is everybody?" Berlie placed a shovelful of dirt on the tidy pile forming on the patio. Bacall ran up and sniffed it, then looked expectantly down in the pit.

"Well, I just picked up Patsy from Elk Glen, where they are about to start murdering trees—Patsy, why don't you go get that petition? Maybe Daddy will sign it."

"Yeah!" Patsy suddenly perked up and dashed back inside.

I settled into the wooden porch swing. "And before that," I continued the Saga of the Carpool Mother, "I dropped Linnea off at Matty Kohlrausch's house so Anna could keep her until I picked up Patsy at two-thirty and Phil at five."

"Good God." He grimaced. "At least you've got it all concentrated in the afternoon." Berlie, the innocent, had been away three weeks: Major carpooling deals had been struck while he was gone.

"Oh yeah? I have to take Phil to swimming at five-thirty every morning except Sunday, Tuesday, and Friday—those are Fran Kublik's days to drive; then, at eight, Linnea, Patsy, and I pick up Crista Galli. I drop Patsy and Crista at Elk Glen at eight-ten, pick up Matty Kohlrausch, and drop him and Linnea at St. O's at eight-forty-five. Then I pick them up again at eleven-forty-five and keep Matt until two-fifteen, so that his mother will keep Linnea when I go to pick up Patsy, Crista, and Pontine Kohler in the afternoon, because there are only enough seat belts for three kids in the Honda."

I paused long enough to take a deep breath and blow it out. There was oil on my fingers from when I had checked the fluid levels at the gas station.

"Then I have a little time to start dinner before I go get Phil at track practice at five and pick up Linnea at Matty's."

Berlie stopped digging and was staring at me like I was a mutant. "Are you kidding?"

I was propelling the swing with one foot and sitting on the other, a method that created an erratic flight path. "No, I'm not kidding. This is the worst carpooling year I've ever had."

He came over and sat down beside me. "So why don't we get you a station wagon? You could haul more kids, and *their* mothers

could drive some of those days instead. Why don't we do that?"
It was an old argument.

"Because three kids in the car is my maximum tolerance limit.
Any more than that would push me past the red line. And because,"
I said slowly, so he would understand each word, "I am not a
station wagon person; I am a *Honda* person."

Years ago I had gone from dealer to dealer, armed with my
dad's firm belief in American products and a 1979 *Consumer
Reports* new car issue. But when all was said and done, I'd settled
behind the wheel of the silver Accord as easily as I used to plunk
down behind the yoke of the old Piper Cherokee. There was something about the Honda's instrument panel—it was logically arranged and it actually gave some useful information—and, I have
to admit it, there was something about the way the grey velour
bucket seat hugged my body, the way my feet touched down on
the pedals, the way the gearshift felt in my hand as I downshifted
coming off a tight curve, that made me feel close to what I had
felt when I'd been in my own cockpit.

Sometimes when I was all alone on a country road, cresting a
short hill at fifty miles per hour, I almost believed I could become
airborne, my compact little craft sailing on until it leveled off just
below the soft clouds that drifted lazily along the horizon.

Let other women lumber around in their overweight station
wagons, I'd say. I might have been earthbound, but I'd outma-
neuver them all in my trusty Honda.

"I am a Honda person," I repeated to Berlie, hoping the message
would at last be understood.

Patsy breezed onto the patio with her petition. "Gee, Dad. Don't
you know that by now?" I guess Patsy was imitating my voice.
Her words came out low and emphatic. "I am *not* a station wagon
person; I am a *Honda* person. . . ."

"An *Accord* person," I added.

"A *hatchback* person," Patsy intoned.

"But a station wagon—" Berlie began.

"You want a station wagon?" I said for the hundredth time.
"Get one yourself." End of conversation. I got up from my seat
and sent the swing flying. It smacked into the wall.

"Dad," Patsy jumped right in. "You won't believe what they want to do to the most beautiful tree in the whole world."

"It's pouring out there." I shivered as I came into the warm kitchen. The red plaid wallpaper and the baskets and copper pots hanging from the rafters took a little of the chill off me, mostly by power of suggestion. My raincoat dripped on the blue-and-white tile.

"I let Phil, Patty, and Jimmy Bock off at the Movie Six Emporium," I said. " 'Crocodile' Dundee. I told them you'd pick them up at ten-fifteen. Is that OK?" Berlie didn't say anything, so I went on. "I wanted some time alone with you to catch up. And we haven't had a chance to talk about the thing with John Jensen—it was really awful."

He stood silently with his hands behind his back. Beyond him I could see a fire crackling in the fireplace in the living room. The ropes had been taken down from the rafters and lay neatly coiled on the hearth.

"You weren't going to go to bed early, were you?" I tried. Why didn't he answer? I could hear the old Regulator clock ticking in the hall.

Suddenly he stepped towards me, waving a handful of magazines in my face. "I found *your* daughter reading *these*, in the middle of *our* bedroom floor!" I could see a long muscle working above his jaw.

I grabbed the magazines before they went up my nose. Copies of *Flying* magazine from 1983. "Linnea? But where—"

"She said she found them in the top of your closet." The muscle was working double time now.

"What was she doing in the top of my—"

"Getting down your old hats to play with."

"But—" Why isn't he yelling at Linnea for going through my stuff? I thought.

"I thought this flying business was settled—over and done with." He looked at me with rock-grey eyes.

"It is." My words sounded like stones hitting the bottom of a well. "How could I fly again?" My arms made a sweeping gesture, taking in the entire house. "This is my airplane. Or whatever part of it the money from the plane bought."

Suddenly I felt like some ninja had throttled the Life Force out of me, and I slumped onto a chair. "God, I hope it didn't buy the laundry room."

Berlie stared at me for a moment and then stepped behind me and began rubbing my shoulders. I guessed all was not lost after all.

"Look, I'm sorry I yelled," he said. "But you know how I feel about you flying. You could get hurt."

I couldn't help thinking about John Jensen hanging from the graveyard tree. *He* hadn't been flying, I wanted to point out—and look what happened to him. But something told me this wasn't a good time to get into that.

"Flying's safer than crossing the street," I said. This, too, was an old debate. I could put it on automatic pilot. "Safer than—"

"You know what I mean."

I knew. And I really didn't want to deal with any of it right now.

I started to leave the room, but Berlie turned me by the shoulders until I was facing him. His hands smelled of sweet garden earth.

Oh, what the hell, I thought.

"That whole thing was just a fluke," I tried. I wished he'd just leave it alone. "Those creeps wouldn't ask me to do business with them. Not with Dad gone."

"Why not?"

I got up and began pacing the kitchen floor. "And besides, they'd have no way of knowing if I started up Topflite Medical Transport again. I'd change the name."

"Of course they'd know. They probably know everything."

"Don't be silly. You read too many spook novels." I stopped in midpace. "Anyway"—I gave him a sly look—"if they know everything, then they know Dad is dead. We kept our end of the bargain, fair and square. We kept quiet about everything. So that's the end of it."

"Fair and square?" The vein had popped out again on Berlie's neck. He picked up the magazines, rolled them into a truncheon, and waved it in the air. "What's fair and square about a couple of 'businessmen' who ask you to fly the body of their dear old mother back to Baltimore, so she doesn't have to be buried in West Palm Beach, where she died from a bee sting? That was some bee sting!"

"But, Berlie—"

"And then, when you and your dad hit a little rough air over Jacksonville, the old broad slips out of the body bag and surprise, surprise, it's a mother all right, but he's got a mustache—"

"Berlie, shhhh! Linnea might—"

Berlie lowered his voice to a whispered growl. "And he looks a great deal like an Arab wanted for the assassination of Senator Colby in the Bahamas, and the bee that stung him was semiautomatic, and it got him right between the eyes!" He raised the tightly rolled magazines and brought them down hard on the kitchen table.

"You think those guys play 'fair and square'?" he continued. "Christ, we don't even know whose team they were playing on. Have you thought of that? Have you ever thought about what happened to your parents? I'm not so sure it was an accident. Those guys could arrange anything."

There it was. After ten years, he'd finally said it out loud. But I was ready for him.

"I've thought about the accident," I said, "and I think that's just what it was—a stupid, terrible accident."

"And besides," Berlie continued as if I hadn't even spoken, "even if those guys weren't in the picture, there are plenty of reasons why you shouldn't fly."

"Name one."

"I'll do better than that," he said at last. "I'll name four reasons why you shouldn't fly: Patsy, Phillip, Linnea, and me."

"What does that mean?"

"You know—the four principles of aerodynamics?" He walked over to the trash can. "Stall, spin, crash, and burn." Three months of *Flying* landed in the trash with a sickening thud.

I winced.

"Well, don't worry," I said. "Even if we had the start-up money, I couldn't fly."

"Oh?" Berlie was halfway down the steps to the basement.

"If I were flying," I called after him, "who would drive carpool?"

I closed the basement door and went to the trash can. Only a little peanut butter had gotten on the May '83 issue.

Chapter Seven

I COULD SEE JENNY MEADE crossing the parking lot at McDonald's with last Tuesday's fog still wrapped around her mind. Was it her thoughts, I wondered, or the cumulative effect of her hideous driving schedule? Whatever it was, she still managed to spot me seated by the rear door, and she gestured "wait a minute." A few moments later she sat down across from me with a large Coke.

"Thank you for coming," I said. Not very original, but when were policemen ever expected to be original?

Her large brown eyes seemed to be doing an inventory of my face as she took a long draw on the soda. "You don't think John Jensen killed himself?" Her tone was somewhere between a question and a statement.

The direct approach; I loved it. Especially in women.

"I want to check out all the possibilities," I said, taking an equally long draw on my coffee while I tried to get a reading on her anxiety level. Two could play this game. For a moment I could see us both bellied up to a bar, taking each other's measure while downing shot after shot of rotgut whiskey in a sleazy Wild West saloon.

"It's Saturday morning. I hope this isn't a lot of trouble, with your kids being home and all."

Her face showed a flicker of annoyance, just for a second, and then she rubbed her hands together. "They're at home, but my oldest, Phillip, is watching them." Her sudden smile was wicked.

"What's so funny?"

"When I get back they'll welcome me with open arms. The only time that happens is when Phillip has to baby-sit the others. After about an hour of that arrangement, I start to look real good to all of them." For a minute she relaxed a little. But then, making a sound like the shattering of small bones, she crunched some ice in her teeth and said, "So, what are you thinking about John Jensen?"

I felt sorry for her children today; this woman was gunning for bear. I wondered where *Mr.* Meade was. Why wasn't *he* watching the children? No use broaching that topic. I could see that for now, it was murder or nothing for Ms. Jenny Meade.

"There's always the possibility that what looks to be suicide, isn't."

She just looked at me.

"How did you know Jensen?" I tried.

She looked away for a moment before she answered, and the edge on her voice softened a bit. "We get—got our firewood from him." She fingered a tiny gold chain at her throat. "I guess I know Holly better than I did John—we get our eggs from her. But John—I can't imagine anyone wanting to murder him. No one could dislike John."

"Any indication he was depressed? Down on his luck?"

She shook her head. "Still," she said, "there was that note." She looked as if she were going to say more, but thought better of it. Something told me that if I prodded her, I'd start to look like one of those bears she was gunning for.

"Very distinctive handwriting," I offered. It hadn't been hard, in the laid-back Clark County Police Department, to quietly acquire the interesting bit of paper.

"Mmmmmm." A meager return indeed.

I tried a new tack. "So, how did you happen to be in the grave-yard Tuesday morning?"

She looked at me with the beginnings of a smile in her eyes. "I go there a lot—it's the most pleasant place I know."

"What do you mean?" I couldn't imagine how she would answer.

But then she said, "Sometimes, when I'm alone, I go because it's a good place to be still. It's a good place to think."

I could come up with a lot better places than a graveyard, myself.

"You look skeptical."

Uh-oh. I'd have to work on the old stoneface routine. I was two years out of practice.

I shrugged my shoulders.

She glanced at her watch. "Look, I've got to go." Her hands flashed a little apology in my direction.

"Would you mind going out there with me one day next week?"

She looked at me a long minute.

"Next week's good."

Whew. I wished I had my new cards back from the printer. I penciled my number on a napkin and watched as she stuffed it in her pocket and dashed out the door. I wouldn't be surprised if my phone number got used to wipe some kid's drippy nose. Well, I could always call her.

But she called me first. Later that day.

"Sergeant Cloud?" I could hear sibling-induced squeals in the background. "Have you talked to Holly Jensen yet? She can help you a lot more than I can."

I doubted that. "I'll talk to her," I said. I wondered if something had given her second thoughts. Did she think I was going to hit on her, a married woman? Not likely.

"Who is it, B.C.?"

"Who what?"

"Who's the woman? Your sap's rising, kid. No pun intended."

With Harry Grimes, the Pun King, you couldn't be sure about that.

"No woman, Harry. Besides, 'now is the winter of our discontent.' Sap doesn't rise in winter."

"It's only fall, B.C. Who's the woman?" A look came over his face. "Not that Meade woman—the one in the graveyard?"

"No, Harry. She's interesting, but not that way."

"That's what they all say."

It was time to change the subject. "So, Harry." I watched the head of the Clark County police lab unwrap a cheese sandwich on rye. He neatly refolded the wax paper and put it back in his paper lunch bag. He'd been driving me crazy doing that for all the years I'd known him. Ten years, maybe eleven.

"What do you do with those things, Harry?"

"What things?"

"All those pieces of wax paper. What do you do with them— use them for the next day's lunch?"

Harry Grimes looked puzzled. "No." He pushed his glasses back up the bridge of his nose and shrugged.

I grabbed the bag, pulled out the wax paper and a smoothed-out Tastykake wrapper, and wadded them into a ball.

"You gotta loosen up, Harry. Life isn't all that tidy—so why should you be?" I tossed the trash ball halfway across the room, into the grey, government-issue garbage can.

"That's what Betty always says."

"You must be loose *sometimes*, Harry. You've got six daughters."

Harry laughed. "Yeah, well . . ."

"So how are things with you and Betty?" Normally, I wouldn't have asked, but I was pretty sure of the answer. Harry had that well-fed, well-cared-for look that a lot of married men have. The grey skin and deadened eyes Harry'd had two years ago, when Betty had asked him for a divorce, were gone.

"It was her idea for me to leave the precinct and move the family out here to the country—one last try at making a go of it. Said D.C. was eating me up. I guess it was. We're doing OK now, though. She's happy, the kids are happy. I have time to do things with the girls."

"And you—how about you?" I watched Harry smooth out his lunch bag and refold it.

"Me? I'm a big fish in a little pond." He brushed an invisible crumb off the table. "It's quiet out here, B.C. Sometimes I miss the pressure."

"Don't worry, Harry. At the rate the houses are being flung up all over the place around here, you'll have plenty to do. You know what Dreyfus would say—'give 'em time; they'll bring the crime.' " I grabbed the lunch bag, held it up to my mouth, and blew hard.

"B.C." Harry reached for the bag, but I blocked him.

Pow! I exploded the bag against my leg, and four patrolmen dropped to a crouch and drew their guns.

I slipped what was left of the bag under the table onto Harry's knee and gave him an innocent grin.

"Loosen up, Harry. That's my advice to you." I nodded in the direction of the red-faced patrolmen, who were slinking back to their seats. "If you don't, you're gonna wind up like them." I felt good. I hadn't goofed around in a long, long time.

"How's this part-time deal working out, B.C.?" Harry sneaked a look around the room before he reached under the table and smoothed out the lunch bag. "Is the work enough or too much or what?"

"It's OK. Goldstein's got me checking out some construction thefts. Right now I'm just making the rounds, setting up contacts. You know."

Harry nodded. For a few minutes we sat looking out the window at a field obviously used for off-duty softball. A man in a grey jumpsuit was mowing the grass and swatting at yellow jackets, survivors of the first frost.

"I've gotta get going." Harry tucked the ruined lunch bag into his jacket pocket and ambled off to the lab.

I was alone except for a cadet in the far corner. Reaching into my back pocket, I pulled out a torn slip of pink paper, smoothed it out on the table, and sat back in my chair.

Please forgive me. I love you Holly.

. . .

Holly Jensen hadn't quite gotten the hang of being a widow. Just to get a feel for who John Jensen had been, I asked her if she'd walk me around the property, an old technique. And as she led me from field to field, from shed to barn, and out beyond the henhouse to the edge of the woods, which were still clinging to the reds and golds and purples of autumn, I could see the glow of anticipation rise and then die over and over as she turned familiar corners, expecting to see a man she kept forgetting she would never see again.

"Of course we were discouraged." She poured a cup of tea for me and then one for herself before she sat down at the pine table. "Who wouldn't be? But that's farming. Last year there was no rain. This year too much. And this summer some idiot in a Ranger took out our harrow just as John was crossing over from the Stotts' field to ours on the John Deere. There's so much traffic on the road nowadays." She turned her hands palms up on the table in a gesture of exasperation, and then suddenly withdrew them to her lap, as if she had inadvertently exposed some private part of herself.

"That's where John was going when he left the house that day. To look at a harrow." She looked at me as if that explained everything.

I waited and sipped my tea.

"So he couldn't have killed himself. He was going to buy a harrow." She sounded as if she were trying to convince more than just me.

He could have told you that so you wouldn't get suspicious, I thought. "Was that his handwriting on the note?" I had to force myself to look in her eyes.

"Yes." Her voice sounded steamrollered.

Automatically the questions marched through my head. Why would he write the note if he wasn't planning to hang himself? If it wasn't suicide and it wasn't an accident, then it had to be murder: Who would have an interest in John Jensen's death?

The phone rang. She practically leaped across the room to answer it, pouncing on the receiver as if the second ring would shatter the windows.

"Yes?" she said softly. "Yes." She turned to me. "Detective Cloud, it's for you." Such a gentle voice.

Of course I'd left her number along with the numbers of the contractors I planned to see later. Why not? Nobody'd ever check.

There'd been another hit at Superior Homes. Twelve cubes of cinder block, for chrissake. It should be simple: Look for the guy with the hernia. Well, I'd just have to come back here later.

"I have to go."

She looked relieved.

"But I'd like to ask you some more questions, when it's convenient." What a joke. When could such a thing ever be convenient?

But she nodded and silently showed me to the door. I could feel her watching me as I eased the car down the rutted drive.

There was time, I told myself. It would make it easier on the woman if I took my time. John Jensen's death wasn't suicide; I could feel it. But if someone had murdered him, he or she would be feeling pretty sure nobody suspected anything. It was most probably a one-shot deal—not likely to be the work of a serial killer—someone bumping off farmers of high-fiber crops, for instance. The soybean slayer. The alfalfa assassin.

But, for now, I had to deal with the cinder-block scrounger. What a priority.

Chapter Eight

I LOOKED at the day's schedule clipped to the visor:

A.M.   **Bank**
               Dry cleaners
               Eggs/Holly's
    12:30   **Lunch/Wendy's**

"Bacall, we've got twenty minutes before we pick up Patsy. You want to go for a ride?"

In the rearview mirror I could see the dog prancing around with a wide grin on her face, her tail wagging her entire body.

The sign on the Old Guard National Savings and Loan flashed "9:55 A.M. 75° 10–21."

"October twenty-first." Just saying the date made my heart catch—not a pain exactly, just one of those warning twinges. "That makes it ten years ago today since Mom and Dad died." I shifted into third gear. "You didn't know them, Bacall. Phillip was four, Patsy was born four months later, and we got you the following May—you and Patsy were pups together. . . ."

Bacall gave a little dog chuckle.

I reached back and scratched her ear. "You would have liked them. Dad and I had a flying business together, and Mom watched Phillip for me—she was so good with him. When she and Dad died in the accident, I couldn't run the business without them. No help, and I was pregnant with Patsy. Who could I leave Phillip and a baby with, except Mom?

"I don't know why I'm telling you this now—after all this time. Maybe it's just the Anniversary Effect. I really miss them, though." Bacall didn't say anything, just laid her muzzle on my shoulder.

"And I really do miss the flying," I said, just to see how it sounded. "But you know Berlie. He'll never understand. Says if I fly again, it'll be over his dead body."

A moan came from the back seat.

"True. I wouldn't have put it quite like that, either."

Frankly, I was beginning to feel pretty mad at Berlie anyway, after that tirade of his the night before. He had the facts right about the Bee Sting incident, but the conclusions he'd come to about Mom and Dad's accident . . . no matter what either of us had ever thought about it, we'd never said anything out loud like that. Maybe all these memories weren't just the Anniversary Effect after all. Maybe Berlie's words had watered a nasty little seed that had managed to lie dormant all these years.

My willow basket, full of eggs, sat in the center of Holly Jensen's pine table. Ever since John's death three weeks ago, we'd been sharing a cup of tea whenever I stopped by for eggs. I began to time my trips so I'd have a while to sit and talk. Mostly, though, I just listened.

I don't suppose any time of life is a fitting time to be a widow, but at twenty-six! Twenty-six was for having children, for asking things like "Where am I going?" and "Who the hell am I?"—not for being a widow.

"I keep asking myself." She twisted her long dark braid around her fingers. "I just keep asking the same question—why did he do it?"

I stirred some honey into the lemon-scented tea and waited.

"I want you to see the quilt I'm planning," she said, jumping up from the table. I'd known she was going to drop the subject of John's death as soon as she brought it up. She always did. It was as if it were a golden ball she longed to snatch from a fire— she could hold on to it for a second, but the pain always made her let go.

She had gone into the front room and brought back a large folded sheet of graph paper, which she opened out on the table, moving the eggs out of the way. Colored squares and diamonds and triangles marched this way and that across the paper, forming a design that reminded me of flowers—or maybe they were bird tracks. I don't know—I always have trouble with things like that.

"Pretty," I said.

"My sister, Kay, and I are going to make it for the county fair." She nodded towards a ceramic-framed picture on the sideboard. Kay's photograph, with her perfectly coiffed blond hair and her perfect make-up and her perfect, serene smile, didn't look like the ladies I'd seen at the fair, waiting to register their quilts in the arts and crafts building.

"Doesn't it take an awful lot of time to make a quilt?" I got to my feet and took up the basket of eggs.

She nodded, walking me to the door. "That's what I've got, Jenny: an awful lot of time."

"Cherokee One-Six-Eight-Niner, cleared for takeoff." I release the brake and shove in the throttle. Trees and fields whiz past as the silver plane speeds down the runway. We hit the little bump about halfway down the line, and we're airborne. I pull back on the yoke.

Suddenly seven brown-and-white steers appeared in my windshield.

"Jesus!"

I jammed on the brakes and swerved the Honda across both lanes and onto the far shoulder of the road. It crunched to a stop against a low bank of mountain laurel. The cattle, stolidly planted in the middle of Benson Mill Road, slowly turned their heads to gaze at me and blinked bulgy eyes as I got out of the car. They looked like they were about to graze on asphalt.

"You big dummies!" I shouted, and started to shake my fist, but my legs felt wobbly and I had to grab the roof rack instead.

"*Mmmmuh*," they said; the nostrils in their big wet noses flared, and their enormous brown eyes rolled back in my direction.

In the distance I could hear the low roar of a Zephyr bus headed our way.

"Get out of the road!" Like an idiot I waved my arms and ran towards them. They stared.

"Go! Git!" I pushed a big furry rear end. Just as effective as trying to rush a four-year-old eating an ice-cream cone. The roar was getting closer.

"Git on! Git on!" I pushed, I jumped up and down, I clapped my hands. Nothing.

"You guys," I wailed, leaning my full weight on the lead steer, "GO TO YOUR ROOM!"

"*Mmmmuh*," the leader said, ambling over to the shoulder and on up the rise. Slowly the others followed, grumbling and farting, the gravel crunching loudly under their considerable weight.

I leaped off the road just as the Zephyr blasted past and disappeared around the bend. The steers marched heedlessly onward into the undergrowth, as helixes of steam gracefully rose from the fresh mounds of cow flop in the road.

It was one of those moments when I'm really glad no one else is around. I shook my head and sat down on the bumper. "*Go to your room?*" I said it out loud. "Take me to the Home, boys: I need a little rest."

"You're lucky you didn't hit one of 'em," said Fast Eddie, at the Honda shop. "You'da been eatin' the engine block. As it is, the headlight replacement'll only cost ya a hunnerd or so."

Eddie had a wonderful way with words. I trudged on into the

chilly waiting room. A man in an ancient sheepskin jacket was attempting to read a 1984 *Newsweek*, while Donahue, on the TV set screwed to the wall, asked a married priest just how he was going to bring Rome to its knees on the issue of clerical homosexuality. I pulled an ancient issue of *Flying* out of my coat and settled in.

"You've had homosexual experiences yourself?" Donahue wanted to know. "You're speaking from personal experience?"

No enemy but winter, I read. *Winter flying dos and don'ts.*

I rattled the pages to drown out Donahue.

"Isn't it true that AIDS could wipe out the entire religious community worldwide?"

There are many ways to start an engine for winter warm-up. We like to use a blanket and droplight.

It was so cold in the waiting room that Fast Eddie could stock blankets and droplights in the vending machine and make a fortune. It was hard to believe the weather had changed so much in three days.

"How many of the priests in your community," Donahue plodded on, "are homosexual, would you say?"

"Do you fly?"

I looked towards the television, but it was the man in the sheepskin coat speaking, pointing to my magazine.

"Oh, yes . . . well, no . . . that is, I used to." I crammed the magazine back into my coat. Reflex.

"Ever fly out of Ganton's Farm?" He had a wiry look about him, a promise that if something knocked him down, he'd get right back up. He pushed a greyish-brown lock of hair out of his eyes with a grease-stained hand.

"Ganton's Farm? No."

"But you know where it is?" As he spoke, his breath formed puffs of vapor in the cold air.

Of course I knew where the little private airport was—off Rainey Branch Road, not too far from Elk Glen. But I always avoided the area, the way a barren woman avoids a hospital nursery. "I know where it is."

"They got some beauties out there—you ought to come out and see them sometime."

Was this a variation on Mae West's old line? I turned to get a better view of him.

He looked the way men do who understand how things work—the *Zen and the Art of Motorcycle Maintenance* look. Mr. Ballow had that look. So had my dad. And so—when he was around—did Berlie.

"How come you're not flying anymore?" He leaned up against the wall like he was part of it.

Who was this guy? Didn't he read Miss Manners?

"Do you fly?" I asked. I didn't want to get into my life story with a stranger while freezing my butt off in the Honda repair shop.

"Me? Nope. Got a medical in 'seventy-four. Sea gull come through the windshield and whacked me right here." He pointed to a normal-looking right eye. "This one's blind as a bat." He shoved his hands into his woolly coat pockets. "I work for Mr. Ganton now. Mechanic."

"You any good?"

"Yep."

"Then how come you brought your car in to Eddie?" I could show him what nosy felt like.

A wheezy voice came through the speaker in the ceiling: "Mr. Stilson, your car is ready." He pushed himself off the grimy wall.

"Got recalled. Something about the catalytic converter. Let *them* mess with the sucker, I say." The door closed behind him. Two seconds later it opened again.

"Hey," he said, sending a vapor puff into the room, "you really ought to come out there sometime." He left again.

Fat chance, I thought. Why rub salt into the wound? I looked around cautiously and pulled out my magazine.

Stilson, I thought. Good name for a mechanic.

The sign at the traffic light had been there for two months, but somehow I had convinced myself it would never happen:

ST. OBTURATOR'S LANE BETWEEN CUMBERLAND ROAD AND ROUTE
40 WILL BE CLOSED FOR IMPROVEMENTS FROM NOVEMBER 1, 1986,
THROUGH DECEMBER 1, 1986.

That day, as I turned the car in the direction of the high school
to pick up Phillip, large wooden barricades blocked the way. I
cursed the State Roads Administration and backed up. The alter-
nate route added ten minutes to the trip. Twenty more minutes in
the car every day, I thought, jamming the car into second.

Suddenly a dull pain radiated from the palm of my right hand.
As I shifted into third, the pain grew worse. Using only the tips
of my fingers, I carefully eased the car into fourth gear. It was
awkward, but it held the pain at bay.

"What's the matter with your hand, Mom?" Phillip flung his
books into the back seat and slammed the door.

"I don't know. It just hurts." I rubbed my hand, but I nearly
went through the roof when I touched the center of my palm. As
we pulled out of the lot, I tried using the fingertip method of
shifting.

"That doesn't look very safe," Phillip said, watching me closely.
"Here, let me do the shifting."

"Phillip—"

"I know how. I've been practicing with the motor off."

I shifted into third and almost went into orbit.

"OK, you can try shifting, but wait until I say *now*, so I can
push the clutch down all the way."

Phillip was glowing. "I will, Mom, I will!" If I'd asked him to
give me his favorite jeans and four weeks' allowance, I knew that
I'd have had a deal, such was his boundless joy.

"Ready to go to fourth, Phil?"

"Yes."

"Now!" We made it.

"Oh wow, Mom. This is really great!" He was fairly glowing.
I tried to remember when I had last felt what he must be feeling.

We parked in front of Dr. Robard's office and headed in for
another go at the wart. All the while, Phillip was babbling on and

on about shifting for himself and "Didn't I do great, Mom?" Then I remembered:

Sitting at the controls of my dad's old Apache and taking off for the first time: That was when I'd last felt that way. A long, long time ago.

My hand got better after a day of guarding it. I sat outside the clarinet teacher's house on a Friday afternoon and thought about my life on the road. Somehow I didn't think that what I was doing was the same thing Jack Kerouac had in mind. Well, I'd see how close to it I could get in half an hour. I backed out of the driveway, onto Gaither Road.

In a few minutes I came to a sign: NEW BARN ROAD. I'd always wondered where it went. With thirty minutes to kill, this was as good a time as any to find out. The road was narrow and twisting, and I hadn't been on it more than a minute when it began a sharp descent through the darkest woods I had ever seen in Clark County. I had to concentrate hard to stay on the road.

As I pulled out of a particularly mean little curve, I saw an apparition in a long white robe standing about a hundred yards in front of me. The tall, cadaverously thin man in sandals and a white sheet was holding his arms out wide and looking heavenward with wildly rolling eyes. He had a long black beard and a huge sunburst of wild black hair, and from his neck hung a cardboard sign with the message THE END IS NEAR!!! marked in crayon.

To my horror he started moving towards the car, his lips soundlessly mouthing curses or prayers—I couldn't tell which. But his robe was fashioned from a contour sheet, and his sandals got tangled in the pouches at the corners. After three steps he went down with a thud.

Out of the shadows, two men in turtlenecks and L.L. Bean parkas rushed down the embankment and jumped on the unfortunate prophet. They bound his hands behind his back and helped him stand.

"Are you all right, ma'am?" one of the men called to me. I nodded, and they disappeared down a driveway on the left. I spotted a sign at the end of the drive.

PTERION ACRES
CENTER FOR PSYCHIATRIC PRIORITIZING
AND IMPULSE CONTROL

"The worst part is"—I poked at my salad—"I'm still not sure if it really happened. The guy looked just like John the Baptist out on a locust binge." It was a miserable feeling, losing touch with reality.

"Of course it was real." Jif centered the Roy Rogers sweepstakes placard on the table. "Those crazies get loose all the time. The man in the cemetery was real, wasn't he?"

"Yeah," Fran chimed in. "What about the hung man?"

I choked on my soda. "You mean the *hanged* man?"

Fran scrunched up her face. "That's what I said."

"No," Jif giggled. "You said the *hung* man."

"Big deal. What's the difference?"

They all laughed. Suddenly I couldn't. The image of John Jensen hanging in the cemetery was not funny. On the other hand, I felt like I had to set Fran straight before she said anything worse.

"See that man over there?" I nodded towards a lineman getting out of a phone truck across the lot. He tossed his hard hat through its open window and wiped a muscular arm across his brow. As he walked quick and easy past our window, a brace of tools swung back and forth on pants stretched tight across his firm behind.

"Now, *that*"—Jif anticipated my line of thinking, as we all turned our heads to watch him round the corner of the building—"is a hung man." She crossed her arms with satisfied finality. "The one Jenny found in the cemetery was a *hanged* man because he hung himself."

"I'm not so sure he did." Everyone turned their attention from the Hung Man to me.

"What do you mean? How else would he have gotten there?" Elena's eyes were wide.

Fran chomped meditatively on her burger. "You think someone else hung him there? *Murdered* him?" The word hovered uncertainly in the air. It was a word used on television programs, a word used to describe things that happened in the city. It wasn't a word you ever needed to use when you talked about the day-to-day events in Clark County.

"The detective on the case," I began, and then lowered my voice, "Sergeant Cloud, was at the funeral—"

"I can't believe you went to that," Jif interrupted. "Why would you—"

"Hold on a minute, Jif," Elena said. "I went with Jenny to the house afterward—I wanted to pay my respects, too." She patted Jif's arm in a gentle, absentminded way. "Let Jenny finish what she was going to say."

I spoke so quietly that they all leaned forward to hear. "He never actually *said* so, but I think he doesn't buy that suicide bit."

"But if the man didn't hang himself, how could anyone make it look like he did?" Elena, in her distraction, was actually eating some of her fried chicken.

Fran got a wicked look in her eye. "What would you do if . . . ?" It was the opening line of a game we'd been playing for years. Something told me this round was going to be a lot heavier than "the most embarrassing moments" sort of topics we usually tackled.

"What would you do if you wanted to kill someone but you didn't want to fry for it?" Fran looked at each of us in turn. "How could you kill him and make it look as if he'd hung himself?"

"Lots of ways." Before Jif had stuffed her car trunk with all fifty-four volumes of the *Great Books of the Western World* series, she used to read three mysteries a week while waiting to pick up kids for carpool. "You could strangle him with a rope in his sleep," she said, "and then take him to St. O's for an instant replay."

"You could poison him and then take him there and hang him." Elena smacked her lips over a chicken bone.

"Naaa." Jif shook her head. "That would show up on autopsy."

"Potassium wouldn't." Elena slathered some jam on her biscuit. I wondered what on earth *she* had been reading lately.

"But the needle mark would."

"Oh. Well."

"Or there's this karate thing you could do"—I reached out and pinched the back of Fran's neck—"that knocks a person out for a little while, so you can do whatever you want with them."

"Sounds hokey to me." Fran brushed my hand away from her neck.

"Probably *is* pretty hokey. On the way home from track, Phillip was telling Steve Bradbury how he'd seen it on Channel Sixty-four. You know, one of those movies where they're speaking Japanese and they give you Chinese subtitles?"

"If it was in Japanese, how did he know that's what it was about?" Elena wanted to know.

I had to laugh. "Easy. He's fourteen."

"Well, we all know the hung—*hanged*—man was real," Fran said. "And I know that the guy on New Barn Road was real."

"How do you know?" I asked.

"Because last week my mother saw Jesus on the offramp of I-95."

"Sounds like a hit tune on WCRN," I observed.

"What's that?"

"The new country and western station in Baltimore." I improvised a few bars for her:

Last week my mother saw Jesus—(plunk plunk)—
On the offramp of I-95—(plunk plunk plunk)

"But she did," Fran said. "And he had the same card—'The end is near'—and the same sheet and everything. It was probably the same guy. So, you see, what you saw was real. What else would it have been?"

"Carpool Fatigue," I said. "I read about it somewhere. It's like shell shock, only you don't get V.A. benefits. They just fill up your gas tank and send you back to the front." I formed the letter *A* with some of Elena's french fries.

"Why do you drive down those weird roads, anyway?" Fran ate the *A*.

"I like to see where they go."

"I've always wanted to know what was down that creepy little dirt road that has the sign for the Elk Glen dehydrator." Elena handed her last piece of chicken to Fran.

"So, why don't you drive down it?" I formed a french fry L.

"It's too spooky looking. Besides, what's a dehydrator? It sounds like a place they take dead cows, to make them into Slim Jims—you know—those beef jerky things at the Jiffy-Stop?"

"Yuck," said Fran.

"You ought to check it out anyway, Elena." I stood up to leave.

"Maybe. Just stop worrying about seeing John the Baptist on New Barn Road," Elena said, patting my arm. "Give yourself a break." She looked up at me with enormous, dark brown eyes. "You've got too many things on your mind. You ought to do something nice for yourself. Something you've really been wanting to do. Give yourself a break."

"I don't know what that would be." I felt really tired. Too tired to think. "What would you do if you wanted to treat yourself?"

"Get my nails done," said Fran.

"Clean out the garage," said Jif.

"Sleep through the night," Elena sighed.

At two-thirty that afternoon I drove all the way down the private lane at Elk Glen Country School before I remembered that the girls had to stay late for choir practice. I had an hour and a half to kill.

"Something nice for yourself." Elena's voice echoed in my mind.

I ran the gauntlet of station wagons, drove back to the main road, and turned left. In eight minutes I was pulling into the dusty parking lot at Ganton's Farm.

Thirty-one airplanes gleamed in the late-afternoon sun. I felt I had finally come home.

Chapter Nine

NO ONE WAS IN the open-sided shed across the drive, and no one answered when I knocked on the door of the trailer marked GANTON'S AIRFIELD: OFFICE. And COME ON IN, said a sign on the door.

"Anybody here?" I called. No answer. The place was comfortably cluttered. There were several desks, a phone, and a bulletin board. A coffee maker and stacks of clean mugs covered the counter next to a humming refrigerator. But it was the wonderfully grungy old sofa along the far wall that made me think of the World War I "ready room" on display at the Air and Space Museum in Washington. I half expected a couple of stringbean young men in leather jackets and silk scarves to amble in and help themselves to hot java.

The back door led out onto a large deck, where someone had left some greasy work gloves and a can of Schlitz. I looked down the grass runway and beyond. To my way of thinking, it was the most gratifying sort of perspective. To the right of the runway were the planes, some of them thoroughbreds, some real dogs, but most of them just sturdy little birds, the kind that would get you there and back without you having to think too much about it.

It was like coming home from two years at a fat farm and having carte blanche at Mama Leone's. I ran down the steps and began devouring every detail of every plane on the line. I was peering in the window of a cherry-red Stinson when someone on his hands and knees backed up against the two front seats and said a word that, although I couldn't quite make it out through the glass, I knew from its delivery was distinctly rude.

"Mr. Stilson." I tapped on the window and laughed at his startled expression. "From the Honda shop, remember? You said to come out sometime."

He crawled over to the cabin door and pushed it open. "Forget the Stilson—call me Bud. Come on board. I was tightening down a seat and lost the damned nut. Maybe you can find it—I give up."

It smelled so good inside the Stinson, I could hardly stand it. Vinyl and dust and the sweet smell of aviation fuel went to my head like Dom Pérignon. I ran my hand over the carpeting. Beneath the seat I could see a tiny glint of metal. I knelt down and reached as far as I could.

"Nice body," he said. I nearly dropped the nut.

"What?" I handed it to him and maneuvered myself into one of the seats.

"The Stinson. It's got a nice body, don't you think?"

"Oh yeah, sure." Mae West must have been rolling. I wondered if my face was red.

"But it's the engine that's a beauty. Listen to this." He yelled, "Clear!" and hit the starter, and my ears were filled with the sweetest sound on earth.

"Ohhhh," I moaned, slumping back against the headrest. "That's *won*-derful." Then, "Oh!" I exclaimed, almost immediately, straightening my spine and drawing my arms tight against my sides. It was *too* wonderful.

"I—I've got to go!" I made for the cabin door.

"Wait," he said and shut off the engine. "Is something wrong? What's the matter? What's your name?"

I was already halfway to the trailer, churning along in my Ree-
boks and wondering how Cinderella had managed in glass slippers.

Feeling a little safer in the car, I drove back to the main road
and tried to settle my thoughts. At the bottom of a hill, I pulled
into a tight curve, and the June issue of *Flying* slid out from under
the seat.

"Get back under there," I said, shoving it with my foot. Just
then, a rabbit leaped into my path, and I swerved and cursed and
four more issues shot out and slithered around under my feet.

What if I've killed it? I thought, looking into the rearview mirror,
expecting to see a twitching lump in the road. This is an omen. I
never should have come out here. . . .

I caught sight of the rabbit moving fast as it cleared the bank
and disappeared into a thicket.

It was an omen, all right. But it took me a while to figure out
what it meant.

It had been raining since 5:30 A.M. I could see that today was
going to be one of those "damp, drizzly Novembers of the soul,"
when every van would cut in front of me, every traffic light would
be red, and every other driver on the road would be picking his
nose.

In the back seat Phillip and Vince Kublik were not asleep enough
to snore and not awake enough to talk about sex. Who could ask
for more? I drove the two semicomatose fourteen-year-olds to
swim practice and hoped they would awaken by the time they hit
the water.

It wasn't a bad time, I told myself, waiting in the car during the
boys' practice. No phone. No kids. Automatically, I pulled out a
back issue of *AOPA Pilot*. But this time when I saw the airplane
on the cover, I could almost smell it; I could almost hear the sweet
sound of the engine. It had been dumb to go out to the field.
Dumb, dumb, dumb. I flipped open the magazine and forced myself
to concentrate on an article.

*A similar encounter with vertigo can arise after taking off
towards a "black hole" (such as a body of water) on a dark night
in VFR conditions when the horizon is not visible.*

"Mom!" Phillip was knocking on the car window. "Let us in." It hadn't seemed like an hour, but there they were, wet hair and all. Back to the real world. I hadn't driven a mile before they'd steamed up the windows. What was it about adolescent boys that made them defeat even the strongest defrosting system?

The boys spoke as if I weren't there.

"Did you see Ali Foster's boobs in that yellow sweater in English?" Phillip panted.

"Yeah. Who could miss 'em? You going to homecoming?" Vince's knees poked through the front seat and into my back. Why do swimmers have such bony knees?

"Nah," Phil said. "I wanted to go with Sandra Wisnewski, but Roy's taking her."

Who was Sandra Wisnewski? Did she get good grades? Did she live nearby? Why couldn't she have waited for Phillip to ask her— had she no taste?

Phillip belched.

"Way to go, Phil. You got some on the window."

"Did you hear about Billy Timmel's mother?" Phillip asked Vince.

I had. It had been a source of yet another "What Would You Do If?" at lunch with my friends last week. "What would you do if you were waiting in the Super Saver parking lot for your daughter to get off the Holy Savior school bus, and a guy comes up to your car and yells, 'Hand over your purse'?" There were the predictable answers, with Jif finishing off: "I'd run over his foot with the car."

But the real incident hadn't gone by the numbers. When poor Mrs. Timmel had quickly tried to pass her pocketbook out of her car window, the shoulder strap had hung up on the gearshift, and the lousy thief had fired a sawed-off shotgun at her, right through the car door. She was in Shock-Trauma, struggling to recover from twelve hours of abdominal surgery, and the stupid jerk who had put her there was probably bragging in some bar in Baltimore about how he had eluded the police on foot, with dogs and helicopters in hot pursuit.

"Bill Timmel told me all about it. They still haven't found the creep." Vince's knees jabbed the seat in indignation.

"Mr. Copley, in Psych, said that the police can tell a lot about a guy like that just from how he acted." Phillip coughed for emphasis. "They can narrow it down to just a few suspects."

Phillip spoke with such assurance, that authority with which all fourteen-year-olds spoke—even when saying things like "If you hold your breath while you're doing it, the girl won't get pregnant," or "The police give you fifteen miles over the limit before they'll stop you for speeding"—that I was almost ready to believe him.

But then he said it. "The guy that shot Mrs. Timmel, according to all the facts they put together, he was a certain type . . . uh . . . what they call . . . *testicular*."

The word hung in the air. I couldn't control my reaction any longer.

"HAH!" My sudden laugh exploded against the windshield and set off shock waves of guffaws in the back seat. The car, pulling into Vince's driveway, shook.

"Testicular?" Tears were running down my cheeks.

"Maybe that wasn't the word," Phillip defended himself between our shrieks. "But it was close to that."

"Way to go, Phil." Vince hooted and pounded on Phillip's arm. *"Testicular!* Yeah, that's it: Anyone who'd do something that nasty would have to have a lot of balls." He backed out of the car and dashed up the sidewalk.

When we got home I rousted the two girls out of bed, made juice and cinnamon toast for everyone, shoved Phil out the door to the bus stop, and put in a load of wash before Patsy and Linnea and I piled back into the car to begin the next round of carpooling.

"You have sleepers in your eyes, Linnea." Patsy's foot tapped an arrhythmic code on the back of my seat.

"Do not."

"Do too. Eye boogers."

"Maaaa-um!"

I switched on the car radio to drown out the bickering. We stopped to pick up Crista Galli.

"A hunnerd bottles of beer on the wall . . ." Patsy's clear voice fought against the radio's volume. Oh hell, I thought.

The other two joined in: ". . . *Hunnerd bottles of beer.*"

It was a long, enumerative drive to Elk Glen. At least Linnea had eventually fallen asleep in the back seat. The inventory would stop when the others got out.

At Elk Glen, the doomed oak tree stood tall and defiant within the ribbon perimeters of the future high school. How long, I wondered, before they cut it down and started gouging a foundation out of the stony earth? I followed an enormous Chrysler station wagon down the drive, watching it slosh and wallow its way over the speed bumps.

The Honda zipped over a hill on Benson Mill Road. The rain, I knew, would be cold and bone-chilling if I were to get out and walk in it. But from the snug interior of the car, I enjoyed the way the droplets on the side windows transformed the trees, with their few remaining leaves of red and gold and copper, into a jewellike scene by Seurat. As I slowed to make the turn at Hilltop Road, I could see the glitter of the raindrops on the wild asters and ryegrass that had gone to seed by the side of the road.

"You should have on a raincoat, Linnea." Matty Kohlrausch was wearing a lime-green raincoat embellished with small navy-blue pheasants, and black galoshes that came up to his kneecaps. His sou'wester hung down over his eyes, primarily because he had it on backwards, causing him to thump into the side of the front seat before he finally felt his way to the back of the car.

"I'll be OK, Matty." Linnea was used to Mister Fuss-It.

"Your feet'll get wet," he warned.

"I'm just going to go right into the school," Linnea sniffed.

"But if there's a puddle, your feet'll get wet and you'll have to sit in wet shoes all day and then you'll get sick."

I tried to pay attention to the discussion on the radio, but the fate of the golden rain frog just didn't cut it.

Of course, there was a minor ocean in front of St. O's doorway, and Linnea plowed right through it. I could see Matty shaking his prissy little finger at the child as she squished up the steps into the building.

· · ·

By the time I'd stopped at the Super Saver, filled the gas tank, and bought replacement windshield-wiper blades, I had fifteen minutes to get home, unload the groceries, and get back to St. O's in time to pick up the children, one of whom, if certain predictions proved accurate, would be deathly ill because of wet feet.

"Matty," I asked over grilled cheese sandwiches and tomato soup, "why did your mother go back to work at the insurance company?"

Although Mrs. Kohlrausch, the mother of five children, couldn't share carpool because of her job, she did get home in time to watch Linnea while I made my afternoon run and got dinner ready. Crista Galli's mother, and Pontine Kohler's, too, had gone back to work, leaving me to take up the carpooling slack. Oh sure, they reciprocated in other ways, driving my kids to evening and weekend activities, even keeping them when Berlie and I had slipped away for a two-day second honeymoon in White Sulphur Springs last year. But I wondered if the complicated juggling of schedules and responsibilities the other women went through was worth the money they earned. Why did they do it?

Matty looked me dead-level in the eye. "Mommy said she went back to work because if she drove carpool one more year, she'd go nuts."

We all traipsed around the mall after lunch to return a sweater Patsy hadn't liked and to find a pair of shoes that Linnea would agree to wear until they no longer fit. I thought about making her sign her name in blood at the time of purchase, but it wasn't the sort of thing other shoppers would condone, unless they had four-year-olds themselves.

Then it was time to drop the kids off at Mattie's house while I made the afternoon run to Elk Glen.

"Pontine," I couldn't keep myself from asking, "why did your mother go back to school full-time?" Mrs. Kohler was working on a doctorate in psychology.

"She said if she didn't get out of the house, she'd go crazy," Pontine replied.

Someone in the back seat was sneaking a Heath Bar. I could smell it. I thought I might kill for it if there were any still left.

"That's what my mom told my dad," Crista added. "And he said, 'If you go nuts, Doris, how would we know?' " The girls giggled.

If the other mothers had stayed home, Pterion Acres might have given us all group psychiatric rates. As it was, I'd probably have to check in solo, flying my Honda and talking with the dog. They'd make me pay full fare.

"The way I figure it," I said as I picked all the onions out of my taco salad, "it'll take me two or three months to go over the FARs—the Federal Aviation Regulations—and another couple of months to brush up on the flying, and then, assuming I've passed my medical, I'll be ready to pass my flight check. But it's the flying time that's going to cost money."

"How much?" Jif had finished a Wendy's special number three and was lining up packets of condiments with regimental precision across the black-and-white mail-order advertisements immortalized in the tabletop Formica.

"A thousand dollars, maybe."

Jif whistled. "Where are you going to get that?"

"A little here, a little there. I can save it up . . . or . . ." I said, keeping my face straight, ". . . I could get an interview with Yupplettes on Wheels."

"You wouldn't!" Fran rose to the bait. Yupplettes on Wheels— Y.O.W.—was a transportation service for children of well-to-do working parents. It paid not-so-well-to-do mothers to see that the kids got to doctors' appointments and were picked up from play practice and all the other places their parents would be driving to if they weren't working in law offices or medical practices, or "consulting"—whatever *that* was.

"You wouldn't," Elena said, pushing around the beans in her bowl of chili. "Sure, we all carpool. But . . ." She furrowed her brow and looked earnestly into my eyes—I was sorry I'd teased them—"but what we do, we do for love. To do it for money . . . well, that would be so . . . so . . ." She made a helpless gesture with her hand.

"I'm just kidding."

They all sighed in collective relief.

"What about Berlie?" Fran was right. What about Berlie?

"I don't know."

"Are things going any better for you all?" Jif carefully folded her napkin into increasingly smaller triangles.

"Not really." I shrugged. "Nothing unpleasant ever happens. We just sort of tiptoe around each other. You know what I mean?"

"I know," said Fran. "I bet when you told him about finding the hung—*hanged*, man, he said, 'That's nice, dear.' "

"Just about." Berlie hadn't thought much of my theories about Sergeant Cloud and his obvious, but unspoken, idea that John had been murdered.

"That isn't one of the 'safe' subjects, is it?" Fran said. "Like 'What's for dinner?' or 'Has anyone seen the paper?' "

"Could it be, Jenny"—Jif fixed me with unblinking blue eyes—"that this flying business is just a convenient way to make something happen?"

I looked right back into her eyes. "No, it's not. I tried to tell you about it before, about wanting to fly." Suddenly I felt like I might cry. I squelched the urge with thoughts of Berlie throwing my flying magazines in the trash. "The feeling's been growing in me for a long time, but I guess I've been trying to ignore it. Now I can't."

"So what about Berlie?" Fran repeated. "How's he going to feel about this plan you've come up with?"

"I've got that figured out, too, more or less. I guess the best thing would be not to tell him until I've passed my flight check. Present him with a fait accompli."

"That might be *très stupide*," Elena said.

I shrugged. *"C'est la vie."*

Chapter Ten

"So, B.C., you got anything on those construction thefts?" Harry dabbed at his chin with a napkin.

"Still laying the groundwork, setting up contacts."

"So are you working on anything else now?"

"Beamer-bammers."

"What?" Harry put down his sub.

"Vandals. They've been sneaking up on innocent BMWs and beating the hell out of them with tire irons. Mostly in parking lots. Broad daylight. Makes a real mess."

"What've you got?"

"Nothing yet. Goldstein just put me on it."

"B.C.," Harry said, stirring his coffee slowly, "you're not doing anything about that guy in the graveyard, are you?"

I smiled. "What makes you ask a thing like that? The case is closed, right?"

"History made me ask it, B.C. A sense of history."

"What if I were? What difference would it make?"

"I don't want history to repeat itself—I like having you working here. I wouldn't want you to cook your goose with this chief too."

It was true. I hadn't been Cimonetti's favorite person.

"Yeah, well . . ." I looked out the window at the trees thrashing in the rising wind. "Don't worry. I'm only thinking about it. Can't get in trouble for thinking, right?"

"Thinking?" Harry stood up to go. "That'll get you into the worst kind of trouble there is."

"I come here to think," said Jenny Meade, resting her hand on a highly polished tombstone as if it were the shoulder of an old friend. "I didn't come here for a while, after I found John." She looked up the hill at a giant oak tree, then shrugged it off to the end of her train of thought. "But I couldn't stay away long."

"It really upset you, finding the body?" Over her shoulder, armies of paper jack-o'-lanterns, skeletons, and ghosts filled the windows of the nursery school.

"Finding *John*, that was terrible. But dead bodies? I'm used to them."

This was a strange woman. How much time *did* she spend in graveyards? "What do you mean, Ms. Meade?" I came up beside her as she began to stroll along the winding path at the base of the hill.

"Call me Jenny," she said.

"Jenny." I'd been calling her Jenny in my mind ever since the day I'd heard her talking to her dog. Should I say, "Call me Tom"— or keep a little distance, professional distance? "Call me Tom." Oh well.

"You're used to cadavers?" I asked.

When she smiled, her cheeks turned red. "My dad and I used to have a medical transport business. We flew supplies and organs for transplants all over the country."

"But that's not the same as—"

She held up her hand. "And sometimes we flew bodies from one place to another. Usually someone who had died in one place but was going to be buried somewhere else."

I could see her watching me out of the corner of her eye as we walked along.

"Dad said they were the ideal passengers: No matter how rough the landing, they never complained." Her cheeks flashed red again, as if they were channel markers for pleasant thoughts.

"What happened to your company?"

The lights went out in the channel.

"My dad died and I couldn't run it by myself."

I saw her hands, which had been swinging freely at her sides, clench into fists just before she shoved them into her jacket pockets.

"You quit flying?"

She nodded. As any fool could see, this was not her favorite topic. But I blundered on.

"Why?"

Her eyes looked like they were scanning a list a yard long. "A lot of reasons," she said, finally. "No plane, for one."

"Well, that'll do it." I wondered if I'd ever get to know her well enough for her to tell me the other reasons—the ones she wasn't talking about.

"This is where I found John," she said, and I realized we'd come to the top of the hill. We stepped into a grove of dogwoods beneath the large oak tree. "He was hanging from that branch." She pointed to a gnarled, evil-looking limb.

Noting the spot, I took her by the elbow and led her out of the grove and partway down the hill. If I'd been alone, I would have stayed up there and looked the place over, worked out the mechanics of the hanging, figured out how hard or easy it would have been. But there were so many vibes coming from Jenny Meade that there was no way I could do any such thing. Whatever was going on with her, it didn't have anything to do with hanging.

"I'm going to fly again," she said, nearly making me jump.

"Oh?" I motioned to a bench and we sat down.

"It'll take some time. It'll take some cash. But I've got a plan. And I'm going to fly."

It sounded like a litany, a wonky chant she had devised in times of stress to give herself comfort. One look in her eyes, though, and I could see it had worked.

"Look at that," she said suddenly, pointing to an enormous obelisk rising in phallic splendor just across the path from us. It had to be the largest monument in the whole place. She read the inscription aloud: "Albert Madden. Nineteen eighty-one. Building contractor." She allowed herself a tiny smile. " 'In death as in life,' it should read, 'letting bad taste triumph over good judgment.' "

"Got something against contractors?" I asked.

She shrugged. "I sure don't like what they're doing to the county. A few more years and the whole place will be completely built over. I wish the whole bunch of them would fall in a hole."

"At the rate they're being hit by thieves, you might get your wish—or at least they'll be *in the hole* if the insurance companies get tired of paying up."

"Good. Maybe they'll go away."

"Watch yourself—I might have to take you in and book you."

"What are you talking about?" She had to know I was kidding, but her eyes were larger, all the same.

"I've been looking into all the construction thefts that have been going on in the county. You wouldn't believe all the stuff that's been lifted lately."

"Harry Homeowner needs a bit of lumber to finish that deck." Her cheeks lit up again.

"That's what I thought," I said, "but the volume's too great on almost every hit."

"Maybe he's building a whole house." She looked at her watch and jumped up from the bench. "Uh-oh. I've got to hit the bank before it closes."

I raised my eyebrows.

"To put money *in*." She gave me a quick smile and a wave and was off before I could pin her down to another meeting. I could hear the Honda's soft growl as it came to life, and then quiet settled in all around me.

Too much quiet. I went to the office and pulled out the construction file and a county map and looked at the variables I had plotted on it.

I had been concentrating on where and when the thefts had occurred. Had they all taken place at the same time of day? No.

Were the sites all in the same area, following an eastward or westward path—was there *any* pattern at all? Nope. I marked the latest hit and stared at the map.

Maybe I needed more variables. I worked on the size of the take. Nothing. There were big thefts and small ones. Gradually, a particle of light dawned.

"Hah!" I said.

Crofton turned around at the next desk. "Something funny?"

"Termites," I said.

"Termites aren't funny." Such a literal man, Crofton.

"The suspects. The suspects are termites."

He just stared at me.

"If small amounts of goods are taken during the day, and large amounts are taken at night, what does that suggest to you?" To Crofton it probably suggested something about the quality of night air.

He shrugged.

"Termites. Someone working on the inside."

"Uh." In a fit of professional admiration Crofton turned around and began typing up an incident report.

But I was on a roll. I made a chronological list of all the thefts and looked at which companies were being hit and how often. No pattern. Then I highlighted what had been stolen each time. I looked at the last entry: twelve cubes of cinder block. I could see Jenny Meade's cheeks lighting up—*Maybe Harry Homeowner's building a house.*

If he were, he'd start with the cinder blocks. I ran my finger up the list to another cinder-block entry. At the very top there was yet another. After the first cinder-block thefts came nails, joists, and two-by-fours, followed by roofing, doors, and dishwashers. It was a long, detailed inventory, and when I got to the next cinder-block entry, it repeated itself in nearly the same order. I scooped up the list and the file and went down to Lieutenant Detweiler's office.

The Clark County head of detectives was a tall, thin man with such fragile, pale skin and faded blond hair that he looked almost transparent. He was addicted to Hostess Snoballs, those golfball-sized lumps of chocolate cake encased in a rubbery fist of marshmallow coated with gritty coconut, which he washed down with a fifty-fifty mixture of coffee and half-and-half. I could almost hear his arteries clogging as we went over the list. But he was a good strategist, and three hours, eight Snoballs, and ten coffees later, we had a plan that had a pretty good shot at success.

"Set aside that other thing you were working on," he said. "The BMW thing, wasn't it? And concentrate full-time on this."

So long, part-time, I thought. So long, Beamer-bammers. And so long, Jenny Meade. At least for a while.

Chapter Eleven

"This head wind is a real pisser. You think the fuel will last to Friendship, Dad?"

"Don't see how, but there's nothing between here and there. Better start looking for a place to put her down."

"You're kidding."

"Not kidding. The minute a good pilot hears a strange noise, what does he do?"

"I know—look for a smooth spot to land. But there isn't any strange—oh, Jesus, what's that? The engine's dead!"

"That's your permission to land. We're out of gas."

"But there isn't any—"

"Right over there. See? Just ride her down easy. Right over there."

"Right over there, Mom! Stop! Mom, STOP!" Patsy and Crista were squealing from the back seat and pointing to a ditch.

I checked the rearview mirror and pulled off the road.

"What is it?" This had better be good, I thought.

"We want to get that wood for Phillip." In the ditch lay several pieces of lumber that must have fallen off a truck.

"Oh, for heaven's sake!"

"But Mom, you know he'll love it."

True enough. I snaked the lumber in between the two girls and on up against the dashboard. When I closed the hatchback, I finally noticed where we were—in front of the Flower Lady's house. The wooden table had been taken in for the winter.

As I pulled back onto the road, a crosswind shook the car and bent the trees in the yard across the way. John Jensen's yard, I thought. Poor Holly. It had been about a month since his death, and I hadn't seen Holly for a week. How much of him had she put away? How much had she allowed to stay? Was there a calendar with John's handwriting on it, noting appointments he'd never honor? Were his clothes still hanging in the closet?

The wind pushed against Holly Jensen's house as if seeking some weak spot. A strong gust beat a lilac branch against the window; Holly looked up. "I'm glad John got all the storm windows fixed last winter," she told Kay. "See? He made them so you could put them up from the inside." They were in the bedroom, cleaning out the closet. "I used to make him laugh by telling him, 'John, you've made this place so tight, we might go to bed and breathe up all the air one night and wake up d—' " She broke off with a grimace. "Dead," she finished.

Her sister put down the garbage bag she had been filling with men's shoes and clothing and came around the bed and hugged her. Holly could feel Kay's tears on her shoulder. Her own tears made dark stains on the raspberry silk of Kay's blouse.

"Come on," Kay said. "Let's take a break and go outside." They went out onto the front porch and sat down on the steps, each woman automatically breaking off a sprig of dwarf hemlock and sniffing its Christmas scent. The porch was large and plain, with a rough-hewn look to it. Two wooden porch swings, each long enough to seat four, moved in the strong breeze.

"The wind's so warm. Hard to believe it's almost November." Holly rolled the hemlock between her palms. "Warm wind like this always pulls freezing weather in behind it."

"What I want to know"—Kay smiled gently at her sister—"is how did you get to feel so at home in the country? I mean, I like it and all, but it's not Bethesda, is it? How could growing up there prepare you for life out here? It's as if John came along and rescued a little country girl who'd been accidentally born into a city family."

Holly shrugged. "I don't know. Just feels right out here. Always has."

From the moment she'd first seen him at the Save the Seals rally at the Lincoln Memorial, it had all felt right. John, with his down vest and shaggy beard and that silly farmer hat. Just like that, she had found all she'd ever wanted. In six months they were married— right here in the front yard. They'd worked so hard since then. Now . . .

They looked out across the front field plowed and planted with winter wheat. Across the road and beyond another field, they could see Rebecca Stott in her garden, pulling up the last of the flower stalks and piling high the refuse of a glorious summer.

"Holly"—Kay turned to face her sister—"are you going to be able to stay on here?"

Holly stood and put her hands in her pockets. "I think so. I sure hope so. We had a fair amount of insurance."

"But with it being suicide . . . ?"

"No. It's OK. The agent said long as we'd had the policies over two years, then they'd pay off in full."

"Thank God for that."

Rebecca Stott must have caught sight of them. She waved cheerfully and dumped another armload of dead plants on the pile.

"I feel so sorry for her," Holly said.

"For Rebecca? Why?"

"Her husband's such a turd."

Kay smiled at her sister's directness. "What do you mean?"

"Oh, he's such a stingy, small-minded, selfish old coot. If he ever laughed, it would crack his face. Just a turd, that's all."

They watched Rebecca tug her straw hat down over her ears as the wind pulled at it, making her old sweater flap like a bird.

"You wonder how a man gets that way, don't you?" Kay said. "I mean, she's such a nice woman—surely he wasn't like that when she married him?"

"I don't know. She doesn't say much about him. I heard he had a hard time as a kid. But he's such a mean old crock now, I can't imagine him ever being different." Holly sat back down beside her sister.

"Men can change." Kay slowly twisted the hemlock sprig. "But she must see something in him—or else, why would she stay?"

Holly shook her head. "I don't think she believes her life could be any better. I don't think she's ever had anything to compare it with."

"But she knew how happy you and John—"

"No," Holly interrupted. "We were good neighbors and all, but when you're working hard all of the time, you don't see folks much. And she'd only come over when Stott wasn't around. To tell you the truth, I've seen more of her since John died than during the whole time he was alive."

They rose and went back into the house.

"Kay . . ." Holly hesitated. "I've been wondering about Frazier."

"You have?" Kay seemed to be holding her breath.

"Well . . . he seems to be avoiding me lately. Since John died, I mean. Do you think he really didn't want to pay for the funeral— that he just offered to be polite?"

"Oh, no, honey. It was his idea, and he wouldn't have taken no for an answer."

"Well, then, is it my imagination, do you think? I'm not sure."

"I don't know." Kay unfurled another garbage bag and began filling it. "Actually, I'm beginning to be a little worried about him myself."

"You are?" Holly sat on the edge of the bed, fingering the Double Wedding Band pattern of the old quilt. "Worried about what?"

"Oh, I don't know. Sometimes I wish he were back on the subs full time. But now he's mostly at the office.

"At the office," she repeated, her voice a ripsaw of sarcasm.

"When he's home, he doesn't talk—just sits and reads Jaguar magazines and books about life on the Riviera—stuff like that. He seems to care about things that are really not important, and not to care about the things that are." She patted a strand of her blond pageboy back into place. "At least when he had sea duty, I was sure about what he was doing—and the homecomings were great."

Holly's eyes widened. "You don't think he's having an—"

"I don't know what to think. I just don't seem to know him anymore." She perched on the footboard and tugged her challis skirt down over her knees. "Oh well, maybe it's just the job. He got another promotion—to project director at Applied Science Associates."

"He's not working today, is he?"

Kay shook her head.

"Then, where is he now?"

She shrugged her shoulders. "That's another thing that doesn't make sense. He said he was going to look at some real estate out in the country. Why would he want to do that? He hates the country. Makes him sneeze."

"Kay"—Holly emptied a drawerful of socks into the bag—"how worried are you? I mean, you're not thinking about div—"

"Holly." Kay held her hand up like a traffic cop, as if to stop the word from coming out. "Let's just say I'm very worried. Very, very worried." She stood up, went into the bathroom, and closed the door.

Holly picked up John's favorite flannel shirt from the pile on the bed. She sniffed it and rubbed her face against it; then she put it back on a hanger and hung it in with her own things.

The hand-painted sign said ELK GLEN DEHYDRATOR—TRUCK ENTRANCE—NO TRESPASSING. Claiborne turned his Mercedes 450 SL down the heavily wooded, narrow dirt road and dodged potholes for a quarter of a mile. Finally, a clearing opened up before him. On the left he passed a small stucco house with diapers and colorful shirts dancing on a clothesline out back. NO TRESSPASSING read a sign at the edge of its driveway. On the right stood a ramshackle barn surrounded by mounds of weeds and cast-off machine parts that seemed to be holding it up. Just beyond were two windowless buildings of corrugated steel, one two stories high, with wooden stairs leading to a door on the second floor, and the other, low lying and mud stained. Between them rose three wide silos slightly higher than the first building.

He glanced at a scrap of paper in his hand and got out of the car. The last building had a small door around the back that creaked when he pushed it. His eyes took a few moments to get used to the dim light. Off to his right, a ratlike movement caught his attention.

"You're early, Claiborne." Barton Stott stepped out of the shadows.

"I thought you might show me around a bit—where's this thing that makes feed pellets?"

Stott gave him a skeptical look—the crafty farmer laughing up his sleeve at the dumb city slicker. He backed out the door and into the sunlight. Squinting, he led the way to a huge horizontal tank elevated fifteen feet off the ground.

"The idea is"—Stott used the world-weary tone of a man who'd performed the same task forty million times—"to dry out fodder and compress it into a more manageable form."

He pointed to a large bin that looked like a steel coal car from a train. Except it was open at both ends and rose up at the far end when Stott pressed a button, just like the bed of a dump truck.

"Trucks take what's left after a field's been harvested—don't matter what it is—corn, oats, alfalfa, anything—and dump it here. Then, when I raise this end"—he pointed past Claiborne—"it all slides down there, and an auger chops it up and forces it up that belt."

Claiborne walked down to the far end and saw a series of sharp steel spikes on a cylinder that fed into a trough with a shining auger the width of his body. A conveyer belt led from the trough up into the horizontal tank.

"Then what?" he said.

"The tank gets real hot—up to two thousand degrees—and the stuff dries out like *that*." He snapped his brittle fingers. "Then it gets chopped up even finer, and it's forced through an extruder.

When it comes out, it's in pellets—like rabbit feed. They ship it out for all kinds of livestock feed." He looked as if he could run the entire operation in his sleep.

A car pulled in the driveway of the stucco house; Stott motioned Claiborne to follow him back to the building where they had met.

When Stott had closed the door, Claiborne quickly glanced around in the murky light and began his pitch.

"I'll get right to the point: I've been looking into this Farmland Protection Program you were talking about at the funeral. Seems to me there are a couple of loopholes in it that could mean a nice cache of money for a person who knows how to work it right."

Stott's eyes glinted in the single chink of light piercing through a gap in the roof. "Yeah?" His breath barely propelled a troupe of dust motes across the shaft of light.

"That's the way I figure it," Claiborne said. "For someone with the right amount of land that's in the right place, someone with the right amount of balls."

"You thinking about me, maybe?"

Claiborne was thinking about Stott's shriveled-up balls banging against Rebecca's silky thighs. Her thighs would be silky, wouldn't they? Even in her old-fashioned dress, there had been something extraordinary about her.

"I'm thinking about you, yes." He smiled to himself. "Let me tell you something about what I had in mind." He smiled again in the dusty darkness. . . .

To his right, on the way back down the dirt road, Claiborne glimpsed a stone structure through the trees. He slowed down. It was a tower—long abandoned, by the look of it—three or four stories high, with Gothic leaded windows and a fairly sound-looking slate roof. He drove on, then took the next right and found himself on the grounds of the Elk Glen Country School. A very old mansion formed the hub of a constellation of mismatched buildings, and in the adjoining field there were signs of new construction. He parked in the lot and casually walked off to the right and into the woods where the tower would be.

It was a beauty. Octagonal, with thick walls of limestone. He picked the rusted padlock on the door, and let himself in.

Rebecca Stott was counting the flower money from the Mason jar when her husband tracked his muddy boots through the kitchen.

"Turned real cold out there," he said, picking up a five-dollar bill from the pile and putting it into his pocket.

Rebecca stared at him—stared right on through him—and went back to her counting.

"Where's my supper?" He stood in the center of the room and sniffed like a weasel.

"It'll be ready in about ten minutes. Cheese-and-onion pie." She got up and began laying down plates and silverware for two.

She felt him watching her through narrowed eyes. He wandered over to the long dry sink, where a cookbook lay open.

"Thought you said 'cheese-and-onion pie.' " His voice, like a door hinge, set her teeth on edge.

"I did." On the table she set a jar of carefully arranged chrysanthemums, all shades of reds and golds and yellows.

"Well, in here"—he jabbed a finger at the cookbook—"it says 'quiche.' Quiche is that stuff faggots eat. What the hell made you think I'd eat something like that? Next thing you know, you'll be serving me these!" He pinched off the tiny head of a dwarf chrysanthemum and flicked it across the room.

She looked him right in the eye and said nothing.

"I'm going out to get some real food. Food for men with balls. You can eat that shit by yourself." He stamped out onto the porch, leaving the door wide open.

"Homo food!" His words rushed into the kitchen on a freezing draft as the truck pulled off into the night.

Later, Rebecca sat at the kitchen table, a warm pool of light shining on the pile of papers beside her hand. She glanced past the lace curtains at the window, checking for headlights, and picked up a document printed in green ink. The deed to the farm—her farm, left to her by her grandmother, the farm she had lived on all her life—was titled to Rebecca and Barton Stott. The retitling, twenty-five years ago when they had gotten married, was the twenty-year-old bride's gift to her hard-working husband.

But it was a gift gone sour. "It may have been your land to start with," he would say, time after time, "but I'm the one runs it. I'm the one knows how to make it pay!"

She looked out the window again, across the driveway and across twenty-five years, years where the warmth of a day's work in the garden would be chilled to freezing as soon as he walked into the room, years when her laugh could be released only when friends, who had first made sure Stott's old pickup was nowhere around, came to call.

When had he changed from the shy, self-conscious man who had worked for her grandparents, the man who had mended fences and watched her weeding the flower beds, the man who had brought her a pup when she was seventeen and had a broken leg? Was it living all alone in that forlorn house at the back of the north field before Gram died that had started it? Or did something from long before—from years spent as the oldest of eight kids in the paper-thin shack down by the river—rise in his soul and sweep away everything of value in him, just like the Patapsco River at spring flood?

Once in a while he still did something that brought to mind the man she had known when she was a young girl: an offer to drive her in to town, two tickets to the county fair. But when she consented to go, she always found herself alone, while Bart disappeared to attend to business he didn't care to discuss. But it didn't matter anymore—he hadn't offered anything in a long, long time.

She unfolded the deed and smoothed it out. For the next two hours she tried to determine how she could legally and quietly get his name off of it. When she finally put everything away and went to bed, she could see a light still burning across the fields at the Jensens'. Poor Holly, she thought, the nights must be even worse for her.

Holly Jensen couldn't sleep. She'd almost made it, but for some foolish reason she had reached out to touch John's scratchy beard, and the coldness of his pillow was like a slap in the face. No use staying in bed, she thought. Might as well get up and get something done.

She could see by the light across the way that Rebecca was still up, too, and knowing that made her feel less alone.

So this is growing up, she thought. This is the real world Kay used to tell her she had to join. It sure stunk. John didn't care whether she read the paper or wore last year's styles—jeans were jeans in his book. Miss Dawson's finishing school had been a crock. But working with John, eating their own stuff, going to bed tired— but *good* and tired—that was all she'd ever wanted. Why had it had to stop?

She was almost through cleaning out the desk in the guest room. She ran her hand over the desk's smooth writing surface. She and John had made it together their second winter in this house. . . . Well, John had done most of the work, but she had fetched the tools and held the walnut planks steady and done an unbelievable amount of sanding and waxing.

A picture of herself in her wedding gown peeped out from behind a stack of bills. The bills, of course, had to stay. But all the little scraps of paper with part numbers, names of seed varieties, re- minders of meetings—"farmer clutter," she called them—all that junk needed to be cleared out. Even John's very last message to her, she remembered, the note they'd found in his pocket, had been written on farmer clutter—on half of a receipt for twenty pounds of feed from Southern States. It was so hard to throw out anything with John's handwriting on it, but it all had to go . . . didn't it? Yes, it did. Except that last note—and the police had that.

Only one drawer was left and then she'd be done. She tugged it open and found a stack of brochures, John Deere mostly, all bound with a large rubber band. Tucked under the band was another list. She sighed and unfolded it. It looked like a wish list for farm equipment—things he'd have wanted if money hadn't been an issue—which, of course, it always had been. Only, there was a second page that was an actual order blank, filled out with some very expensive items. And a third sheet had the next five years set off in paragraphs, each describing a major improvement project they had talked about doing "someday." The descriptions were very detailed, Holly thought, as though he had actually intended to carry out the projects. She blinked back the tears. He had taken a pencil and marked a large *X* across the page. Well, that really summed it all up, didn't it? She gathered up his dreams and dropped them in the trash.

Chapter Twelve

Tuesday, Dec. 2

Deliv. envelopes
P.U. eggs

"I just don't know what to think, Jenny." Holly paced back and forth, making the blue-speckled dishes rattle in the hutch. "Most of the time," she said, "I feel like my life is a movie that sometimes I'm watching, and sometimes I'm not." And then she proceeded to describe a scene in the "Holly Jensen Story." Her account was so vivid, I felt as though I were watching too.

She told me about Rebecca Stott and her nasty man and about the trouble she thought was brewing between her sister, Kay, and her husband. From what I remembered of Frazier Claiborne from after the funeral, I suspected Kay probably had good reason to worry.

Claiborne must be a very private man, I thought. That kind is hard to live with. And he'd certainly looked like he was up to something. I wondered what.

Holly's voice brought me back to the sunlit kitchen.

"Sergeant Cloud was out here again." Her news surprised me. "You should have seen how upset he got when I told him I'd thrown away most of the stuff in John's desk." Holly's eyes grew large. She picked up two diamond-shaped pieces of calico and began stitching them together.

"I can't say I don't have a pile of questions about the way John died," she said.

She looked up from her work and then back down again. "But mostly—well, you know"—she smiled apologetically—"mostly I've been trying to understand why he did it. And, of course, there's no way to do that. He just didn't have a reason."

She put down her sewing and went to the window. "But Sergeant Cloud's line of thinking is just as ridiculous. There's not a soul on earth that would have wanted to hurt John." She shook her head at the idea.

"Anyway, I told him not to worry about the papers I'd thrown out—they were still in the trash can by John's desk. He put them all in a big envelope and went off whistling. The whistling made me cry."

She smiled sheepishly. "I was glad he was already driving off. John used to whistle." She sighed. "It's stuff like that that gets you. Just little things that sneak up on you and smack you in the face."

"I know what you mean." I got up to go. "Do you think he'll be back—Sergeant Cloud, I mean?" I hadn't heard from him for a while. I wondered what he'd been up to.

"I don't know. I don't think he's supposed to be working on this, you know?"

I nodded.

"He's a funny man," she said. "He looks so rough and tough, but when he asked me all those questions about John—oh, I don't know." She shook her head. "He reminds me of one of those Indians I've read about—you know—the kind that asks a rabbit's forgiveness before he kills it for supper."

"He *is* an Indian," I said. "Didn't you know?"

Holly shook her head. "Oh, jeez."

I wanted to ask her more about Cloud's questions, but I had to get home and start a nice dinner: Berlie was home for a change. I carefully backed up the car in Holly's drive and reminded myself to hit the Super Saver for some fresh grapefruit.

The trunk of the Honda was full of envelopes, some stuffed, some not. Ever since I'd worked out The Plan, my scheme for really getting airborne, I had been taking on any kind of job— "piecework," they called it—to feed the savings account I had opened in my name. It was impossible to fit any regular job into my carpooling schedule—even part-time work wouldn't accommodate my ridiculous driving obligations. But piecework filled the bill.

In November I had delivered phone books. Now, in December, I drove and stuffed envelopes, stuffed envelopes and drove. When Phillip complained about life's latest injustice—an essay assignment or a new zit—my customary wit's end response, "Stuff it!" took on whole new layers of meaning—for me, anyway.

The only one (thank God) who seemed to notice my new activities was Bacall, and she was not at all happy about them. Piecework, whether phone books or envelopes or reams of coupons to be hooked on doorknobs from here to Ulyssia, took up too much room in the car and left not even one little corner for a dog. A good dog. A quiet dog. A dog who told me she would do *anything* for a ride in the car. A dog who had made her feelings known by regressing into puppyhood.

"Bacall!" I walked into the kitchen and picked up the remains of Linnea's snow boot.

Bacall looked around to see who I could possibly mean.

"You! There's nobody else here."

"What's the matter with Bacall?" Berlie said. He was trying to readjust after a week in Cleveland.

"What do you mean?" I knew perfectly well what he meant.

"She's bonkers. Look at her—she's ten years old and she's chasing her tail. Stop that!"

Bacall had paused to chew on the leg of the solid maple table.

"She's mad at me for not taking her for a ride."

"So, why don't you take her for a ride?"

"The kids have gotten too big. There's not enough room any-more." I said a little prayer that Berlie wouldn't look in the hatch-back and find the trunkload of envelopes. I really wasn't ready to deal with his opposition until all the elements of The Plan were in place.

Berlie poured himself a Dubonnet on ice, sat down at the kitchen table, and watched me chop onions. "You'd have plenty of room if you got a station—"

"Don't start with me, Berlie." I waggled the knife in his direc-tion, dropping a few chunks of onions on the floor. Bacall was on them in an instant and scarfed them down.

"Oh no! Look out—she's headed your way." I knew what was going to happen next.

Berlie didn't. "So?"

Bacall walked over to Berlie, peed on his foot, and crossed the room to the basement steps, galumphing down into the darkness without so much as a backward glance.

Berlie stared at his left shoe and the puddle surrounding it. "First Cleveland, and now this. What in hell's going on?"

I patted a big wad of paper towels around his foot. "It's the onions. Every time she gets hold of raw ones, her bladder goes kerflooey." I dumped the wet towels in the trash and handed him another fistful. "Here. I've got to pick up Phil. Watch the stew for me, will you?" I nodded towards a pot on the stove and grabbed my jacket and purse.

"Wait," Berlie said, and dashed down the basement steps—*squish-thump, squish-thump* all the way to the bottom. In a mo-ment he reappeared, dragging Bacall by the collar. "Here," he said. "Take her for a damned ride."

Bacall leaped into the car in a single bound.

"I know it's been too long," I said to her. "But I've made six hundred and fifty dollars so far. I just hope nothing happens to screw it up. That's my worst fear . . . now that I've allowed myself to hope." We waited for the light at Route 40 and St. Obturator's Lane. The roadwork was completed, and the barriers had been taken down. I couldn't see any difference.

Bacall sneezed and looked out the car window.

"I mean, I worry that the furnace might die or some other disaster will hit and eat up my stash."

Bacall continued to stare out the window.

"Oh, come on. I'm sorry you haven't been able to come along lately. Try to understand."

A belch rang out from the back seat.

"It won't be forever. I promise. Anyway, when I get the plane, you can come with me on every trip."

Bacall's ears pricked up. She tilted her head to one side.

"Yes, up in the air. In the plane."

Bacall panted softly in my ear. A comforting feeling, if you don't mind the damp.

Chapter Thirteen

"BERLIE?" I CALLED FROM THE BEDROOM. I put on a pair of the heavy woolen socks Berlie used to guard against the steady chill of caves and pulled a bright, Peruvian-style sweater, thick as a rug, over corduroy pants. It was cold enough to convince me that winter was here to stay.

"Berlie?" I passed bedroom doors closed tight against Sunday-morning intruders, and went down the stairs. There were no signs of life except for a newspaper that seemed to have detonated upon contact with the living room floor. The components of a carbide lamp lay in a tidy line across the kitchen table, and the sharp smell of acetylene filled the air, as if a modernized Mephistopheles had come to snatch an overdue soul down to Hell.

"Berlie!" I called down to the basement.

"What?"

I could hear him ratting around under the basement steps. "What are you doing?"

"I'm *mffuhffmmmffumff.*"

I went down the stairs and found him, his rear end sticking out of a pile of sleeping bags. He had on his beloved sweat suit, the grey one turned a permanent brown by cave mud.

"You're *what*?"

He snaked out from under the pile. "I'm planning our summer vacation." He held a stack of AAA tour guides in his hand.

"Oh." I let him lead me into the family room half of the basement, where I sat down on the grey velvet sofa.

"How does Mount Rushmore sound to you?" He plunked the North/South Dakota tour book in my lap.

"Mount Rushmore? In the Badlands?" I blinked up at him as if someone had just awakened me with a flashlight.

"Close. Buffalo. Indians. And we could head west and see Yellowstone if you want. What do you think?"

"How would we get there?"

"Oh." He stepped over the chrome-and-glass coffee table and sat down close beside me. "We can take our time driving there. I have three weeks I need to use up before the end of July."

I didn't like the way he was avoiding my eyes. Suddenly the light dawned. I turned and gave him my most piercing look.

"Don't even *think* of hitting up any of your buddies. I'm not staying with any cave men. Think of the children—they could be warped for life."

"What do you mean?" He knew full well what I meant. It was entirely possible for a caver to travel the whole length and breadth of the country without ever staying in a motel. All he had to do was call up another caver and announce he was going to be in the area, and, like a particularly earthy chain letter, he'd be passed from friend to friend along the cavers' underground railroad.

"We don't go unless we stay in motels. Real ones, with our own beds and our own bathrooms."

"But—"

"No buts." The first time we had stayed with cave men, I had found out what an uninhibited lot they really were. Of course you have to drop some of the niceties of social behavior when you're crawling head-to-ass in the gloom of some slimy cavern. But when they got back to their own houses, they didn't seem to readjust.

They walked down the halls naked—"Just going to hit the shower for a second, Mrs. Meade—won't be a minute"—and scratched themselves right where they itched, and discussed things at the table that canceled out the noncaver's appetite.

"Think of the children," I added. "It's hard enough to try to get them to be normal as it is."

"Oh, all right. Motels all the way." He lowered his head as if he were either going to sink into a depressed state or butt me like a goat.

He made a direct hit below my left shoulder, his head quickly sliding down to burrow into first one breast and then the other.

Well, I thought, I'd been complaining that we weren't on the same wavelength. I supposed this was one way to do some fine tuning. Berlie's way, anyhow.

"*Mmmuh.* Your sweater's itchy." He sat up and looked at the bright pattern, sliding his hand up underneath the front. "Where'd you get it?"

I grabbed his wrist and watched his hand struggle under the wool like something from an old Peter Lorre horror movie. "Fran made it for me. Great sweater, isn't it?"

"Tell her to make the next one angora." He gave me a sudden smile. "Jenny, girl, I've been thinking about this since you came home from the grocery store yesterday in those pink slacks." He put his entire head under the sweater, toppling me over and stretching me out along the length of the sofa. The guidebooks slid off my lap and onto the carpet—Berlie's Tactical Error Number One.

He had unhooked my bra when I caught sight of the book lying open a few inches from my face. "*Jewel Cave,*" the dog-eared page read, "*one of the longest caves in the world, it is still being explored.*"

I pulled myself upright so fast that Berlie fell between the sofa and the coffee table.

"What'd you do that for?" He made a quick lunge at me—Tactical Error Number Two—but I stooped to pick up the tour guide and he grabbed thin air.

"Berlie"—there was no point hiding my suspicions—"what are you up to?"

He moved a little closer and grinned. "Well, I was just about up to your left tit, and I was almost—"

"That's not what I meant." I pushed him away. "Look at this. 'The Spelunking Tour . . . follows unimproved passageways and is only for the most hardy.' " I gave him my fiercest carpool look. "*You* are going caving on *our* vacation."

"Well," he began, but I didn't give him a chance to finish.

"*Well*'s just a hole in the ground," I sniffed—it's easy to be trite when you're pissed—"and holes in the ground are what you can damn well stay out of, at least on our vacation. You need to spend what little time you have with your children. They hardly see you now—and you expect us to drive around looking at stone presidents and herds of buffalo being stalked by herds of stupid humans with stupid cameras, while you're off somewhere getting stuck in some tunnel covered with bat shit?"

"Guano," he said quietly. "Bat guano. And I've never gotten stuck in my life."

"There's always a first time." I poked a finger into his belly. "You're not getting any younger, you know."

He looked hurt. "Of course not. Who is? But look here—" He got up and went into the laundry room and came back with a wire coat hanger. "I can still fit through any tight spot—" He pulled the hanger into an O and held it over his head. In a few seconds he had worked his arms and head through the hoop, and had it halfway down his chest.

I didn't know whether to laugh or to cry.

I laughed. He always could make me laugh; I'd give him that. Holding the hanger steady for him, I leaned over and bit his behind as he wriggled it, with great effort, past the wire.

"Hah!" he said. Then, "Ouch!" as I bit him again. We tumbled onto the sofa.

"But, Berlie," I said from somewhere under his armpit, "I'm serious about this."

"Oh baby—me too!" He held me so tightly I couldn't move at all.

"About the caving. I'm serious about the caving."

"Aw, hell. Can we talk about it later?" He looked at the clock on the VCR. "At ten-fourteen, maybe?"

I relaxed a little in his arms. "Ten-fourteen? For sure?" I knew that if he promised, he'd make good on it.

"Absolutely."

I nibbled his ear.

"Jenny," he said softly.

He let go of me only long enough to dash up and lock the basement door.

"Get ready, Miss Jenny!" he called as he ran back down the stairs, flinging off clothing right and left. "Here comes Caaaave Maaaaaaan!" And he made a joyous swan dive onto the sofa.

At ten-fourteen the conversation went much more smoothly.

"It's not only the time you spend in caves, Berlie." I was frying bacon, and kid noises were coming from upstairs. "It's the danger, too." I waved my hand before he could speak. "It *is* dangerous. You keep going on and on about me flying, but flying's about forty times safer than what you do down in those holes."

Berlie abandoned the carbide lamp he had taken apart to clean and got out a carton of eggs and a pottery mixing bowl. "You're saying flying's safe? Come on—suppose your engine quits?" He broke an egg on the edge of the bowl with particular force.

This obviously wasn't going to be a good time to bring up The Plan.

"I can land without an engine. I've done it. But what do you do if you're going down some hole and your rope breaks?"

Someone slammed a bathroom door.

"Bounce?" He dropped a whole egg into the bowl and laughed.

"Come on, Berlie. If it's a long fall, you get to say, 'Oh, shit!' If it's only forty or fifty feet, then all you get is 'Oh—' "

He fished out the unbroken egg and cracked it. "What about midair collisions?" He smacked another egg against the rim of the bowl.

"Look, if you keep your head out of your ass and fly where you're supposed to, you do OK. And besides, most of the airports

I fly—" I corrected myself, "*flew* out of weren't that busy. It's not the problem the papers make it out to be." I turned the bacon over with a long-pronged fork.

"Oh yeah? What about—"

"What about if the cave *caves in*? Interesting expression, don't you think? What about that?"

"Now, most caves are really very stable. Most caves—"

"But you don't go in *most caves*, do you? No, you have to go in *wild* caves—and that's just what they are. That cave you and Andy are mapping—you don't know how stable it is, do you? Of course not!" I waved the long fork in the air for emphasis. "You don't know, because NOBODY ELSE HAS EVER BEEN IN IT!"

At that moment the bacon gave an enormous *pop!* and I jumped back from the stove—too late. My forearm felt like it had been napalmed. Berlie rushed to my side and peeled my fingers off of the burn.

"Let me see. God, that's awful." He held my arm under the faucet and turned on the cold water. It helped some. I leaned up against him, not for support, just for the comfort.

Phillip clattered into the kitchen and draped himself all over a chair—an accident waiting to happen.

"What's for breakfast? I'm starving."

"Set the table, Phil. Your mother's just given an inch of flesh so that you might have bacon." Berlie rushed to get between the lamp parts and the Pack Rat. "Leave the parts where they are, son."

"I've been wondering, Dad." Phil picked up the gasket and quickly spun it around on his index finger just before Berlie snatched it back. "What would you think about me maybe going on a caving trip with you sometime?"

Berlie's eyes lit up. "I'd think it was great." His voice deepened dramatically, as if he knew someone was eavesdropping and he wanted to be sure they heard. "I'd get to spend more time with you and all." He grinned. "But your mother here"—he nodded his head in my direction—"she thinks caving's too dangerous."

"Aw, Mom." Phillip gave me an exasperated look.

I turned off the cold water and dried my arm with a towel.

"What I think is, when it comes to danger, working in this house is number one." I dumped the eggs into the hot skillet.

"True, true." Berlie was eager to agree. He began putting the lantern parts back together.

"But *caving*," I said the word, trying for the same tone a preacher would use to say *fornication*, "*caving* is next on the list."

"How about driving?" Phil chimed in. "Driving's pretty dangerous, and you do it all the time."

"Phil's right," Berlie said. "Driving's more dangerous than caving, and—"

"Keep out of this, Phillip." I slapped a plate of bacon and eggs down in front of him.

Phillip stuffed his mouth full of eggs before he spoke. "And a perfon in a car haf a greater chanfe of biting the duft"—he finally paused to swallow—"than they do in an airplane. So flying's safer than driving." I slipped him another piece of bacon.

"Phillip's right. I'd be safer if I stopped cooking and driving carpool, and started flying again."

My son looked at me as if he were an extra who'd accidentally walked onto the wrong movie set.

"Yeah, Phillip, stay out of this." Berlie almost had the lamp reassembled. "What he meant to say was, you'd be safer if you quit cooking bacon—it's bad for the heart, anyway—and got a bigger, more substantial car. Like a Taurus station wagon, maybe. Or a Bronco, with roll bars and—"

I took a quick glance down at the counter and grabbed the first thing that came to hand. It was heavy and awkward, but it gave me great satisfaction to throw it at him with all my might.

But by the time William Davies's *Caves of West Virginia* knocked over Berlie's chair, Berlie and his lamp were halfway around the corner, with Phillip not far behind.

Chapter Fourteen

Such a bear you send me, Black Cloud. Mary Tall Dog and Jim Cree, Wiley and Jack Lame Deer, lots people come to see it. They say it is more like a bear than a bear is. When will you come home to name it?

Love,
Aunt Wiyanna

Sometime. Maybe next year, I thought. Not now. Cold weather was seriously moving in, and I wanted to get the construction case wrapped up before building activity slowed down for the winter. Besides, once the snows came, even a really stupid thief would think twice before he left an incriminating trail of footprints in the whiteness.

I stuffed Wiyanna's note into the pocket of my jeans and watched Harry Grimes scan the lunchroom before he spotted me and came over to my table.

"B.C., how's it going?" He brushed some crumbs off the chair before he sat down heavily. "You get those construction thefts nailed down?"

I looked at him, checking to see if that was the first shot in a pun war. Evidently not; he looked pretty innocent. I explained my theory of the house-building thieves, neglecting to tell him where I had gotten the idea. I didn't want to get into another argument about Jenny Meade, although I made a mental note to call her. Just to thank her for the lead.

"So I told Detweiler I had a pretty good idea what would be stolen next, but I couldn't pin down which site would be hit. So that let out the possibility of a stakeout—it would take too many cops. Anyway, Detweiler is a real techno-nut. He wanted to go for electronic systems instead of visual surveillance. I said, 'What the hell—as long as I supervise the deal.' "

Harry folded the wax paper from his sandwich and put it in his lunch bag. "Did it work?"

"Sort of." I had to laugh. "We've been experimenting with all kinds of sensing devices. The first one was a photoelectric cell that sets off a signal in the patrol cars."

"I heard about that," Harry said.

"Bet you didn't hear the whole deal."

Harry raised his bushy grey eyebrows. There wasn't much that didn't get around the station.

"We figured two-by-fours would be hit next, so at two sites we set the sensors high on the stacks of lumber, so strolling opossums and raccoons wouldn't trigger them. Jack Layton and me were cruising in the area, and when the alarm went off in the car, we raced out to Bennett's Landing, and there was a ten-point buck staring us down in our headlights.

"The next try was with a motion-activated signal. We caught two forty-pound groundhogs screwing each other's brains out. They never even knew we were there. Later that night a Saint Bernard set it off.

"So now we're setting up an infrared sensor. I can't wait to see what *that* gets us." I rose to leave.

"Probably a couple of humans screwing their brains out." Harry folded up his lunch bag and tucked it in his pocket.

. . .

The once-grey carpet around my desk looked as if it had sucked up almost as much coffee as the people who worked there had, and the fluorescent lights bathed the whole room in flickery blue. I pulled out a file marked JENSEN and extracted the manila envelope that contained the papers from John Jensen's desk. "Farmer clutter," his widow had called them when she had given me the pile.

I dealt the contents out across my desk as if playing a variation on solitaire and reared back in my chair to assess what I had: I had a shitload of receipts for feed and farm equipment, articles clipped from farming magazines, lists of chores and supplies to be bought, and catalogs for all kinds of machinery.

I leafed through the articles: manure management, "Corn Today," wheat-base options (whatever *they* were), and "At Last! A Safe System for Handling Insecticides!" Pretty run-of-the-mill, except for that last one. Insecticides. The old pseudosuicide alarm was ready to wail when I reminded myself that insecticides would have shown up in the autopsy.

"Harry?" I said into the phone. It couldn't hurt to check.

"What kind of insecticides?"

I read off the names in the article.

"The boys downtown, they'd find any of those, no problem."

That was that. I looked at the catalogs; nothing remarkable except for an occasional item circled in red—disks, harrows, a corn planter.

John Jensen had been a list maker, but he wasn't one to invest in anything so extravagant as a notepad. Most of his memos were jotted on the back of receipts—except for two sheets of notebook paper and a completed order blank from one of the catalogues. One sheet listed farm equipment and the other looked like a list of projects for the house and the farm. It was the second sheet that caught my attention. Down through "second story for chicken coop" and "new roof for the barn," across "plant stand of pines/ Benson Mill boundary" and "shore up Arvis's porch," ran a darkly penciled X. It canceled out everything on the list. Had it been an acknowledgment of reality, or an act of despair?

I pulled out the pink scrap of paper in my shirt pocket and

moved it among the receipts and lists on the desk until I found some that matched the color: Southern States receipts for chicken feed, seed, poultry dip, and such. I unfolded the scrap and read the old-fashioned handwriting:

Please forgive me. I love you Holly.

Wednesday, Dec. 10

Bakery/P.U. cake
Groc.
5 yds gingham for Linnea's costume
Library/6 bks overdue!!
P.U. vac cleaner prt/rtn floor polisher

I brushed the snow from the top of Charles Eckert's tombstone (B. 1906, D. 1972, "BELOVED BROTHER") and sat down to think about weather, schedules, and the transience of life. But the granite was too cold for my behind, so I slid to my feet and wandered up the knoll, keeping to the path so I wouldn't trip over footstones hidden beneath the snow.

The snow that had just started to come down now fell on yesterday's five inches, softening the harsh edges of the graveyard. At the bottom of the path I turned and looked back across the rows of tombstones, towards the old church. With the thousands of shades of greys and whites, it was like stepping into the foreground of an impressionist painting. Beyond the crest of the hill, the merest sliver of red—the door of the church—glimmered through the falling snow.

The flakes were large—the way snow looks when it's about to stop—but I could tell it was going to keep on coming down all day. My built-in barometer, Dad had called it—an ability to sense minute changes in pressure. "Seems like the only time you need to look at the altimeter, girl, is when you set it," he used to say. Anyway, the snow would continue—if for no other reason than that there were so many things on my schedule that day.

At least Mrs. Kohlrausch was going to pick up the little ones from St. O's, at eleven-forty-five. And no matter how much it snowed, St. Obturator's wouldn't close early. It operated under the smug assurance that neither rain nor snow nor gynecologist appointments would stay the mothers of the Episcopal parish day school from completing carpool.

Elk Glen, on the other hand, had a reputation for early dismissal unequaled in all the county. They closed for snow; they closed for heavy rain, for high winds, and bad plumbing. They had even closed, in the autumn of '85, for crickets. But it was the Closing for Mildew that had really made them legendary. When the same damp spell that had brought the invasion of thousands of crickets into the classrooms later caused a tide of mildew to wash over everything in the mansion—from the damask wall coverings to the ornamental plasterwork on the ceilings, from the antique Persian carpets to the pre–Civil War library—something had to be done. The "something" consisted of the entire staff, dressed in sweat suits and wielding Pepsodent toothbrushes, scrubbing or dusting everything in the building with a very expensive substance that smelled suspiciously like Clorox, but which the historical society had insisted they use. The process took two weeks, during which it continued to rain, mothers went mad, and the board of directors decided it was time to finally hire an architect for the proposed high school building, which could be used as a backup in just such an emergency as this.

Keeping this in mind, I headed over to Elk Glen, anticipating the inevitable closing. Bacall was waiting for me in the car, a victim of the grounds keeper's silly prejudice against dogs in the grave-yard—"Dogs like bones just a mite too much, Mrs. Meade."

The Elk Glen parking lot had only teachers' cars in it—all of them backed into their spaces, ready to make a quick getaway the moment the *s* word was spoken. Snow.

"Let's go play," I said, crumpling the "TODAY" list into a tiny paper snowball.

Joyful puffs of dog breath clouded the windows. The car shook with her delight.

The snow was coming down more heavily now, filling up the

footprints trailing across the parking lot into the school annex, where a skinny woman was taping construction-paper Santas to the door windows. Bacall was too large to get out of the back seat without the front one being pushed forward, but she was trying anyway. Her head and one shoulder were stuck outside the door, and the rest of her body wagged with impatience inside the car. As fast as the giant snowflakes fell on her nose, her hot pink tongue slapped upwards to capture them.

"OK, Bacall." I grabbed the blue nylon leash dangling from her collar. "We have plenty of time." As I pushed the front-seat lever forward, Bacall sprang from the car as if shot from a rocket launcher. I barely had time to close the car door before we were off towards the woods, with Bacall in the lead like a furry snowplow, sending up double plumes of snow two feet high in her wake.

Once we were within the woods, Bacall settled down to the more serious business of being a retriever. She sniffed. She listened, cocking her head to one side. She looked under bushes and up-turned logs and scanned what little of the horizon was still visible to her through the silvery branches of the trees.

Slowly, we made our way deeper into the silent woods, until we were within sight of the old stone tower that used to be the chapel for the manor house—or what used to be the manor house but was now Patsy's school. What a shame they couldn't find a use for the tower, I thought, with its carefully laid stones, the intricate patterns in the leaded glass, the carved wooden door that—

I pulled Bacall up short on the leash and shushed her, holding my finger to my lips. The tower door had creaked softly as it opened, and a woman in a limp tweed car coat slowly backed out. She was hatless, and the snow quickly dusted her silver-and-black hair. She seemed to be looking up, perhaps at a staircase inside. With a nod of her head she closed the door, slipped her bare hands into her pockets, and headed off around the far side of the building and out of sight.

"Imagine being out in this weather with no hat or gloves," I whispered.

Bacall harrumphed.

We waited a few moments and then went up to the tower. The

prints from the woman's crepe-sole boots were sharp and crisp, except for the ones she had made coming in, which were now almost filled with the new snow.

As I turned to head back to the lot, Bacall stopped dead in her tracks and pointed. I fell right over her, nose first, into the snow. Bacall held her point.

"Retrievers aren't supposed to point, dodo. What is it?" I raised up on my elbows and looked. The faintest of impressions, tracks made perhaps two or three hours ago, led from the direction of the parking lot to the tower. A tall man, I thought, by the size of them. We followed the trail back to the lot, but the tracks were lost in a confusion of station wagons and beaming children. School had been canceled.

"Well," I said as the dog leaped into the car and we queued up behind the last station wagon, "I guess someone's found a use for the tower after all." I smiled to myself and wondered who.

"This is fun." Patsy, Crista, and Pontine giggled as the long procession of heavy cars slithered and slid down the Elk Glen drive. A thrombus of BMWs and Volvos blocked the exit onto Benson Mill Road. I turned the Honda sharply to the left just before we came to the seething mass of uselessly spinning wheels and cut through the unplowed snow to the "old road"—a disused carriage path that led through narrow stone gates onto Benson Mill Road.

The fields were beautiful with the snow. Someone was plowing Holly Jensen's drive with a tractor, and across the main road I could see the Flower Lady gracefully making her way to the mailbox, walking along a tire track, with arms extended for balance like a high-wire artist, lightly placing one heavy boot in front of the other as if she were wearing the most delicate of satin ballet slippers. As the Honda passed, she reached the mailbox and ducked to look inside.

"Look, Mom, look! There's the Flower Lady!" Patsy pointed in excitement. But by that time, all we could see was the back of her— her colorless, old tweed car coat and her silver-and-black hair pulled back into a braided bun that was wet from the falling snow.

Chapter Fifteen

THE MOON SHONE VERY BRIGHT. Its reflection off the ice-glazed snow lit up our bedroom like the tower beacon at Dulles. Nothing made me madder, knowing that I had to get up at 5 A.M., than being unable to get to sleep. Wasted time. Berlie could go to sleep anywhere, anytime. He was asleep right now, on his back, snoring.

"Roll over." I put my hand under his shoulder blade and pushed up until he turned onto his side.

"Gimme some of your carbide, Patsy," he said, without waking up. "Pick up that beaner—it may still be good."

Why should he be the one to sleep so soundly? He could sleep until seven. I rolled away from him and burrowed down under the covers.

The house looked so peaceful as I slowly circled above it in the old Cherokee. With the snow, in the moonlight, it looked like the best part of my cousin's train layout when we were children: little houses nestled in a layer of cotton batting, Fels Naphtha making everything sparkle and stink at the same time.

The engine made a steady, reassuring drone as I rose higher with each turn. When I could see the lights of the runway, I banked and started dropping down. No traffic at this hour. The Cherokee descended and I put her down easy on the snow-paved field. The glazed surface crunched beneath the wheels as I taxied over to my tie-down. My mind ticked off the checklist as my hands shut down the plane. I could do it in my sleep:

    Retract flaps; turn off radios.
    Turn off lights; position throttle to 1000 rpms.
    Pull mixture control to full lean.
The engine stopped.
    Turn off magneto switch; turn off master switch.
    Secure controls.
I unlatched my seat belt, snaked it around the yoke, and slid the buckle into the lock.
    Release brakes; tie down all three points.
    Set chocks against the wheels.
When everything was completed, I locked the cabin door and set off for the trailer. But when I was halfway down the field, I stopped, turned, and looked back at the little bird one more time.

Before I could turn again, I must have been sound asleep.

Holly Jensen switched off the light over the kitchen table, went down the hall, and climbed into bed for the second time that night. Reading hadn't worked. Mint tea hadn't worked. Maybe it was the bright moonlight or the coldness of the bed or the crowds of unwelcome thoughts scratching about in her mind, like cockleburs down leather hiking boots on a long trek.

Overhead she could hear a small plane flying west towards the fairgrounds. Holly pictured the quilt she hoped to have finished for next year's judging. Kay had helped her pick out the colors: peach, teal, silver, and mauve—all pale and soft, imprinted with tiny flowers. But the design had been her own idea: bouquets of daylilies bordered by rows of tiny triangles—"flying geese," they called them. It was going to be a fine quilt. She and Kay were making pretty good progress.

"Why do I have to do all the little triangles?" Kay had wanted to know.

"Because you're more patient than I am." When she smiled, Holly could feel the muscles in her face. Had it been that long since she had last smiled?

"Too patient." Kay pushed the needle through the calico with long, delicate fingers.

"What do you mean?"

"I mean with Frazier. Maybe I'm being too patient. I keep waiting for this 'phase' of his to peter out."

As she picked up a diamond-shaped piece of calico and began joining it to another, Holly watched Kay from the corner of her eye.

Kay was such a good wife for Frazier. When he'd been in the Navy, she'd been the perfect officer's wife. She had thrown the right parties, worn the right clothes, and known the right people. And on top of all that, Kay was a real person—a caring person. Surely Frazier knew how lucky he was.

"Do you really think Frazier's having an affair?" Holly asked.

The words made Kay flinch. She pressed her lips together and drew in her breath. "What else could it be? He's fifty. I'm forty. We've been married twenty years." She sighed. "It's in the numbers."

"Oh, come on now. Mom and Dad were married *forty* years and Dad never—"

"Frazier's not Dad." Anger, for a brief second, flashed in Kay's eyes. "He's not anything like Dad."

Holly wanted to put her arms around her sister's drooping shoulders, but something told her to wait; there was more.

"I already told you that he's been spending a lot more time at the office." Kay's voice took on a mocking tone. "*At the office.* At least the time with the Reserves is for real. And the trips connected with the research at work . . . I think. But he goes out at all hours 'to check on some real estate.' And he's been bringing me flowers. What would you think?"

"I'd think, 'What a nice guy, to bring me flowers.' John always brought me cordwood." She thought of the firewood, cut, split, and neatly stacked at the side of the house. If his calculations had been as good as in the past, there'd be just enough to last through the winter.

"I saw him picking up a bouquet once in a while at Rebecca's table, before the cold weather set in," Holly said. "Now he goes to the florist?"

"I think he gets them from the Safeway. They smell like sour milk—you know, the Safeway uses one of their old dairy cases for their flowers." She put down her sewing and hugged her arms to her sides. "I hate to burden you with this—you've got your own . . . well . . ." She grimaced. "Really, Holly, what do you think?"

Holly thought that her brother-in-law seemed very different lately, his usual self-assurance grown to catbird proportions. "I don't know, Kay. What would you do if you knew for sure he was having an affair?"

Again her sister flinched. Holly tried to think of a euphemism.

"I think it's the not knowing that I can't handle. The doubts." Kay picked up two little triangles and began sewing again. "I'm thinking about hiring someone to watch him." She looked expectantly at her sister's face.

"A detective! Like on TV? Oh, Kay, that's gross!"

"Well, that answers that." Kay ran her fingers through her hair. "Too tacky, huh?"

Holly grimaced. "Oh, I don't know. It's just . . . you know. Hiring a detective—that's something *other* people do, people you read about in the papers. Couldn't you just ask him?"

"Oh sure. 'Frazier, are you having an . . .'" The word seemed to catch in Kay's throat.

"—fooling around," Holly said. "'Are you fooling around?' No. I don't suppose that would work with Frazier. He can't even tell you what he does at work, so why would he tell you what he does at play?"

"He does, though—tell me what he does at work."

"But I thought it was all top secret. Defense contracts and all that."

"It is. But sometimes he talks about it. They're getting a big project ready right now—they call it 'Red-Det-Op.' Frazier's the project director—he's their top sub weapons expert, you know—and it has to be ready by June."

"So he'd have to be putting in a lot of extra time?"

"Yes." The word came out slowly, as if towing heavy freight behind it. "But not that much time. There's too much of a pattern to it. Frazier's a very organized man."

Kay fingered the piece of calico she was holding. "I know just what she'd be like, too." Her words jabbed fiercely through the still air. "Some little waif he thinks needs rescuing. That's what he'd go for."

"But, Kay, you've never been like that—in need of rescue."

"I know." The words were leaden.

Holly reached out and touched her sister's knee. "Oh, Kay."

"Well." Kay stared at the long strip of triangles she had joined together. "I'm just thinking about hiring a detective. I haven't called anyone yet." She held out the strip to her sister. "If you made a quilt of just these things, what would it be called? The design, I mean. Would it have a name?"

Holly smiled. "That's an old, old pattern. It's called Wild Goose Chase."

"Oh." Kay picked up another triangle and then set it down. "Let's hope that's the quilt for me."

Wild Goose Chase. As the bed at last began to feel warm, in her mind Holly pieced together such a quilt for her sister. But the bright colors she began with—red and blue and purple and green—gradually faded, until all she was left with were patches of black and white and grey.

Across the road, Rebecca Stott carefully got out of bed and drew the heavy lace curtains against the moonlight. But the shadows they created on the rose-patterned wallpaper and the worn Oriental carpet made her more awake than she already was, so she got up and opened them again. At the end of the drive the old maple tree looked bereft without the wooden table that stood beneath it during the growing season.

The skeletons of the summer's flowers had long been uprooted and piled for compost, the gardens had been turned and covered with mulch, and the table had been stowed in the shed. She climbed back into the iron bed, where Barton Stott, sleeping, breathed in the cold night air in a manner, she thought, typical of the way he lived his life: taking a great deal in without seeming to give very much back.

With her back to him, she prayed for sleep, but it wouldn't come. She thought about the seed catalogues on the kitchen table. She pictured herself filling out the order blanks, adding dozens of new varieties while keeping all the old. She imagined the day they'd arrive: going out to the gardens and turning the soft soil over in her hand, breathlessly laying the earth open to receive the gleaming seed.

Barton shifted slightly, sending a puff of stale air over her shoulder. She drifted back into the garden, but now it was autumn. She was counting off by rows the strange events that had sprung up last fall and were continuing to grow thick and fast, even into the winter.

It had started with a note in the money jar. She had gone down to the road to pull the table behind the tree and to collect the day's receipts. There was twenty dollars—not bad for October—and the note:

> Your flowers are beautiful. Tomorrow, might I have some of the little red ones, and some blue, for my wife? It's our anniversary.

How sweet, she had thought. And the following day there was another note thanking her, requesting another bouquet for the weekend. Every three or four days a note would appear, asking for certain flowers and for information about their names and how they were grown. She tried to answer each question carefully, but some of the flowers had originally come from her grandmother's garden, and she couldn't remember what they were called. She was tempted to make up some names but decided it would be dishonest of her. Even though she kept an eye on the table, she never caught a glimpse of the writer.

That's how she had grown to think of him, *the Writer*, until the last day in October, when the note read:

I have sea duty for three weeks. The flowers will be gone by then, won't they? Under the table is a thank-you for all the loveliness. But I'd rather thank you in person. Could you meet me at the fairgrounds November 22 at 12 noon? It would please me so much to think that you might.

She didn't know what to think. She nearly forgot to look under the table. A package wrapped in brown paper was duct-taped to the bottom. Thank God Barton was out at Elk Glen, running fodder through the dehydrator. She took the package to the shed and opened it. It was a book about wildflowers—*A Countryman's Flowers* by Hal Borland. The pictures were so beautiful they made her want to cry.

In the end, curiosity got the best of her. She had pictured him first as the Writer, a gentle old man buying flowers for his wife. When she learned he was a sailor, her image of him changed. He must be much younger, tanned, and with sea legs. Possibly with sea shoulders as well, and a belly flat and hard from hoisting the mainsails—real flesh on his bones, not all shriveled up and stringy from years of being mean and—but then, she was going only because they shared a love of flowers. Just an innocent afternoon spent talking about purple loosestrife and butterfly weed. How sweet to talk of the things she really cared about without someone trampling all over it.

The warm wind that had blown the entire day and night before their meeting had stopped sometime on the morning of the twenty-second, leaving a steely-grey wall of cold pressing down on the countryside, like the grip of a selfish old man. Rain would be moving in next. Rebecca pulled on cord knickers, knee-high boots, and a heavy Norwegian sweater and climbed into the old Jeep she used mostly to haul manure. She could hardly ask Barton for the truck.

The fairgrounds were completely deserted when she got there— no cars, no people, no nothing. She panicked. Was this a trick? Something Bart had dreamed up to use against her? No. He was incapable of writing such notes, and he didn't know anyone who could write them, either.

She had wandered down past the open-sided cattle barns, counting off the breeds—Ayrshire, Holstein, Guernsey—and was just about to turn and head back to the Jeep, when a tall man stepped out of the last barn and beckoned to her.

"I've got violets . . . and pinks . . . and sweet baby's breath," he called, like a street Arab selling something she had longed for for thirty years.

That first meeting there had been followed by many picnics in the Brown Swiss barn, with Chinese food in paper cartons and wine in crystal glasses, fresh straw and long underwear to fend off the cold, and rain dripping from the corrugated roof, splashing up redolent memories of the gentle animals who had patiently stood there last summer, waiting to be judged.

When the snows finally came, he had led her to the old stone chapel in the woods near the Country School, and, spreading out a beautiful Navajo blanket on the upper floor of the tower, had made her feel that her life had truly and finally begun.

Winter, instead of being the time of the year when her life lay as dormant as the fields, had become as spring. She saw herself through his eyes, and she liked what she saw.

And each time they met, it mattered less to her that she was married—or that he was.

At their first meeting it had been a shock to realize who he was, that he was Holly Jensen's brother-in-law. But then he had explained that his wife had been traumatized by a childhood experience, and although they loved each other dearly, it was as if they were brother and sister. She had long ago given him permission to find the kind of love he needed elsewhere. And now, at last, he had.

Rebecca chose to believe him. She didn't expect him to leave his wife. She was just going to take the time with him for what it was.

Stealthily, so as not to rouse the tight-clinched figure sleeping beside her, she stretched out the length of her body and went to sleep.

Chapter Sixteen

"I CAN ONLY GIVE YOU a dozen eggs this week." Holly placed a steaming cup of cranberry tea in front of me.

"How come?" I yawned prodigiously. "Excuse me; I had trouble getting to sleep last night."

"Me, too." She pushed a jar of honey towards me. "I think it was the moon. Too bright. My neighbor was saying the same thing."

"Mrs. Stott?"

Holly nodded. "I think Rebecca has trouble sleeping, moon or no moon. I see her light on at all hours. Sometimes I even see her roaming around outside."

I could picture her in a long white nightgown, an Emily Dickinson figure drifting up and down the ruined rows of flowers in her garden by the light of the moon. Then I imagined her in a long cloak and hood, making her way through knee-high snow to the tower in the woods, the door opening to her knock, and two strong arms reaching out to draw her inside.

"They just don't seem to want to lay," Holly said.

"What?"

"The hens," she said. "They aren't laying very well. Must be the cold weather."

"Oh." Trying to sound casual, I said, "Tell me more about your neighbor Rebecca. We buy flowers from her stand all the time, but I've only seen her once," I lied, "after the . . ."

"Funeral," Holly finished flatly. She stared at her hands and smiled. "Rebecca is the kindest, gentlest person you could ever meet. A little spacey, maybe, but really neat."

"Spacey?"

"Oh, you know, sometimes, talking to her, it's like she's from another world."

Holly tried to hide a yawn. "This is her tea you're drinking. She grows herbs as well as all those flowers. You should see some of the beautiful wreaths she makes out of them."

"And her husband?" I couldn't help asking. "You said he wasn't very nice."

Holly scrunched up her face. "That turd? Like I was telling my sister: He's a mean old coot. I wish he'd dry up and blow away."

"He's that bad?"

"Probably worse."

"How is your sister?"

Holly grimaced. "Not so good. I was telling you last month about her worries?"

I nodded.

"Well, now she wants to hire a detective to follow Frazier."

"That's what I'd do—find out once and for all."

"I don't know. Asking a perfect stranger to pry into your life . . ."

True. Then a thought came to me. "She could ask Detective Cloud—you know him—a little, anyway. And I think he's only working part-time right now. Maybe he'd do it."

Having a pretty good idea what a detective would find out about Frazier Claiborne put me in a bad mood. I left Holly to deliver Patsy's science fair project. Someone had littered the ditch beside the Flower Lady's field with soda cans. Jesus, I thought. A whole six-pack. I hoped whoever did that got stuck in traffic about ten miles from a bathroom.

It took me a while to unload Patsy's project and carry all of it down to her classroom—fourteen bean plants subject to freezing in twenty-degree weather. They had been fine as long as they were under the blanket in the car. But now that I had an armload out in the air, they showed signs of mortal distress. It took fourteen trips to carry each one in under my coat. I felt like a kidnapper working for the Jolly Green Giant—all to prove for the one millionth time that plants move towards light. Phototropism, I snarled to myself—who needs it?

I have to get ahold of myself, I thought as I headed back towards home. Bad moods make bad drivers. When I came even with the Flower Lady's ditch, I did a double take: The soda cans were gone. Imagine that—a reverse litterbug. Maybe there was hope for humankind after all.

I glanced at the list on the visor and changed course for the bank. The line was long at the drive-in window. I pulled out a book and started reading.

> No person may act or attempt to act as a crewmember of a civil aircraft—Within 8 hours after the consumption of any alcoholic beverage; While under the influence of alcohol; While using any drug that affects the person's faculties in any way contrary to safety; or While having .04 percent by weight or more alcohol in the blood. . . .

"Eight hours from bottle to throttle; no pills that give thrills; point oh four, stay on the floor." Every time I studied the FARs, I marveled at the corniness of the old pilot mnemonic phrases, still ringing in my head from when I was an eighteen-year-old student.

Just behind me a horn honked. I looked up to see that the Datsun in front of me had inched forward, leaving a car length between us. A scrofulous Ford Fairlane was just about up my tailpipe.

"What's the big hurry, you old fart?" I inched the Honda forward. "There are three cars in front of the Datsun anyway." I picked up the FARs again and tried to concentrate.

The guy in the Fairlane honked again.

All three cars had gone through the line, and it was my turn at the window. I took out enough money to pay the flight instructor for my first brush-up session.

Carter looked awfully young for a flight instructor, but Bud Stilson had spoken highly of him. Before we got in the plane, he spent a good bit of time questioning me about my previous experience and my attitudes towards flying. I liked that. He seemed impressed with how up-to-date I was on the FARs. Well, sure; I'd had plenty of time to study them, waiting around in my car.

"Looks like you've done a lot of my work for me, Mrs.—Jenny." He pointed to the cloudless blue sky. "Only thing left is for us to get up there and blow the cobwebs out. Shouldn't take long."

We crunched through the frozen grass to a Mooney waiting just outside the door. "Don't worry about the smell," Carter said. "Bud's been working on the fuel selector valve."

But I barely heard him. As soon as my back hit the seat, my feet went to the rudder pedals, my hands to the yoke, and the plane became an extension of my body. The ailerons moved up and down on *my* wings; the engine, when I switched it on, roared within *me*—I could feel its pulse in my veins. I had to force myself to study the position of the instruments—the Mooney's instruments were arranged differently from my old Cherokee's. And then we took off. "Slipped the surly bonds of earth." The poet Magee was right.

Beneath us the petty features of the land grew smaller and smaller until there was nothing but a winter expanse of dull brown, with occasional patches of dirty white and smoky green to relieve the monotony. But above and all around us, we were enveloped in limitless blue possibilities.

When we were through with the banks and turns, Carter asked me to do stalls and recoveries. Then, as we descended to approach Ganton's Farm for some practice landings and takeoffs—"touch and goes"—I caught sight of the mansion and the tower at Elk Glen. Patsy was down there, I thought, learning about gerunds and the associative property of addition.

"Could we make one more circle before we do the T and Gs?" I asked.

Carter smiled. "Want to go over your house?"

I nodded. How hokey could I get?

"Everyone wants to do that. Wouldn't be a first time out if you didn't."

We were over the countryside right then, with fields and stands of trees flowing gracefully along the curves of the land. But off to the right the hard glint of Ulyssia spread out its asphalt fingers reaching ever farther in all directions—the land of the orange signs. I concentrated on the terrain directly in front of me: I could see the Franciscan monastery with its red-tiled roof. Farther to the east was the steeple of St. Obturator's and the gravestones in their irregular rows. To the north a ways was Mt. Pisgah. A long line of school buses wound around its drive like a giant yellow snake. And just off the starboard wing was our street, Tragus Court, with its four houses arranged in a semicircle, as if to ward off some suburban version of an Apache raid.

We turned and headed back to the field. The T and Gs went pretty well, considering how long it had been since I had last landed.

My last landing, I thought. The day I had flown my parents' bodies back from Raleigh, after the accident.

Suddenly the excitement was gone. All the good feelings were gone. As quickly as I could, I made arrangements for my next session with Carter and hurried off to the car, leaving the young man standing next to the Mooney, probably wondering what the hell was going on.

It had been such a stupid accident. Mom and Dad had been driving through the gentle hills beyond Raleigh—it suddenly struck me how much the hills around here were like the ones there. They were on their first vacation in five years. A tractor-trailer had brushed by them as if they weren't even there, knocking their car down an embankment, where it burst into flames. Witnesses said there had been plenty of room for both vehicles—a lane for each— yet the truck had moved over, flicked them off the road, and kept on going as if nothing at all had happened. Trying to get my parents out of the car, other drivers had been too busy to take down the truck's license-plate number. What would it have mattered? It wouldn't have brought them back.

But the idea of the accident kept coming back to me. The Honda and I had become airborne weeks before the anniversary of my parents' death and before Berlie had confronted me with his worries about the incident with the body bag. And I knew that these events and the flying fantasies—even my decision to fly again— were all connected. Only a fool could ignore it. So of course I tried.

The next flying session went much better. It had been natural, I told myself, to run through all those old emotions. But this time I was all business. We flew out to Frederick to get gas, and Bud came along to pick up a part for a plane he was going to work on.

"Wait'll you see her, Jenny," he said. "Well, she's not much to look at now—she took a nasty spill—but by the time the rally rolls around, you won't believe your eyes."

"What rally?"

"The annual trip to Ocean City. The Clark County Flying Club goes every year, on Memorial Day. You'll be right up there with 'em by then. Won't she, Carter?"

Carter turned to Bud and shouted over the engine. "She could pass her flight check right now, as far as I'm concerned. I don't know what's holding her back."

"Money." I threw out the lead balloon of reality.

"Oh, yeah," Bud yelled. " 'If God had meant for man to fly, He would have given him more money,' " he quoted the old adage.

God, I thought, pilots have got to be the corniest people on earth.

"What's this plane you're getting a part for?" Carter asked. "I didn't see any new planes on the field."

I leveled off at forty-five hundred feet, below a broken overcast at seven thousand.

"It's being delivered tomorrow. Cherokee Six."

My stomach did a flip.

"Yours?" I asked. How would he fly it?

"No. I'm just getting her back in the air for the owner."

I concentrated on the excursion to Ocean City, counting the months. By May, I said to myself. I might make it by May.

Below me, the silver ribbon of the Monocacy River shone in the grey light of a winter day.

You can avoid facing certain issues only so long, and then you reach a point where it's no longer possible. For some people, it's when their ulcers perforate, or when they find themselves walking down Main Street in their underwear. For me, it's when I start dreaming about it.

Only this time, it wasn't a dream. It was a short article back on page A23 in *The Washington Post*, announcing that Marcia Colby, after trying for almost ten years, had succeeded in getting elected to the post her late husband had held before he was shot by a terrorist, in the Bahamas. Senator Marcia Colby, D—Iowa, would begin her term of office this month.

The widow of the man whose assassin slid out of the body bag over Jacksonville. Could I ignore that? Maybe. I read on.

Senator Colby was in town this week to speak with area farmers about the upcoming battle over the latest farm bill. She would be addressing the Clark County Farm Association tonight at eight-fifteen, Building B, at the fairgrounds.

No use waiting for the dreams to begin; I figured I might as well get on top of it now.

I scanned the schedule on the visor.

P.M. 8:00 PTA—Elk Glen

The baby-sitting was already in place: Phillip was riding herd. Maybe I could cut the PTA meeting and talk with Senator Colby a few minutes after her meeting.

Arvis Dutton gave me her phone number. Her voice, on the line, sounded gutsy with a motherly overtone—an interesting combination. If I were from Iowa, I thought, I'd probably vote for her.

"Senator Colby, I'd like to talk with you about the man who shot your husband," I said. No use beating around the bush.

Can you hear a shiver? There was such a long silence, I couldn't be sure. But one thing was for certain: When she finally spoke, the motherliness was gone, but the guts remained.

"What are you talking about?"

It was hard to explain, but I tried. What had happened in the plane was complicated in itself, but her final question was the one that really threw me.

"Why didn't you come forward at the time?" Ice was practically forming on the phone line.

"Could we talk about this in person, Senator Colby?" I said. I was getting uneasy about saying so much over the phone—the legacy of a childhood spent watching reruns of *The Untouchables*.

I was too nervous to pay much attention to the meeting itself. Arvis Dutton in his perennial corduroys, his bald head gleaming angelically in the harsh light of the 4-H building, introduced Marcia Colby—not as the widow of a murdered U.S. senator, but as a highly vocal opponent of the newly proposed farm bill.

Marcia Colby was a knockout. Long, flaming red hair framed her round, serious face and cascaded down the back of a mauve, teal, and grey tweed suit of soft wool. Her voice had none of the harshness that many prominent women adopted, as if to say to the world, "There's a job to be done, and I'm just the man to do it."

The crowd, though mainly male, included a fair number of women. Comments rippled up and down the rows of uncomfortable folding chairs, just as they had at John Jensen's funeral. In fact, except for the lack of a coffin, it was pretty much the same group. After Senator Colby completed her fifteen-minute description of the bill, discussion—if you could call near pandemonium "discussion"—began. In a few moments she raised both her hands, and, to my amazement, everyone quieted down, and the rest of the meeting proceeded in an orderly and effective manner. By the time it was over, committees had been organized, and everyone there was ready to charge out and storm the Hill.

I waited to one side until just about everyone had left. A few clutches of people were gathered near the door, but the place was about empty except for one man who sat watching the Senator as she extricated herself from a conversation with a worried-looking farmer in grey work pants.

When everyone else had finally gone, the man got up and stood beside Marcia Colby as I introduced myself.

"This is Gary Fenton, Mrs. Meade. His office at the State Department has had a special interest in my husband's case."

I shouldn't have been surprised, but I was. Gary Fenton was about my age, blond, with almost colorless blue eyes and the wiry, compact body of a gymnast.

"I've been thinking about what you asked me on the phone this afternoon, Senator Colby," I began. "I don't have any excuse for waiting so long. But my explanation has to do with my family . . . the threats those men made—we weren't even sure whose side they were on or anything." I stole a glance at Fenton. "When my father and mother died, I never made any connection between it and your husband's death—I just figured that was the end of it. Now I'm not so sure. I'm sorry. There really is no excuse."

She turned to Fenton. "I think Mr. Fenton has a few things he'd like to ask you."

He did. And by the time he was done, it was eleven-forty-five, my daughters had been bullied into bed by their power-crazed brother, and I had been appointed in absentia, at the PTA meeting, to head the one-woman search committee for the Elk Glen official sculptor for the new high school.

Chapter Seventeen

"DETECTIVE CLOUD, you don't know me." The voice on my workshop phone was soft, but with an edge of determination. "I'm Kay Claiborne; Holly Jensen is my sister."

I laid down the sandpaper I was using on a little deer figurine. Was this the break I needed? *Someone* finally throwing out some information that would actually lead somewhere?

"Yes, Ms. Claiborne?" My blood was starting to rev up.

"My sister said you were only working part-time. I wondered if you would take on a . . . a . . ."

I waited. Finally she drew a breath and spit the words out.

"I need someone to watch my husband. I think he's having an affair."

Shit. The dregs of P.I. work. I was on my way up again—not down and out. I didn't need this.

"Ms. Claiborne—"

"Of course, I couldn't talk with you now. Could we meet somewhere this afternoon? Maybe Hagerty's, in Ulyssia?"

On the other hand, she might tell me more than her sister could—or would—about John Jensen. You never knew.

"Hagerty's. OK. Three o'clock?"

At three o'clock I saw her come in the door, look around the room, and then cross to where I was sitting. She was good-looking in a subdued sort of way. Her shoulder-length blond hair was curled under at the ends—not a hair out of place—and she wore a mohair coat of many shades of green, purple, and black. It looked so soft I almost reached out to touch it. But something about the way she held her shoulders and back told me that even if I'd known her for twenty years, that would never be the thing to do.

She sat down in the cavernous pine booth and slid along the seat until she was opposite me. I had thought about stringing her along until I got some information about the Jensens, and then turning down the surveillance detail. But when she lifted her head and looked at me, the pain and self-doubt in her blue eyes were too intense—and too familiar—for me to ignore.

"Why do you think your husband is having an affair?" No use dancing around.

She looked down for a moment, as if the fault lay with her. As if she'd been the one sneaking around, telling lies, shutting the other person out. Why did women do that?

"He's changed," she said.

The official explanation—every single time.

"But, then, he's changed before, and it didn't mean he was having an affair." She twisted her wedding band, a thin circle of gold surprisingly plain for such a well-dressed lady. "But this is different."

"How is it different?"

She looked me in the eye. "You probably want to know the ordinary things—that he seems to be working odd hours, that he sometimes speaks on the phone in a voice so soft I can't hear him, that he avoids making plans that involve the two of us being alone together. But some of those things can be explained by his line of work." She told me what little she could about her husband's job.

"But it's what I see in his eyes that has me worried." She picked up a spoon and studied its smooth surface. "Oh, not all the time," she said. "Some mornings, though, when he thinks I'm asleep, I watch him getting dressed. There's a look of excitement, anticipation. Something I haven't seen in years. Not since we were first married and his Navy career was just getting going."

Sounded like an affair to me. I could probably wrap up a report in less than a week. But I was looking for more than the sordid details of the love life of John Jensen's brother-in-law. I had to be careful how I went about any extra interrogation.

"Has anyone else noticed a change in your husband?"

"Oh, yes. Holly was worried about him too. She felt he was mad at her."

Aha. There was my foot in the door.

"Ms. Claiborne, I've got to be at a meeting this afternoon. Can we meet here tomorrow, same time? I'll need to get a little more information from you."

She nodded.

And here came the pitch. "And I'd like to talk with your sister too. If you don't mind."

"Holly? Sure. It's OK with me if it's OK with her."

When things are easy, it makes me worry. I needed time to think out my next move.

"I guess it's a possibility," Holly Jensen said. I was glad she had agreed to see me on such short notice. "Anybody *could* have an affair . . . if they wanted to." She flung her long, dark brown braid back over her shoulder.

Not Jenny Meade, I thought. The signals just weren't there.

"But some want to more than others," I said. When I'd first arrived, she'd been struggling to carry one of the porch swings down the front steps. It was heavy, even with the two of us carrying it. But by the time we got to the barn, it weighed a ton. Oak. It had already outlasted its maker, John Jensen. And it would probably outlast the rest of us as well. The second swing was no lighter.

"Frazier's always liked women," she said. "He seems to feel more at ease with them than most men do—not that he isn't just as at ease with men. Mr. Smooth, John and I called him." She poured me a cup of cranberry tea. Her kitchen smelled of homemade bread. "But I've never suspected him of having an affair before. Now . . ." She twirled the end of her braid. "I guess I can see what Kay's getting at . . . maybe."

She went to the counter and brought back a basket and set it on the table. "It really steams me, though. If it weren't for Kay, God knows where Frazier'd be today. Swabbing decks or something. She's helped him in everything he's ever wanted to do."

She lifted the tea towel in the basket, uncovering a shiny round loaf of pumpernickel. With her long fingers she broke off a chunk of bread and pushed the basket over to me. "Not that he isn't smart or that he wouldn't have made good anyway. But Kay really speeded things up. She knows all the social stuff—who to have over for drinks, who to invite for beef Wellington. You wouldn't know it to look at him now, but Frazier had a lot of rough edges when Kay met him."

"You came from the same background Kay did. Don't you miss all that, out here on the farm?"

"Miss it? All that phony horseshit? You gotta be kidding. This is the best place in the world to be. This is *real*." She stretched her hand towards the kitchen window. A red-shouldered hawk resting on a fence post glanced briefly in our direction and then lifted itself slowly into the winter sky.

It was a sad story, I thought, sitting in Hagerty's the next day, listening to Kay Claiborne's account of a marriage gone dry. I could see them at the beginning, the eager young couple eating up the days and months, almost instinctively climbing from rank to rank in the maze of Navy protocol. For Kay Claiborne, it was a question of breeding; the daughter of Rear Admiral Spencer had learned the ropes very early in life. For Frazier Claiborne, it was a question of sheer determination and natural intuition.

"His family couldn't even find time to make it to his first commissioning ceremony ten miles away in Portsmouth." She sniffed. "Just as well—they would have all shown up drunk anyway. He always said I was his real family. His only family." She turned her face away.

Damn it, she's going to cry, I thought. But when she turned

back, her eyes were dry and filled with an almost ferocious sorrow.

"Sergeant Cloud, I just want you to find out what's going on. I can't sleep; I can't think straight. Half the time I think I'm just imagining all this. Half the time I know I'm right. I need you to find out the truth."

There was a long silence before she finally spoke again.

"When can you start?" She ran her finger around the rim of the martini glass as if she expected it to ring a Baccarat tone, a sound Hagerty's wasn't known for. "Following him, I mean. How soon can you really start getting some information?" She took two sips and pushed the glass away.

"You've given me all I need to know. I'll start Monday, if that's all right." I scooted to the end of the booth and got up. "One more thing, though: This morning your sister said that in her opinion, anyone could have an affair—if they wanted to."

She shrugged her pretty shoulders and blinked.

"Do you think John Jensen might have had one?"

"Oh, no." She shook her head, making her smooth hair swing from side to side. "Not John. You didn't know him."

"But could he have maybe *wanted* to?"

She nailed me with those fierce blue eyes. "Not in a million years."

Chapter Eighteen

"Changing course to Three-Five-Five degrees. Hold on to your hat."

The plane banks steeply to port. The navigator, who had unbuckled to check out something in the storage area, slides across the floor and crashes into the cabin paneling.

"Bacall, I told you to look out. Are you OK?" I glanced in the rearview mirror at the indignant dog. "I'm sorry. This looks like it's going to be a wild-goose chase." Bacall and I had just come from the studio of Piers Gunnaffson, an artist specializing in chainsaw sculpture. I was looking for someone to do a large statue to stand outside the new high school building at Elk Glen.

"What better way to personify the disparate elements of Clark County?" Pearl Osburgh, chairman of the building committee, had suggested in an accent that was, from what I could tell over the phone, the synthesis of East Baltimore and all the Katharine Hepburn movies she had probably sneaked into as a child. "The purity of design distilled into fine art and the rough, elemental tang of the local outdoorsman."

"What the committee wants," Fran had told me the morning after the meeting, "is Saint-Gaudens in a gimmee cap."

"What's a gimmee cap?" I asked.

"You know, those hats the good ol' boys wear, with JOHN DEERE and SOUTHERN STATES and DEKALB above the bill. They go to the booths at the county fair and say, 'Gimme cap,' and that's how they get 'em."

I thought of John Jensen's hat, where it had rolled up against the tree. DeKalb.

Fran had fished around in her purse for several business cards and had given them to the newly elected chairman of the sculpture search committee—me.

"Anyway," she said, "I think the building committee may have stumbled onto a good idea in spite of themselves: Can you think of a better art form for some of those kids, the ones whose favorite movie is *The Chainsaw Massacre Part Eight*?"

I looked at the first card.

PIERS GUNNAFFSON
RT. 4, TROCHLEAR NOTCH, MARYLAND
Objets du CHAINSAW

Piers Gunnaffson was a very successful sculptor and a source of constant ferment within the already well-fermented Clark County artistic community. But I could tell that his chainsaw sculptures were not what the building committee had had in mind when they settled on that particular form of expression.

"I am in my American period now." Gunnaffson had said it reproachfully, as if I should have already known. Before me rose an eighteen-foot totem pole whose individual components—"animal godlets," Gunnaffson had called them—were all unmistakably male and appeared to be at the very point of engendering little godlings. Such a statue wouldn't last ten minutes at the new high school before the students would equip it with prophylactics—and probably freshman beanies as well.

I looked at the note Gunnaffson had scribbled for me as I had taken leave of his studio. "Try Tommy," he had growled. "He's probably more your style."

The address was in Revenge, in the eastern part of the county. A vicious-sounding town, Revenge had been innocently named for the most prominent family in the area.

I looked at my watch, then checked the schedule on the visor. "We have just enough time to make it, if there's no traffic." I turned onto Hilltop Road, and a squirrel, remarkably fat for this far into winter, streaked across the pavement in front of the car.

"Look at that, Bacall. Bet you'd like to get ahold of him, wouldn't you?"

Bacall thumped her tail against the inside of the car.

"Heh!" Her wet nose poked my neck for emphasis.

We watched as the bushy little rodent scampered away.

"Too bad, pooch. We don't have time." I stepped on the gas.

"I miss him so much," Holly said quietly as she stitched down the long stem of a patchwork daylily. She said it in the same tone she would have said, "I have a green sweater," or "I think we're out of milk." In fact, every detail of her daily life seemed to have the same weight to her. Because nothing was as important as the fact that John was gone, everything was exactly the same. If the pump quit or she couldn't find a pin, what matter? Each was just one more loss—just the way things were.

"I know. He was a very special person." Kay set aside the little triangles she was joining and poured more tea into the mug in front of her sister. The mug logo read, "Cargill: When you think of fertilizer, think of us."

"I know this sounds stupid . . ." Holly looked at her sister.

"No." Kay shook her head. Maybe at last Holly would begin to open up—get it all out. "Go on."

"Kay, I've gone back and forth, back and forth on this, and I just don't believe he killed himself."

Oh hell, Kay thought. "But, honey, what other explanation is there? He didn't have an enemy in the world. Nobody would ever have wanted to kill him."

"That's true. But something must have happened. He got up at four o'clock in the morning to go to Hanover, to look at a harrow. We'd needed a new one forever. He wouldn't pass up the chance—it was a real bargain. Something must have happened. Maybe he was stopped by robbers." She drank down the whole mug of tea.

"But, Holly." Kay felt so bad. They had been through this a hundred times since Cloud had started poking around last fall, and it never got them anywhere. "Was anything missing? His wallet? The truck?"

Holly looked down at her hands. "No."

"And how did he wind up in the cemetery?"

"They could have made him drive there."

Kay drew a heavy breath. "But what about the note?"

Holly twisted the wedding band on her finger. "They could have made him write it."

"But why?" Kay couldn't keep her voice from rising. Until her sister got over this idea, she just wasn't going to be able to start a new life—any kind of life at all. "Why would they want to kill him?"

Holly got up and put another piece of wood in the stove. She shrugged her shoulders. "Crazy. Psychopaths. People kill for no reason."

Kay gathered up the teapot and the mugs and carried them into the kitchen. When she came back she said, "Holly, let's go away for a while. Let's go down to Sanibel Island and watch the sandpipers."

They looked outside at the muddy fields and the dirty patches of snow along the edge of the road. Sleet clattered against the windowpanes.

"What about the farm?"

"There's nothing happening right now. And your neighbor, Mr. Dutton, would take the chickens over to his place."

That was true. She had gotten rid of most of the livestock, and there were only five hens left in the henhouse. Arvis would be glad to take them. "What about Frazier?"

"Oh." Now it was Kay's turn to look at her hands. "Well." She opened a needlepoint tote bag sitting beside the sofa and pulled out a man's navy blazer, a needle, and some thread. "He'll be all right. I don't think he'll miss me."

"Aren't things any better?" The world might look flat to Holly Jensen, but one thing stood out in the greyness: the dull glow of another's misery. It was as if she had acquired a special radar—a sorrow detector. She could spot a person in pain at any distance.

Kay shook her head. "No. Everything's worse. We don't even . . . I don't understand it. We used to be so good together. He says it's the project. But that's just an excuse. Your detective, Cloud, says he'll have a report by the end of the week. But I'm not sure I'll be ready to hear it so soon. Or maybe I will."

With three fingers Kay grasped the spare button on the inside of the jacket, the way Holly had seen Mr. Gill steady the balls of a young sheep in the neutering demonstration at the farm show, and with a quick little snip of her sharp-nosed scissors, she cut it free.

She positioned the button and began sewing it onto one of the sleeves. The pewter, wrought in the shape of an anchor within a circle, gleamed in the lamplight.

They sat in silence for a long time, the only sound the spatter of the sleet against the window and the ticking of the banjo clock in the hallway. Holly got up slowly, staring into her sister's eyes as if some grave news had interrupted the program normally playing there. She went down the hall and into her room. Kay could hear her speaking softly into the phone. When she returned, ten minutes later, she was carrying a suitcase.

"What's that?" Kay said.

"I'm ready." She stuffed the quilt pieces into an old army surplus backpack and slung it over her shoulder. "Let's head south."

The best thing about running a chainsaw in Revenge is that nobody bothers you about it. Nobody complains about the roar of the machine, about the piles of logs in your yard, or the language you use when you wrestle a two-ton tree section into position for cutting. How could they, when the neighbors rev their ATVs at midnight, when their own yards showcase rusting Edsels and Impalas, and the air itself is always blue with greetings shouted from friend to friend as they all stand on their porches getting beers from the refrigerators?

The second-best thing about running a chainsaw in Revenge is that nobody ever comes around. So when I looked up from a runaway beech log after delivering a thunder roll of obscenities and I saw Jenny Meade standing there, she might as well have been Saint Peter or the Lone Ranger: I was that surprised.

"Tom Cloud." Her eyebrows nearly disappeared up into the hood of her parka.

This sort of thing had been happening too much lately, I told myself. I'd be thinking about something at work, a suspect, maybe, or a witness in a trial long ago, and then, Bing!—the guy would walk past me in Sears. Just then, I'd been thinking about the Jensen case, going over and over the details, looking for the one thing that would justify reopening the official investigation, when who turns up—in my back yard, for chrissakes—but Jenny Meade? If I hadn't known better, I'd have thought I was losing my mind.

"Jenny Meade." I hadn't seen her since our talk in the cemetery, but I was still thinking about what life in the Meade family must be like. Letting go of the runaway beechwood, I straightened up and took a step forward.

"Tom. I didn't expect . . ." She pulled a piece of paper from her pocket and held it out to me. "You were recommended to me by Piers Gunnaffson." She explained her reason for coming to see me.

Before, when we'd been together, we'd always been on her turf, so to speak. Now it was my turn. I took her into the shop and started to show her around.

She looked about, curious and almost embarrassed, as if she'd accidentally walked into my bedroom. "I only pictured you as a cop."

"And if you prick us, do we not bleed?" I had meant to make her laugh, but the effect was the opposite.

"Tom, I didn't mean—"

"I know. I'm teasing."

One eyebrow went up.

I changed the subject. "The lead you gave me—it's going to work out."

The other brow shot up.

"The one with the construction thefts. Remember? We were talking in the graveyard?"

The eyebrows came back down and she smiled. "Yes?"

"You said the thief might be building a house. I went over the kinds of materials being stolen and the order they were taken in, and it looks like you could be right."

I told her about the sensors we were using, about the ground-hogs, the deer, and all the rest of the false starts. "I think the infrared is going to get 'em."

She smiled.

"Jenny, let me show you my *other* work."

Her delight with the pieces in the workshop, the way she ran her hand over them, as if they were silk and she had expected only burlap, began easing my mind out of the frenzy I had worked myself into earlier, alone with my thoughts in the yard. I felt the muscles in my neck slowly releasing their grip on me.

"—and this one, of the mother and child, is really wonderful." She was quiet for a moment, her hand resting on the figure. She picked up a life-sized chipmunk. "You didn't do *this* with a chainsaw?"

"No." I laughed. "Not the small ones."

Together we worked out an idea for a large sculpture for the front of the new high school out at Elk Glen: It would be a child reading a book, with an adult looking on—just the thing for the beautiful forked cedar that had been curing in the side yard ever since the week I'd moved in.

I had been concentrating on the project so hard that her parting words, as she rushed to her car to pick up one of her kids, caught me off guard.

"Do you think John Jensen killed himself?"

Maybe fate *had* sent her—to tell me to quit mooning around about the family I'd never have and to really get my butt to work on a case that might have a surprise or two.

"I told you. That's what the report said."

"Oh, come off it." Her bluntness was refreshing. "You don't think so, do you?"

I folded my arms across my chest, knowing an attempt to stonewall was useless—she'd keep cutting until she got to the heartwood. "No. But I don't have anything to go on—except his widow doesn't think so either. But there's no use questioning her again: She told me all she could right after it happened. I could go out there again, but it would be a wasted trip."

And that's just what it was. When I pulled into Holly Jensen's slippery driveway at dusk, the house, glazed shut with a thick coat of freezing rain, was dark, and nobody was there.

Chapter Nineteen

"DON'T YOU THINK it's funny that when four people who spend all their time in their cars get a little time off to have some fun, they get in a station wagon and drive somewhere for two and a half hours? And in February, yet."

Our semiannual trips to Reading, to "hit the outlets," were as productive as ever in terms of bargains found and group therapy accomplished. But for me, this had become the Year of the Killer Carpool, and the idea that we would voluntarily be members of an adult carpool was a little strange.

"Jenny." Jif turned and hung over the front seat of Elena's blue Volvo station wagon. "Don't be such a party pooper!" She launched into a sad monologue about her son's grades in geometry, which led to a group discussion on late bloomers in general, and adolescent boys in particular.

"Jenny, you're awfully quiet. This is your favorite subject." Elena looked at me in the rearview mirror.

"I think I've made a big mistake," I began, "and I'm not sure what to do about it." And then I told them the whole story: about the flight of the Bee Sting and the guy in the body bag; the threats from the men at the airport; my suspicions about my parents' death; and my talking to Marcia Colby and the man from the State Department.

"Wow." Jif was completely turned around in her seat—the only person I knew who could do that and not wrench her tits off on the shoulder harness. "How come you never told us any of this before?"

"I don't know. I guess I just blocked it off in some corner of my mind and pretended it never happened."

"Like the cask of amontillado." Jif and her Great Books.

"But when Berlie used it as a reason for me not to fly . . ."

". . . you had to find out the truth," Jif finished for me.

"Only now . . ." Fran paused long enough to shake her head.

"Now," I said, "I wish maybe everything were still bricked up behind the wall."

Friday, Feb. 13

A.M. 10:00 Take valentines and cupcakes to Patsy's class
10:15 Take Berlie's boots to shoe repair

I drove down the hill that overlooked Holly Jensen's farm. I missed sitting at her table, listening to the fire crackle in the stove. But I hoped her trip to Florida was doing some good. She had said that Sergeant Cloud's questions, the day he had taken the stuff from John's desk, had been rolling around in her head, making her feel paranoid. More than once she had caught herself looking at good solid friends with something uncomfortably close to suspicion.

I knew what she meant. Gary Fenton had had the same effect on me. Fenton the Fed, I called him, although I wasn't sure that State Department personnel were actually "feds." He had contacted me twice in the same week after my meeting with Senator Colby. I was beginning to see hidden motives in the checkout girl's

"Have a nice day," and I kept watching in the rearview mirror to see which cars turned left when I did.

I had turned over all the files to the new owners when I'd sold Topflite Medical Transport. But first I'd set aside the notes and paperwork on the Bee Sting flight. After so many years, it had taken me hours of searching before I remembered where I'd stashed them—in the shoe box with all of our old income-tax returns. I gave them to Fenton.

Fenton the Fed wasn't much on giving out information, but I got the impression that his department wasn't responsible for dispatching the assassin—neither literally nor figuratively—nor did they have anything but the foggiest idea who actually had. But maybe that was just the impression he wanted me to have. Like I said, after talking to him, I was seeing faces in the wallpaper.

I passed Holly's fields, and Rebecca's. I hoped I was wrong about this affair business. I liked the Flower Lady, and if all Holly had said about Rebecca's husband were true, I wished her some happiness in her life, wherever she might find it. But I liked Holly's sister just because she was Holly's sister, and I didn't want to think of her husband and the Flower Lady taking a roll in the hay—or pursuing any other agricultural interests, for that matter.

In a haze of suspicion and unkind thoughts I turned right at the corner of Hilltop and Benson Mill Road, causing Patsy's cupcakes to slide across the floor of the trunk. At the end of Rebecca's field was a 7UP can, and there were two more along the wooded stretch of road. I was almost afraid to look any farther.

Three more cans stood on the big rock that had a little pine tree growing out of it—one of Patsy's favorite landmarks. Had Fenton spooked me, or was something strange going on?

On my return trip, the cans were still there. I had let my imagination run away with me; I'd been Fenton-foozled. As I turned the corner of Hilltop I could see a shiny Chrysler New Yorker in Rebecca's driveway. Well, I thought, at least it wasn't the sort of car Frazier Claiborne would drive.

If Frazier hadn't been out of town on business, Rebecca wouldn't have been home Wednesday morning—their usual time together—

when the man from Masterson Development Corporation showed up behind her shed. She'd been out there checking on the compost and nearly jumped out of her skin when his long shadow fell across the pile as he raised his hand to tip his hat.

"Sorry, ma'am," he wheezed as he lifted his wool hounds-tooth check fedora. His shoes, very expensive, she guessed, were nearly submerged in the newly thawed mud that covered the ground and driveway. "Just looking around the property. I was told nobody'd be home."

The man's tongue flicked out to wet his lips. "Hope you don't mind." His voice and hands bespoke a man in his late fifties, but his smooth baby face looked fresh and hopeful, as if he were drawing his lifeblood from some secret, rejuvenating source.

A dart of fear caught her in the chest. Did anyone know about her and Frazier?

"Why would you be looking around my property?"

"Oh." He reached into his coat pocket and pulled out a card. "Jim Carson, Masterson Development Corporation." He held the card out to her.

"My property is not for sale."

A cloud of consternation crossed his face. "Isn't this the Stott property? Corner of Benson Mill and Hilltop Road?"

Rebecca's mind was racing. There had been a spate of phone calls lately, people asking for Barton, people whose voices were unfamiliar to her. Dehydrator business, he had said. But they didn't sound like farmers or feed brokers—they sounded like Ulyssia people, people with a lot of words but not much sense. She had been too busy painting the front room and the kitchen to give it much thought.

"You have the right place, but it's not for sale."

"But I—" he began.

She took two steps forward, not sure what she was going to do. The pitchfork resting against the shed caught her eye, and she reached for it. "Who told you this place was for sale?"

"Why, Bart told me." He took two steps backwards and glanced at his car.

" 'Bart'? Not 'Mr. Stott'? I don't know what *Bart*"—she spat the word out—"told you, *Mr.* Carson, but the place is *not for sale!*"

The man's countenance suddenly changed from something close to fear to cloying sweetness, the kind of look some people use with very small children—or with crazy people.

"Oh. Well. I understand, Mrs. Stott. I'll be going now. Have a nice day."

As he slipped and slopped through the mud to his car, she saw him sizing up the fancy millwork on the front porch, a design her grandfather had drafted and cut himself. Could his vision penetrate the thick walls to reveal the old Oriental carpets and her modest legacy of fine antiques in the parlor?

Now, she thought, I know where his odd youthfulness comes from: He must suck it out of the land, once people let him get his hands on it.

When his car was no longer in sight, she opened the door of the shed and stepped over the sill. The single window was too dirty to let in much light, but the dimness pleased her. She sat down on a bale of straw next to the potting table and let the place steady her thoughts.

This was where she used to come as a child—to work out her problems, her worries, and disappointments. In the unbearably hot days of late summer, her grandmother would hang armloads of herbs and special flowers from the low rafters, and they would slowly dry out, the changes in them almost as subtle as the gradual rounding and smoothing of Rebecca's angular young body.

On the wall behind the potting table the smaller gardening tools, some of them eighty years old, hung between double pegs. The shovel, spade, pitchfork, rake, and hoe hung on the wall by the door. How many more seasons would she feel the smoothness of their handles against her palms? How long before some auctioneer motioned towards them—"an odd lot"—and they wound up on the wall of some overpriced restaurant that used to be someone's flyblown dairy barn?

She scooted back farther on the bale and eased her shoulders against the wall. She used to bring her guitar out here, in the years before she knew Barton, and sing and play in the gathering darkness, with the sound of the crickets and the tree frogs and the birds that sing at dusk waiting just outside of the shed, like a soft summer blanket placed at the foot of the bed in case the night grew too cool. What was that song she had sung, in the years before the music had gone out of her life? Only the first few lines would come, but even thinking about the old songs made her feel better.

Come all ye fair and tender maidens;
Take warning how you court your men.

She laid her head against the wall and looked up into the rafters, searching for the words. What she saw, along the top of a beam, was the translucent grey skin of a black snake, five feet long.

At midnight, when she heard the sound of her husband's boots on the stairs, she turned on the light and sat up in bed, pulling the covers tight about her. It was so cold in the bedroom she could see her breath. In the winter she always wore layers of flannel— a nightgown and several shirts—and woolen socks and sometimes even mittens to bed. He wouldn't let her use an electric heater to make up for the inadequacy of the old furnace: He claimed it might cause a fire. She doubted he could even imagine the joy of being warm.

"You sick or somethin'?" His voice sounded like a rat sliding down a tin roof.

"A real estate man was here today." Masterson Development Corporation might not exactly be a realty company, but she was playing a hunch.

"Oh? Which one?" He peeled off his trousers and stood in his long underwear, scratching himself.

Which *one*?

"What's going on, Barton? I thought we were going to sign on with the Farmland Protection Program. We've got the papers and everything."

He took off his socks and threw them into the corner. "Just looking out for number one." He got into bed.

"Number one? Where do I fit in?" She could feel his bony arm reaching down to scratch his balls.

"Heeheehee," he said. Another rat down the roof. "I guess that makes you number two. Heeheehee." He laughed at his bathroom humor for a long time, shaking the bed. "Number two," he repeated drowsily and slunk off to sleep.

"He's going to sell my farm." Rebecca wasn't telling Frazier in order to gain pity; she was just trying to explain the despair she was feeling in spite of his presence. She didn't want to depend on him, either. Frazier put his arm around her as they lay on the Navajo blanket. More words of the song came back to her, its melody trailing in and out of her thoughts.

> *Be careful how you court your men.*
> *They are like the stars of a summer's morning.*
> *They first appear . . . and then they're gone.*

Well, she thought, when they're gone, they're gone.

She stretched her body against his solid strength and tried to explain what the farm meant to her, how it had shaped what she was, how "owning it in memory" would never be enough.

She told him what the lawyer had said when she had asked him about the joint title: "There's no way you can change it without him knowing, Mrs. Stott. And if you divorce him, you'd probably have to sell the farm to give him half. Unless he agreed to sell you his half." Well, he wouldn't. And even if he did, where would she get that kind of money?

"But, Rebecca," Frazier had said, "he can't sell anything without your signature. You talk as if your farm is as good as lost."

She pulled herself to a sitting position, drawing his topcoat up to her neck for warmth.

"I had a trunk," she said, "a mahogany trunk. My grandfather had had it shipped all the way from Burma when he was a young man. A wedding present to my grandmother. It had elephants of all sizes carved on it, and it was inlaid with ivory and mother-of-pearl." Her fingers could almost feel the delicate designs along the borders as she described it.

"One day a woman came up to the house for some flowers, and she saw the trunk and offered me eight hundred dollars for it. I told her that it wasn't for sale, but Bart told her to come back in a few days. When she came back, she got the trunk."

"But—" Frazier looked at her in disbelief. "If you loved it . . . ?"

"That's the way Bart can be."

"He doesn't beat you!" Frazier's neck became taut steel.

"No. He can be much worse than that and not even lay a hand on me."

They lay very still for a long, long while. She could almost hear Frazier's mind pacing up and down its own corridors. And then they made love again.

"I hear you wrapped up your first assignment." Harry Grimes stirred his coffee and wiped off the plastic stirrer with a napkin.

I couldn't help smiling, even though it had been a crappy morning. "Yep. Those construction thefts turned out to be inside jobs— or a variation on the theme. Guy with Conger construction had a buddy at Superior Builders who had a buddy at Walton Homes. You get the picture."

"You nail 'em yourself?"

Let the pun war begin, I thought. "It wasn't really detective work. I got an idea about how to catch them, and it worked. You might say we lumbered into the culprit."

"What do you mean?" Harry eyed me suspiciously.

"I was going home after setting up a sensor in West Wiggins— we only had two that were working—and in front of me I see this flatbed trailer going down I-70 with a load of two-by-fours."

"So?" Grimes said. "Were they speeding?"

"Nah, but it was three in the morning. And the tractor had 'Superior Homes' on the door—strictly a local outfit. Who makes lumber deliveries at three in the morning? I followed them out to Newton, where they unloaded the stuff. I tracked the driver for three days, and then he made another hit. Conger Builders, over in east Ulyssia. We only nailed two at the site, but when we drilled them, they folded"—I gave him my most wicked smile—"like a house of cards."

"God, Cloud. Show some self-respect." Grimes was pun-stunned.

"OK." It felt good to laugh again. "Anyway, there were six of 'em involved, and they were building themselves each a house—had a twenty-acre tract way out in Newton, near the county line. They were working on the third house when the shit hit the fan. Great big places, too—five hundred thou, easy—maybe more. It would've been a real exclusive development when they got done." I laughed. "They could've called it 'Pirates' Cove.'"

"Cloud." Harry rolled his eyes.

"'Robbers' Glen.'"

"Cloud."

"'Filchers' Fields.'"

"I give up." Harry walked out of the lunchroom. I buttoned my jacket against the cold and went home to work up a report on Frazier Claiborne.

The Claiborne assignment wasn't nearly as difficult as "Filchers' Fields" had been, but it wasn't as straightforward, either. Frazier Claiborne *did* have irregular hours—in a very regular sort of way. He *always* arrived at work at 7:30 A.M., but he left at odd times. Keeping track of him at Applied Science Associates would have been troublesome because of the security around the place—ASA was crawling with defense contracts. But the single access road into the complex and Claiborne's habit of leaving only on the hour made things easier.

I couldn't figure out why he had made two trips to the Elk Glen dehydrator in one week—or any trips, for that matter. But it became unimportant after the second visit. Wednesday, it was. It was a bitter-cold day, a day, as Grandfather used to say, when the birds fall frozen from the sky. Only it wasn't frozen birds that came plummeting to earth; it was Kay Claiborne's grim truth.

After Claiborne left the grounds of the dehydrator, he turned right on Benson Mill Road and then took the next right—onto the grounds of the Elk Glen Country School. Was he lusting after a schoolteacher? I wondered. I waited long enough so he wouldn't see my car following him and got to the parking lot just in time to see him melt into the grey woods next to the lot. He didn't look around—he made his way through the trees as if he owned them. On a little rise, just beyond sight of the lot, he came to an improbable stone tower. It reminded me of something from a story Aunt Wiyanna had told me years and years ago.

I waited, crouched behind a large limestone outcrop, until I could almost hear Grandfather's laugh knifing through the crystal air: "On such a day the buffalo stands very still—so his frozen balls do not clank together and shatter into a thousand pieces. Don't move, Black Cloud, don't move!"

By the time Claiborne returned from the tower, I *couldn't* move. He'd been gone a few minutes when I saw the massive door open again, and a woman slipped out into the cold. She drew her worn car coat tight against her body and headed down a slope, deeper into the woods. If she held her direction, I calculated, she'd come out on Benson Mill Road.

Slowly, so as not to shatter anything, I rose from my hiding place and went back to the car, revving the heater up to high. I got to the end of the school's drive just in time to see her cross the main road and enter a stand of pines. I pulled out onto Benson Mill and then angled off the road as far as I could on the westbound shoulder. I locked the car and raised the hood and then quietly, thinking of Uncle Red Cloud and his ill-tempered lessons in tracking, I slipped into the pinewoods and began to follow her.

Stretches of open fields alternating with narrow remnants of woodlands made the job fairly simple. But the woman was nervous and continually looked around her like a winter rabbit. Still, she was traveling in a straight line, more or less, and I could hang back and follow her without much guesswork.

In less than twenty minutes she came to the edge of a large cultivated field, skirted it, and let herself in the back door of an old stone house. Looking beyond the house and the field in front of it, I was startled to see the familiar outlines of Holly Jensen's farmhouse in the distance.

"You mean you didn't have an idea of where your game was headed, Black Cloud?" my uncle's voice droned in my mind. "You must think like your quarry; you must know where you are headed."

Put a sock in it, Uncle Red, I thought as I made my way back to the car.

The next day I caught sight of the woman's face as Claiborne led her from the tower to his Mercedes. Although her black hair was shot through with silver, the expression on her face was that of a little child—one that had suddenly been handed a present. She looked up at Claiborne with delighted expectation. It made me think of Cinderella. Claiborne, I could see by the look in her eyes, had turned her drab world into sparkling waltzes and satin and silk.

Well, I thought, sitting at my kitchen table with pencil and paper in front of me, Claiborne has been waving his magic wand in someone else's castle. I picked up the pencil and began writing the report that would probably turn a sweet woman's carriage into a pumpkin and her horses back into rats.

Chapter Twenty

Friday, Feb. 20

P.M.   1:00   Lunch/Angelita's

IT WAS AN IMPOSTER of a day. Everybody knew it, but nobody cared. Here it was, the dead of February; it had snowed fourteen inches last Thursday, and today it was 68 degrees, the sun was shining, and the lilac buds were trying to open. Tomorrow or the next day it would be back down to thirty, but today everyone was all stirred up with the crazy hopefulness that only spring can inspire. Everyone but me.

I did try, though, to get into the spirit of things.

"It may be February in Endicott Mills," I said, "but it's spring-time in Dr. Masseter's Porsche." I didn't have to wait to get everyone's attention. "Last night when I was bringing Phillip home from Scouts, I saw Masseter weaving all over Benson Mill Road, playing touchy-feely. Whoever she is, she's a blonde. What a jerk." I looked to Elena for confirmation, but Elena didn't seem to hear me. To my surprise, she looked absolutely radiant.

"I told you so," Jif crowed, "the day you told us about his little red sports car. I told you he was going to hell in a hand basket."

"You won't believe this"—Elena's eyes sparkled with an almost forgotten fire—"but I've met someone." The Masseter affair flew out the window.

"Who? Where?" We tried to modulate the volume of our voices from a McDonald's level to one more suitable for Angelita's—"Home of the Flaming Fajitas." It took some effort.

"Carpool. I met him driving carpool." She stopped to munch a nacho. "I was waiting outside the elementary school for Mitchell's origami class to let out when this huge sheepdog leaped out the rear window of the station wagon in front of me. Then this really nice-looking man got out and tried to catch the dog, but the dog wasn't having any of it. Well, finally I got out of the car and flagged the guy down as he raced by. I said, 'If you just wait a few minutes, your problem will be solved.'

"He said, 'What do you mean?' And I said, 'Just wait; you'll see.'

"While we waited, we talked. He's a writer for the *Baltimore Sun*. His wife died three years ago, and he has a daughter in backgammon class. Anyway, just then, all the kids in the after-school enrichment program came out and the dog went into action. It had every one of them rounded up and standing by Jim's car—that's his name—Jim. When the dog came up to him for congratulations, Jim grabbed him and put him in the back seat."

"How'd you know the dog would do that?" Jif swept our nacho crumbs across the hand-painted tiles of the tabletop and brushed them into a napkin.

"Sheepdogs. If they can't find a sheep, they'll herd kids—or anything else, for that matter. Anyway, that was yesterday, and we went out to dinner last night, and, well, I think this might just be something."

"Oh, wow," Fran said. She signaled the waiter. "Another round of daiquiris," she said. "Time to celebrate."

"A celebration?" the waiter said. A sly grin crossed his face. "Ah, I understand." He hurried off.

I really was pleased about Elena, but it was hard to cover up my other feelings. The fake palm trees, terra-cotta floors, and adobe walls were really getting depressing.

"I've got some good news too." Fran hoisted her knitting bag into her lap and pulled out a brightly colored sweater in a geometric design. "I was about the fifth car in line at Elk Glen on Monday, and I was sewing this together when a car pulled up beside me and a woman in a suede suit and jewelry from head to toe got out and asked to see what I was doing. To make a long story short, she followed me home and looked at all the things I've been making and, well"—Fran paused to flash an excited smile—"I'm working on consignment for her shop—The Natural Unicorn."

"That's fantastic," said Jif. We all agreed. "Maybe we should order doubles—I may have something worth celebrating too."

What was this, a Pollyanna festival? Everyone turned to look at Jif.

"I've been thinking about going into business," she said.

"What, a job? What would you do with the kids?" I knew the Ludloffs could afford child care, but juggling their schedules would be incredibly difficult. Of course, there was always Yupplettes on Wheels.

"Into *business*. For myself. I'd be working out of my home." She lined up our empty cocktail glasses in a row along the aisle edge of the table.

"Oh shit—not Amway!" I put my hand to my heart. This was too much. "Please, tell me it's not Amway."

"Not Amway. What I'm thinking about is a closet-organization service."

"A what?" Fran nearly knocked over the drink the waiter was setting in front of her.

"Closet organization. You know how awful some people's closets are?"

We all mumbled noncommittally and avoided eye contact.

"Well, for a fee, based on square feet, I'd come in and make order out of chaos. Even help people decide what to throw out." She turned her drink around so the edge of the napkin was parallel with the edge of the table. "At least, I'd start with that. Then I could do kitchen organization and eventually time management."

The rest of us sat there, trying to imagine it—a world without clutter. Above us a stuffed parrot on a perch slowly turned in the air currents.

"Well, it's a great idea. And you'll be perfect for it."

"What about advertising? How are you going to handle that?" I stirred my drink with a disgustingly cute jalapeño-shaped swizzle stick.

"That's about the only thing I'll need start-up funds for. I'll buy two-, maybe even four-column ads in the county papers and put coupons in those mailers you get and placards in shop windows and put fliers in the mailboxes—Jenny, could I hire your services for that?" She finally stopped for breath.

"I'm out of the delivery and piecework business." I set down my glass with a ringing finality.

"You mean you've got enough money to finish your flying lessons?" Fran looked so happy for me, I could have cried.

"No. I mean there'll never be enough money to get back in the air, so why bother?" The last thing I wanted to do was start crying in Angelita's. It would be so embarrassing.

"What do you mean?" Elena put her hand on my shoulder.

"I mean that last night the roof started leaking, and even though the man said he could patch it enough to hold it 'til spring, come April they'll have to rip the whole thing off and put on a new one. It'll cost three thousand dollars. It's just a drop in the bucket, but the thousand I've saved up will be one thousand less we'll have to borrow against the house."

Before anyone could say anything, five waiters came dancing around the corner, singing "Happy Birthday to You" to the tune of "La Cucaracha," the little black balls on their sombreros bobbling back and forth like troupes of Bolshoi-trained gerbils. Just as the song ended, they stopped at our table, and a two-hundred-and-fifty-pound gay ranchero stepped forward and plunked down a giant enchilada impaled by five blazing sparklers.

"And who's the birthday girl?" he said, looking expectantly from face to face. When he got to me, I burst into tears.

"There, there, sweetie," he said as the waiters turned to leave. "We all have to get old sometime."

Everyone at the other tables was staring. I took a deep breath and used the Kleenex Jif gave me.

"I'm glad things are working out for you all," I said and tried to smile. "But my life right now—it's just one big flaming fajita."

Chapter Twenty-one

Saturday, April 18

"BERLIE, PLEASE DON'T GO DOWN THERE." I stood looking down into the pit that would eventually become the basement of Elk Glen's new high school. I knew I was wasting my breath.

"Look where they put the dynamite." Berlie was rubbing his hands together as if he were about to dig into Thanksgiving dinner. "Look at the grooves they made in the rock."

It had taken bulldozers and dynamite to hollow out the foundation from the boulder-infested field. Patsy had laughed about the broken windows in the old school, but I had wondered about the wisdom of holding classes during the blasting. "It's OK," Berlie had said, "if you know what you're doing."

Who ever really knew what they were doing?"

Overhead, a Cessna 210 circled lazily in the sky, like a hawk with a full belly just out for the thermal ride. I sat down on an uprooted monolith and waited in the dappled sunlight while Berlie descended into the hole.

"You'll get muddy," I called down to him. "If Patsy sees you down there, she'll die a thousand deaths."

Our children were used to seeing him muddy—he kept an old shower curtain in his car to sit on after caving expeditions—but the kids would rather drop dead than to have friends see their father covered with slime and grinning like an idiot.

"Patsy's petition saved the tree. Did I tell you they're going to build the school around it?" I could see him picking up objects from time to time as he walked about the excavation. He put some of them in his pocket.

I wasn't sure he'd heard me. "The tree will be in a sort of courtyard. The signatures from Ted Kennedy and John Glenn were a help. But I think it was the one from Paul McCartney that did the trick. What do you think?"

He didn't answer.

"Oh, Berlie, come up out of that hole!"

Chapter Twenty-two

Monday, May 4

A.M.   Change oil

THE ONLY TROUBLE WITH CHANGING THE OIL YOURSELF, I observed as I pulled into the Clark County Sanitary Landfill, was that you had to find a place to get rid of the stuff you drained out. Well, at least no one at the dump would complain about the way my car smelled. Indeed, it might be perfume to their overworked noses. The woman at the gate had to give me a map of the dump to direct me to the oil-recycling tank. A map of the dump: What would archaeologists make of that in five hundred years?

Ever since the roof on the house had gone bad, it seemed to me that the forces of gravity had increased to a level that was insurmountable. I thought of the chart my dad and I had used—the one with various factors used to calculate how much takeoff distance would be needed under certain conditions. The way my life was going, no matter how mild the temperature, how favorable the winds, no matter how long the obstacles I had to clear, my little craft would never be light enough or strong enough to become airborne by the end of the runway. The rest of my life would be spent taxiing back and forth behind the yellow holding lines.

Something moving along the edge of pit nineteen caught my eye. I looked, hoping it wasn't a rat. It was a raccoon. I hadn't seen a live one in ages. In fact, the only local wildlife my children had ever seen, except for the rabbits that harried Berlie's garden and the lousy squirrels that raided the bird feeder, were the dead animals they had spotted beside the road. They'd seen opossum and skunks, foxes and raccoons, even an occasional deer. All dead, the life bludgeoned out of them by the continuous stream of cars going back and forth, back and forth, on stupid errands.

"Erica Tempell thinks she is so-o-o hot." Crista Galli sounded as if she were thirteen years old instead of ten.

"I know. Like, she keeps wearing those same three sweaters from Benetton's. Like they were something special or something." Pontine Kohler, whose voice usually had a sweet giggly sound, could have passed for Rona Barrett today.

I looked in the rearview mirror at them. Oh no—had puberty reared its ugly head so soon? "Does everybody have their seat belts on?" I asked. Sometimes I felt as if I had died and been reincarnated as one of those recorded voices that comes out of the dashboard in swank Japanese cars.

Patsy, sitting next to me in the front seat, gave me a world-weary look. "Ye-e-es, Mother."

This is it, I thought. Puberty. Why did it have to come now? Why did it have to take these sweet children and turn them into nasty little beasts for indefinite stretches of time? And why did Phillip have to be in its grip at the same time Patsy seemed to be revving up? They were four years apart! So much for family planning.

"Like, did you see what Betsy did in P.E. today?" Crista started the ball rolling again.

"Yeah." Pontine gave an ugly little laugh. "Like, when she came out of the locker room, everyone had, like, already gone out on the field. So she, like, went back in the locker room and, like, hid. Like, I guess she was, like, embarrassed or something."

"Yeah," said Patsy. "But, like, did you hear what Sandy Simpson did?"

This was driving me crazy. "Don't say *like* when you don't need to."

Patsy looked at me about as long as she would at a housefly and went on with what she seemed to think was a hilarious narration. "Like, Sandy went and, like, told Mrs. Humper that, like, Betsy was still in the locker room. And Mrs. Humper, like, went in and found her, and Betsy, she, like, cried for the rest of the day." The girls all laughed.

I wanted to, like, puke. "You girls seem to be getting a lot of pleasure out of someone else's misery. That's not very nice, is it?"

"*Maa-um.*" Patsy ground the word out into three or four syllables. "You, like, don't understand." She seemed to be addressing some cretin. "Betsy Parker is, like, *so-o-o* hoss."

Whatever that meant. My only hope lay in tuning them out. It was May in Clark County, and what was left of the countryside was lush and green. Tiny shoots of corn striped the fields, and the cows looked bloated on new grass. The trees just barely waved their branches, as if shifting to get more comfortable under the unaccustomed weight of their fleshy young leaves.

I drove past the gate of the Franciscan monastery. I always turned my head in that direction with the unreasonable expectation of hearing bells or the ghostly sound of ancient plainsong. The field beyond was newly plowed, but I couldn't tell what was just beginning to come up. The next field was the Flower Lady's. Rebecca Stott's.

Six or seven black trash bags lay helter-skelter in the ditch between the road and the field. Some animal—probably a raccoon—had torn one open, and egg cartons and cereal boxes and paper towels were strewn all around.

"Look at that," I heard myself saying to the girls. "People have come out here and thrown their trash in the Flower Lady's ditch. What a mess."

We turned the corner onto Hilltop Road and passed the two mailboxes, STOTT and JENSEN, nestled together on the same side of the road, like tin widows seeking solace.

"I'm surprised she hasn't cleaned it up," I continued, although I knew no one was listening. "She always keeps her place so neat."

"Like, maybe," Patsy said in the quiet, gentle way I had feared was gone forever, "maybe she's feeling sick or something."

I reached over and patted my daughter's knee. "Like, maybe you're right, sweetheart."

At the end of the week, after surviving a schedule blacked in with sports practices, play practice, doctors' appointments, music and art lessons, and a field trip to the National Zoo, I had clocked a record sixty-five hours of carpooling. I staggered into the kitchen just before dinner Friday evening and threw my keys down in front of Berlie, who sat at the table reading a *Bob & Bob* caving equipment catalogue.

"I hate the word *like*!"

Berlie raised his eyebrows and read on.

"I *hate hormones*!"

He glanced up for a microsecond, then looked back down at the print.

"And I *hate* CARS!" I stomped out of the room.

Berlie didn't even have the decency to wait two seconds before he called after me. "You wouldn't feel that way, honey, if you had a nice big station wagon."

I slammed the bathroom door behind me.

Even with the sound of the water in the shower, the whole neighborhood probably heard my scream. Primal. I turned off the shower to hear what the reaction would be.

"Dad," I heard Phillip say, "you'd better cool it with the station wagon."

"I don't know why she's so pigheaded about that. Do you?" The two men were probably shaking their heads.

I turned the water back on.

"Pigheaded!" I yelled. "I'll give them pigheaded! They don't—"

Bacall had pushed open the bathroom door with her nose and

was staring at me, her muzzle pressed against the glass shower door. At least someone was concerned.

"Come out of there, Bacall," Linnea said, pulling the dog back out into the hall. "Mom's just talking to herself."

She said she had come to my workshop to check on the Elk Glen project. But it was nine o'clock Friday night, a time when the mothers of Clark County were driving their little darlings to parties, dances, or the movies. Besides, it was easy to read Jenny Meade's face. Or it would have been if only she'd stopped racing around the shop like a Tasmanian devil. If I hadn't known better, I'd have thought she was wired.

"What's going on, Jenny?"

She looked at me with horses-in-a-thunderstorm eyes. "I don't know. I don't know. I can't slow down. I just . . ." She threw her hands up in exasperation and then used them to cover her face.

I put my arm around her shoulders and firmly led her into the kitchen. The smell of her hair made me think of lemons and—oddly enough—horses. But her coat smelled like gasoline.

"You been sniffing high test?" I sat her down at the table. She looked at her coat and shrugged.

"I got gas all over myself at the Shell station today. The damned pump wouldn't work and wouldn't work, and then—pooom!—it worked." Her voice was clenched high in her throat, but her wild eyes seemed to calm slightly as she watched me fix tea.

"I'm going to make you something to eat. OK?"

She nodded absently. "I know what it is," she said. "I've been on the road too much. This is what happens every time. I get *'rollin', rollin', rollin','*" she sang the theme song from the old *Rawhide* television show, "and then I can't stop."

" 'Head 'em up! Move 'em out,' " I called as I scalded the teapot, dumped in one of Aunt Wiyanna's huge homemade teabags, and filled it with boiling water. I got some lettuce, carrots, and baby snow peas from the refrigerator and started a salad. When it was ready, I plunked down a large bowlful for each of us and poured the tea. She ate as if she were hungry. Or maybe it was nervous energy.

"Did you have dinner?"

She shook her head.

"You want to talk about it?"

She did. She'd been behind the wheel almost nonstop, her husband had been away, her kids' schedules were impossible, her plans for flying weren't working out the way she wanted them to, and nobody cared about the environment.

"Whoa," I said. "You want to try that last one on me again?" She had calmed down a lot, but I poured her some more tea anyway.

She laughed a little, at herself, I guessed. "Trash. Idiots are throwing trash all over the place. You should've seen out there by Benson Mill and Hilltop today."

Out where Holly Jensen lived.

"Garbage all over the place. Nobody cares anymore."

Holly Jensen would care. Well, maybe not right now, I thought, not for a while longer. But you could tell she'd really care about things like that. I could picture her in some protest march in the sixties. Too bad she'd missed all that. Well, maybe not.

"That reminds me," Jenny broke into my thoughts. "I saw something out there. . . . I want to see what you think about it."

"Shoot."

She massaged her right hand with her left absentmindedly, the way the old people did in the winter. "In the woods, along the way to Elk Glen, there were these cans. First they were there; then they weren't."

By the time she'd finished her story, I had grown worried about Jenny Meade. Not because of her state of mind. Aunt Wiyanna's calm-down tea and my mother's go-to-sleep salad had begun their work on her. I was worried because it was possible that Jenny Meade had bumped into something again. Something more dangerous than John Jensen's dead body.

Chapter Twenty-three

Thursday, May 7

"I KNOW WHAT." I tried to sound enthusiastic, in spite of the effect record levels of tree pollen were having on my eyes, nose, and head. "Let's go out and look at the airplanes." I carefully made my way past the clumps of cars in St. O's parking lot.

"Does my mother know you're taking us to a strange place?" Matty Kohlrausch wanted to know.

How do they stand that kid? I wondered. He was an eighty-year-old man trapped in a four-year-old's body. What would he be like when he was forty? He probably wouldn't live that long; somebody would strangle him before then.

"You like airplanes, Matty," Linnea squeaked. The tree pollen had gotten her, too. In fact, everyone at home was sniffling and snorting and complaining that the insides of their heads didn't seem to fit the outsides anymore. Spring. "And besides," Linnea added, "we can pick some flowers for our mommies while we're there."

"My mother wouldn't want me to get dirty."

Your mother, I wanted to say, would be ecstatic if you got down and wallowed like a hog, you obsessive-compulsive little creep.

I didn't know what had gotten into me. Matty wasn't all that bad. In a way, he was kind of sad.

"I won't get dirty, will I, Mrs. Meade?"

"No, Matty. Not unless you want to. But it would be OK if you did." No one in *our* family had ever had a fear of dirt. Must be Berlie's genes.

It occurred to me that my tolerance of life's petty annoyances was dangerously low. Fenton the Fed had been around again. He was long on questions and short on answers. I didn't trust him. What was worse, after a few minutes with him, I didn't trust anybody—even myself.

Well, maybe a trip to Ganton's Farm would make me feel better. Maybe it'd make me feel worse. Maybe I didn't really care.

The last thing I wanted to see was those damned 7UP cans— only this time they were Dr Pepper. Same number, same position. I wondered what Fenton would make of that. Maybe I'd tell him tomorrow at the meeting he'd set up—after I dropped Phillip off at Dr. Masseter's for a ninety-minute torture-the-teen appointment. Fenton would probably make me think that the woods were full of spies cavorting in the undergrowth, naked except for their plastic-laminated government IDs dangling from chains around their necks.

We pulled into Ganton's parking lot next to the trailer, and the kids hit the gravel at a run.

"Whoa, there." They stopped. "Stay up here near the office, and don't climb on any planes. And don't"—I shook my finger at them—"go near the runway." I pointed to the long expanse of grass beyond the trailer.

I found Bud underneath the Cherokee, fiddling with a wheel strut. He had put a whole new skin on her, rebuilt the engine, and was now working on "the small stuff," as he called it—even though nothing on an airplane was "small stuff" if it crapped out on you in the air.

"Hey," I said.

"Hey yourself." He looked up and nodded. "Where've you been so long?"

"I told you about the roof."

"Yeah. So?" He put down one wrench and picked up another.

"So, it knocked me for a loop. Set me back a notch."

"Mmmmmm-mmmmmh. I didn't have you figured for a quitter."

Quitter! I could feel my face getting red. "If I could remember which one of your eyes didn't work, I'd hit you in the other one."

He stopped working on the strut and squinted up at me. The sun must have been at my back.

"I'm not a quitter," I said.

"Oh, yeah? Carter says you'll be ready for him to sign off your biennial flight review in less than three hours—that's maybe three hundred dollars, three-fifty tops—and you'd be ready to go. You willing to let three hundred and fifty bucks get between you and flying?"

My breathing grew rapid and shallow. Calm down, I told myself.

"I can't get it right now. I told you, we had to borrow for the roof, and—"

"Where were you going to get the capital to start up your business? How were you going to get Nightingale Transport off the ground?"

I wished I hadn't spent so much time talking to him about my plans for a new medical transport operation. I sat down in the grass and tried to make my breathing slow down. It took a while.

"I was going to borrow it. Against the house."

"So borrow the three-fifty." He pulled a flattened sandwich out of his back pocket and offered me a bite. Peanut butter and jelly. It smelled like WD-40. I shook my head.

"I can't borrow it. Not before I get my credentials in order. Berlie would—"

"Forget Berlie. He doesn't understand. Borrow it from me."

I wasn't sure I'd heard him right. "But I—"

"You could pay me back by the end of June, couldn't you?"

"The end of June?" School would be out, I thought. Yuck. More driving.

"Or the end of July. By the time I get everyone ready for the rally, I'll be rolling in money."

"The rally?" I felt like Little Sir Echo, but there was no helping myself. The whole conversation had a suspiciously dreamlike quality.

"The aeroclub rally. End of this month, remember? They all go to Ocean City? Maybe even this old girl will make it." He patted the Cherokee's empennage. "So how about it? Three-fifty until the end of July?"

I could hear the sound of an approaching aircraft. A Cessna 210 was coming in over the last row of trees. "Well, OK, I guess—" From the corner of my eye I could see Linnea and Matt picking violets next to the deck behind the trailer.

The plane was slipping and yawing all over the place.

"Who is that coming in?" I asked. "What's the matter with him?"

Bud looked up. "Oh, that's Reynolds. He does that every time. Looks terrible, but he cleans it up at the last minute."

The plane set down in midfield, but continued taxiing at almost full speed. He was headed straight for the trailer.

"Linnea!" I screamed and took off at a dead run. "Linnea!" But my voice was drowned out by the sound of the engine.

I tackled both children at full tilt and all three of us slid under the deck on our bellies. We heard a slight thump, and then everything was quiet.

We crawled out into the sunlight. Bud was standing at the open door of the Cessna, pointing to a nick on the corner of the trailer, waving his arms, and shouting unusual obscenities.

I stared at the two children. Slowly, against all odds, a laugh worked its way up. Linnea and Matty looked like salamanders glistering with mud.

"You guys OK?"

They nodded.

"A little dirty, though," I said. I looked at Matty to check his reaction.

"Not half as dirty as you are, Mrs. Meade." He actually giggled.

I didn't need to see my clothes—I could feel the mud soaking clear through to my underwear.

"Mommy," Linnea croaked, "you look just like Daddy."

From a few lousy soda cans, Fenton created reams of notes. I was sorry I'd told him. On the other hand, I thought, maybe I could use it to get a little hard information out of him, for a change. If I'd known what he was going to say, I wouldn't have asked.

"Your parents were murdered, Mrs. Meade."

Everything stopped. My heartbeat, my thoughts—even, it seemed to me, the noise from the restaurant tables all around us.

"Murdered." I watched my friends' eyes go wide and then soften with shared pain.

"Well, now you know." Fran patted my arm and dabbed her eyes with a McDonald's napkin. I had called them together for an emergency breakfast meeting. The pancakes and hash browns and McMuffins lay untouched at our elbows.

"The fact that it was ten years ago probably doesn't make it any easier, does it?" Fran handed me a napkin, too.

I shook my head.

"The State Department guy—he's the one who told you?"

I nodded.

"Does he know who did it?"

"He's not saying, except that it's the same people responsible for the guy in the body bag's death." We sat there for a long while, just pushing food around on our plates.

"Have you told Berlie?" Elena broke the silence.

"I can't. Not until we get some other things worked out. Besides, he's out of town right now."

"How'd you get the guy to tell you?" Jif made a tower of little jelly tubs next to the salt and pepper shakers. "I thought you said he was real closemouthed."

"He is, but I gave him some information he seemed to think was valuable."

"You mean about the Bee Sting guy?" Fran said.

"No, about litterbugs." I told them about the cans, how they appeared and then disappeared. "What do you think? Am I crazy?"

Elena laughed. "Of course. Who isn't?" The smile faded. "The guy acted like it meant something?"

"He took an awful lot of notes. I'd never seen him do that before."

Elena blinked her big eyes. "He must think it's some kind of signal system or something."

"I told Cloud about it too. But he didn't say anything, really."

"Well, it's probably a way to let someone's lover know when the coast is clear." Jif added another jelly tub to her tower.

I thought of the Flower Lady and Holly's brother-in-law, and a tiny shiver went up my back.

"What's the matter?" Elena said.

I hadn't wanted to tell them before, about Love in the Country. It was one thing to examine the obvious facts concerning Dr. Masseter and his midlife crisis; but to fling around idle speculations about people I didn't even know—that was serious business.

But I couldn't help it. I was in bad shape and my judgment was also. So I told them. About the tower and the footprints, at least. I didn't mention anyone's name—or the indirect way Holly was probably involved. After all, she was my friend, too.

"Jenny," Elena said as Jif started to clear the table, "when are you going to tell Berlie about your parents?"

"I can't tell him anything right now; he just left for a week in Dayton." I could feel her eyes pressing me against the back of the booth. "I'll tell him."

"Just don't wait too long," she said.

I could see what she meant, but I couldn't see me coming out the winner once Berlie had that information. For once in my life I was willing to wait, to "coast on the level"—at least until I had the flying certification in my pocket. With a little luck, maybe that would be pretty soon.

"Don't wait too long." Elena wasn't smiling and neither was anybody else. Sometimes, I thought, life would be a lot easier if your friends didn't know you so well.

So maybe it was time for a professional opinion, an opinion

from someone who knew me pretty well but wasn't exactly a friend—at least not the way Elena and Fran and Jif were. I decided to drive out to Revenge to see Tom. Besides, I reasoned, the last time I'd been out there, I'd forgotten to check on the Elk Glen sculpture.

I was unloading a fine maple log from the bed of the truck when Jenny Meade pulled into the yard. She watched me wrestle the maple to the ground and then circled around it as if she might bid on it at an auction. She had one of those preoccupied smiles that women get when they look like they're listening to someone at a party, but they're really wondering whether they unplugged the iron at home.

"You OK?" I didn't buy the nod she gave me, but I decided not to challenge her. "You come to check out the Elk Glen project?"

"Yes," she said and sat herself down on the log as if she'd stay there until she'd taken root. "I want to tell you a story," she began. It made me think of firelight on cool Montana nights a long time ago. "And I want you to tell me what you think."

I straddled the log and sat down, leaning forward to ease my back. She swiveled around to face me, throwing one blue-jeaned leg over the maple and resting her hands on her knees. My guess was she'd be as at home on a horse as she was in one of her airplanes.

"That time, in the graveyard, when I told you I wanted to fly again, you asked me why I had quit in the first place."

I nodded.

"I said I'd quit because I didn't have a plane, and that's true. But something happened on one of our last flights that may have had more to do with the demise of Topflite Medical than I knew about at the time."

It was as odd a story as I'd ever heard. I could see how the pieces might seem unrelated as they were happening. How two ordinary citizens, a man and his daughter, could be told by government agents—or people they *thought* were government agents—that it was in the country's best interest that they forget about the notorious body they had unknowingly transported to an international airport. How her parents' dying in a car accident was just one of those freak things.

"Well, what do you think?" she repeated. "I guess I *was* in danger then, like Berlie said, damn it." She tossed her head, then looked me level in the eyes. "Do you think I might be in any danger now?"

What did I think? I wasn't in the habit of telling people what I thought. At least not on the job. And for as long as I could remember, I'd been on the job. I'd come to think of people as victims, informants, witnesses, or suspects. Sometimes one person fit more than one category. But they could all be put in a category. It wasn't nice, but it was necessary.

Or was it? Jenny Meade was a friend. And she had a problem she'd brought to me. Maybe it was time for me to create a new category.

"I think you'll never know who killed your parents, Jenny, and that makes things tough. You'll never get anything out of a guy like Fenton. If it was his side that killed them, you're probably OK, because Senator Colby knows your story too. If it was anyone else"—I shrugged—"I guess it could go either way. Your best bet is to keep your eyes open."

What a crappy answer. I wondered if I could get Fenton to talk to me. My contacts at the State Department were a little old, but they still might work.

"Come on in and have some lunch." I rose from the log. "Belgian waffles with raspberry butter and whipped cream."

Her sweet, sad smile nearly broke my heart. "I can't," she said, looking at her watch. "I have to be somewhere." She took my hand and pulled herself up.

"I know it's tough," I said, "hearing the truth about your parents' death ten years after the fact. It's like they just died again, isn't it?"

She gave me a surprised look. But the surprise was on me: As she passed me to get into her car, she stopped and flung her arms around me in a quick, warm, head-burrowing hug.

"Thank you," she said. And then she was gone.

·   ·   ·

The call came at 1:45 A.M.

"Phillip's broken out with the chicken pox, Mrs. Meade." Mr. Pinter had taken the Boy Scouts camping on his farm. His voice was gravelly from interrupted sleep. "He feels to me like he's got a fever, and none of the boys will let him back in the cabin because of his spots. He'll be waiting for you just inside our front door."

"I'll go," I sighed in Berlie's ear. "You have to get up at five-thirty to make the plane to Buffalo." Was this getting written down in a good-deed book somewhere? If not, I was going to roll back over and go to sleep.

I grabbed Phillip's old Garfield comforter and a pillow and started the car. Traffic's better this time of night, I told myself. A full moon lit up the countryside with a cold, unforgiving light. Turning the corner of Hilltop and Benson Mill, I noticed a pickup truck parked along the shoulder. A man was getting out. Maybe he had thrown a hubcap. I gave him a wide berth and continued on to the Pinter's turnoff.

At the end of an axle-breaking dirt road, I was greeted by my feverish son. He shoved his gear into the hatchback and rolled himself up in the comforter. "Thanks, Mom, for coming to get me," he said weakly, and then he was out—sound asleep in the back seat.

The truck was gone when we came back by. Must have found the hubcap. But something about it didn't seem quite right. Maybe it was just the moonlight. I tried to picture the truck in my mind as I drove towards home. A black Ford, no frills, none of those ridiculous huge wheels that raised the body four feet off the road. Just a plain black truck.

There was something, though. It took me a moment to figure it out. The damn thing was clean. No mud. Clean as the day someone had signed on the dotted line. And the man, too. Something not quite right.

I pulled into the garage, hauled Phillip out, and guided him up the stairs to bed. He never woke up. It was like herding a wet noodle.

I crawled back into bed in my sweat suit and wrenched my share of the covers away from Berlie. The man with the black truck faded in and out of my consciousness. He wore jeans and the usual plaid shirt, but his shoes were clean—no mud, no cow shit. They had actually shone in the moonlight.

Imagine that, I thought sleepily. A farmer with shiny shoes. I saw him again in my mind as he got out of the truck.

"No hat!" I shouted.

Berlie sat bolt upright and yelled, "Low bat? Where?" He looked around in panic. "Where?" He slowly slumped back down onto the pillow.

"No hat," I repeated, more or less to myself. "No gimme cap. What kind of farmer'd go out without his gimme cap?"

"Don't worry about the bat," Berlie muttered. "Mouth's too small to bite you, anyway."

He rolled over, taking the covers with him.

OK, Fenton, I said to myself. You've got me thinking like you, damn it.

I crawled out of bed and rummaged in my purse for the number Fenton had told me I could call "anytime, day or night."

I could tell by the incredibly flat, controlled tone of Fenton's voice that he was so excited he was about to pee himself. Great. I'd given him one dead terrorist, several soda cans, and a spotless Ford pickup; all he'd given me was a broken heart. What a deal.

Chapter Twenty-four

"OK, JENNY." Fran's knitting needles were clicking like castanets. "Let me get this straight: You saw a guy parked on Benson Mill Road in a clean pickup—"

"And clean shoes and no gimmee cap," I added.

"And Mister State Department got real excited about this?" Jif folded her napkin into a triangle.

I nodded. "Fenton the Fed, at three in the morning."

"You think it has anything to do with those soda cans?" Fran clicked her needles double time.

"I don't know. I'd rather hold on to the trysting-lovers theory for that one."

"I don't think Fenton would get excited about someone's nookie notices." Elena made a lurid gurgling noise with the straw in her soda.

"*Nookie notices?*" Jif snorted.

Elena ignored her. "You just need to catch up on your sleep. You're still thinking about your parents, aren't you?"

I shrugged. "Tom Black Cloud is probably right: I'll never know who was responsible for their death. The tracks have been covered too well. I just have to be careful, but get on with my life. I can't argue with that."

Elena nodded. "How's Phil doing?"

"Poor Phil. He's miserable. I don't know why he didn't get the chicken pox before, when the other two kids had them. I've never seen so many pox on one body."

"That bad, huh?" Fran shook her head.

"He says he's even got them where the sun never shines."

"Reminds me of a folk song," Fran said. " 'In the pines, in the pines, where the sun never shines . . .' " she sang in a clear, sweet soprano.

When I got home, I sang Fran's song for Phillip.

"Sing it again, Mom," he said weakly. "It takes my mind off the itching."

I sang that damned song for two weeks.

"Listen to this, Mom." Phillip, his hair dripping wet from swim practice, was in the back seat, reading a book about caving. All that remained of his chicken pox were shadowy round marks all over his body. He looked like a leopard.

"What, Phillip?" It was hard for me to pay attention at six-fifty in the morning.

"Listen to this—it's about safety in caves: 'Never light a fire underground. Bat guano is flammable and has been known to explode.' " He laughed hysterically.

"What a way to go." I had to laugh. "How would you like that on your tombstone? 'Here lies Phil with his little hatchet/He'd be alive if it weren't for bat shit.' " When he stopped laughing I caught his eye in the rearview mirror. "Seriously, Phil, are you really ready to go out with Dad to Winkleman's Cave?"

"Sure, Mom. Jeez, it's just a little one. Dad says there's not much climbing."

It was a stupid question to ask a fourteen-year-old. As far as he was concerned, he was ready for anything. Still, Berlie was a good teacher. I knew he'd be careful with him.

"Why don't you come along, Mom? Dad would love it."

"No thanks."

"Why not?"

"In a word, *claustrophobia*. In another word, *guanoblas-tophobia*."

"What's that?"

I pulled into the driveway.

"Fear of exploding bat shit."

Friday, May 22

"So when do you pass your flying test?" Jif set the lemonades in a row.

"The instructor couldn't schedule me until June eighth."

"June eighth?" they all crowed in unison.

"Can't you take it sooner than that?" Elena buttered a biscuit and took a bite.

I shook my head. "The biennial takes a long time to run through, and Carter just took on a lot of new students. He couldn't fit me in any sooner." I rummaged through my salad for more garbanzos. I had to admit, now that my goal was really in sight, I was feeling much better about a lot of things.

"It's OK. I'm busy with a job anyway." I nodded towards Jif.

"My most trustworthy advertising distributor." Jif gave me the thumbs up.

"Did you get any responses from this last batch of fliers?" The word made me flinch, even as I spoke it.

"*Did* I?" Jif readjusted the alignment of the cups and pointed to me. "This woman has a knack for finding the best areas to deliver to. It's like she has this built-in radar that tells her where the most disorganized people live."

It wasn't that difficult. I just looked for places with Mercedes 500s. Or houses with swing sets in the back or little riding toys out front. The rich and the fertile—two hotbeds of unbridled disorder.

"Got to go," I said, rising from the table. "I'll try to get this last batch out today, Jif."

The inside of the car was stifling. I rolled down the windows and pulled quickly into the traffic to get the air circulating again. I could barely touch the steering wheel, it was so hot. I was halfway up to the light on Route 40 when the car lost power. Just for a moment, as if it had taken a deep breath to cure itself of hiccups. A pause so slight that I wasn't really sure it had happened.

I went on with my deliveries, out in Mt. Pisgah Estates, an old, established neighborhood where the residents had been piling up clutter for decades. I avoided the new enclave of ostentatious houses that stuck out like a goiter off to one side of the development. There, the residents parked their Audis and BMWs after a hard day's work, to come in and sit on bare living-room floors and eat dinners off unpacked boxes of books until they could afford the kind of furniture that would really "go" with their enormous houses. House-poor. They had nothing for Jif to organize but their priorities, and they wouldn't think of letting her do that.

On the way home, as I was coming up St. O's Lane, the car did it again. I put my foot to the floor, but the Honda just coasted to a stop. Dead. *Nada.* I guided the car as far off the narrow old lane as I could, set the brake, and turned on the flashers. I locked the doors and trudged off to the Shell station. Thank God I was less than two miles from the place. And thank God I didn't wear little froufrou shoes—I'd have been crippled by the time I got there.

"I bet it's the fuel filter," I told the station owner. "Remember, Grady? That's what it was the last time the car did this." We watched as the tow truck brought the car in.

"May be. But I can't get to the job till tomorrow morning." He shrugged apologetically. "I'll call you when I'm done."

I made the calls necessary to get everyone picked up for the afternoon, and set off on foot for the house. Where was Berlie when I needed him? In Peoria, that's where.

"That Honda's getting old, Mrs. Meade," Grady called out to me as I passed the last service bay. "You should get a new car. How 'bout a Porsche?" He grinned as I shook my head and kept on walking.

"*How 'bout a Porsche?*" I repeated to myself. Men. At least he didn't say station wagon.

The next morning I called Grady. "Not ready?" I couldn't believe my ears. "The car's not *ready?*" Grady was sorry. It needed a fuel filter all right, but this was Saturday, and they couldn't get one until Monday morning.

I sat down and tried to picture two days without a car. Life without wheels. There were rides to arrange—a fine web to be cast out and carpooling debts to be snared and drawn back in. But, then, it was a weekend. Berlie had come in from Peoria late last night, and he and Phillip, a major user of my driving services, had left on their caving trip early this morning and wouldn't be back until Monday night, Memorial Day.

Memorial Day! I called Grady back. It was Memorial Day for Berlie, for Phil's school, and for the federal government, but thank God it was not Memorial Day for auto parts.

I checked the calendar. It was not Memorial Day for St. O's, either, or for Elk Glen Country School, until the following weekend.

The phone rang.

"I've got something I want to talk to you about." Bud always came right to the point. "It's an idea I have. Don't much like to talk on the phone about it. You know."

I knew. For someone who liked to talk as much as Bud did— tale after tale about flying, about his boyhood on a hard-luck farm in Idaho, sometimes about his corner of the Korean War—you'd think he wouldn't become so tongue-tied on the phone.

"I won't have a car until Monday." I looked at the calendar just to be sure. All clear.

"Monday. OK, then. Make it after three—I have to get some parts for Ganton earlier on."

"Sure, I'll be out after I pick up the girls from school."

I hung up. I should have asked him if it was about the loan. I wouldn't be needing it. I'd rounded up most of the money already, working for Jif. With a little dip into the grocery money, I'd have it all by June eighth. And by then—

"*Watch that Mooney off the right wing, Jen.*"

"I see it."

"I ever tell you about the time . . . ?"

I rolled out my biscuit dough and smiled, thinking of one of Bud's stories. I cut out the fat, round shapes, buttered them, and set them in the oven. I looked at Monday on the calendar again:

> **A.M.** **Fran carpool**
> **P.U. car**
> **P.U. girls**
> **Bud/after 3:00.**

Monday might be a pretty good day after all, I thought. The girls would be off in school, the men would still be gone, and I'd have my car back.

Later, a knock came at the screen door as I was cleaning up the breakfast dishes.

"You should keep your door locked," a voice said.

I dried my hands and peeped into the foyer. It was Tom Black Cloud.

"Maybe it *is* locked," I said, reaching out for the door handle.

"Not the screen—what good would *that* do? The regular door should be locked."

"It's warm today. You don't want me to deplete the environment running the air conditioner, do you? Besides, it's a safe neighborhood. Nothing ever happens here."

He gave me a funny look, but I couldn't read it.

"No neighborhood's safe," he said.

"Oh, Tom, come on in and have a cup of tea and quit being a cop." At that he smiled, but he stayed on the front porch.

"No, I'm on my way to the mountains, to camp. I just wanted to tell you . . ."

I came out on the porch and shaded my eyes against the bright sunlight.

". . . I did some checking around over at the State Department."

My heart skipped a beat.

"And I don't think you have to worry about starting up a new business. No one's going to bother you."

"But you said"—my mind was racing—"that means you think someone there—"

"Not exactly. Don't think that. I can't tell you what *did* happen. But the upshot is, no one involved in this Bee Sting business is going to get in your way. They can't."

"Can't?"

I could see I wasn't going to get any more out of him—today, anyway.

I sat down on the step and waved as he backed his car out of the driveway and headed off for the mountains. I looked around the court at the three other houses, at the tall trees gathered along the streambed below, a dense, gentle cloud of witnesses rustling slightly in the soft breeze. It was quiet. The lawn mowers weren't out yet. Or the weed-whackers. It was too quiet for anything at all to happen.

Chapter Twenty-five

Sunday, May 24

SUNDAY MORNING while I was making pancakes, the girls surfaced from TV Land after three hours of cartoons. They wanted to go to the mall.

"We have no car." I watched my daughters' faces go blank with amazement. Where had they been yesterday? Or the day before?

"No car?" Patsy was the first to finally realize the implications. "You mean we can't even go to the Donut Nook?"

I shook my head.

"No movie tonight?"

"Not unless you can get a ride."

"Can't we go to Erol's?"

The local videotape-rental emporium would have to do without them.

"No Cold Stuff?" Linnea finally got the idea. They couldn't even take a drive to the ice-cream stand on Gideon Lane.

Patsy and I shook our heads in unison, like windshield wipers.

"Well, shit." Linnea started to walk out of the room.

"Linnea!" I grabbed my youngest and swung her around.

"Boy, Linnea, you're gonna get it now." Patsy had discovered something more entertaining than cartoons.

"We don't use those words, young lady." I sat down and drew Linnea closer to me, eye to eye.

"Daddy does."

Patsy looked at me and waited.

"Well, Daddy hangs around with a bad crowd. That's why you have to be careful about the company you keep. Stay away from unsavory types."

"You say them words too."

Patsy was holding her breath.

"I'm a grown-up. Grown-ups shouldn't say those words, but they can if they have to. When you're a grown-up, you can say them too. If you have to."

"I have to now."

I looked at my tiny daughter—the one who loved flowers and grass and trees. The one who always smiled when a breeze touched her face. The one who nearly got run over by an airplane while she was picking flowers for her mother.

I pulled her onto my lap and gave her a hug.

"Not half as much as you'll have to when you're a mother."

"Think of it as being snowed in," I said, after the fifth or sixth complaint about the car. "Except we can go out if we want to."

"You can go out in the snow," Linnea observed.

"But we can stay out longer—we won't get cold."

"I thought we were going to Gettysburg." Patsy stomped across the kitchen.

"Look, girls." I intercepted Patsy and sat her down in a chair next to her sister. "We can do the things they did in the old days, before they had cars."

"We'd have a horse." Patsy wasn't going to give up.

"The horse is needed for plowing." Two could play this game.

"But I wanted to go to Gettysburg."

"What's Gettysburg got that we haven't got here?"

I could see the wheels turning in my daughter's head.

"The battlefield." Patsy looked at me.

"So, what's the battlefield? Just a big place with fields and trees and hills—just like here."

"But a lot of people died there. It's important."

"You want a lot of dead people? I know just the place. We'll pack a picnic lunch and hike over there." What a great idea.

"You mean the graveyard? Aw, Mom. Not the graveyard. Why do you always—"

I quickly uncovered the electric mixer and got some butter out of the refrigerator. "We'll need some cookies for this picnic. Come on, girls. Let's get started."

"Cookies!" Linnea hopped down from her chair. "Yay!"

Patsy hesitated for a moment and then shrugged. She went to the pantry. "Oh, all right. But they have to be chocolate chip."

It was a little like being snowed in—except it was a beautiful, sunny day and the birds were singing. We spent the morning planning the food and making it. Patsy, as oldest frontier child, was allowed to make a solo trip to the Jiffy-Stop for cold sodas and potato chips. By the time she got back, she was singing too.

"I'm getting hungry," Linnea announced.

"Then let's pack up our stuff and get going."

It wasn't much more than a mile, and along the way we took turns calling out the shapes that the cumulus clouds had formed.

"That's an elephant."

"And he has a rabbit on his back."

"No—now it's changing. See. It's a crocodile with an extra-long leg."

"Yeah, but over there—there's a gigantic gerbil."

"And a teddy bear."

"And some mashed potatoes."

"And an airplane."

"An airplane?" Patsy asked. "I don't see any airplane."

"Over there. A real one." Linnea pointed off to the left.

It was a Cherokee Six. I shaded my eyes and followed its path to the west. I thought it might be Bud's Cherokee. Was the owner taking it out for a shakedown? Bud would be in it, too, taking mental notes and grumbling about the cost of parts. I looked hard to see if it was him, but the plane had too much altitude.

At the top of a long hill, we crossed Cumberland Road and went past the high stone gateposts of St. Obturator's, past the Victorian manse and the church, and down the little path into the cemetery. The leaves, a more serious green than they had been a few weeks before, fluttered amiably in a light breeze. Linnea smiled as it brushed her cheek.

"You girls pick the spot for the picnic." I watched them scampering from place to place. With the parishioners all gone home to their pot roasts, we had the place to ourselves.

"Read me this one, Patsy," Linnea demanded.

" 'Our beloved brother, John Mason, 1887,' " her sister read.

They ran over to Allen George, flanked on either side by his six wives. Patsy read out all of their names. "Oh, brother," she said.

"Oooh." Linnea was on her knees, petting a small stone figure. "Look at the little lamb. Isn't it cute?"

"Linnea, get away from that." Patsy's young face formed a frown. "That's a little kid's grave."

"Nuh-uh." Linnea put her arms around the lamb as if Patsy might try to take it away from her. "It's just a little lamb, is all."

She shrugged off her backpack, sat down in the grass, and looked around her. "Where's Mommy?"

I was at the very bottom of the hill, looking at a grave under a willow tree. I hadn't meant to go there—I always regretted it when I did. But something had pulled me in that direction. "Sarah Louise Johnson. May 13, 1972–June 10, 1984. God took our angel to be with Him." "Twelve years old," I said aloud.

In front of the marker, five helium Mylar balloons were staked to the ground. "Happy birthday," they proclaimed. Two little plush teddy bears wrapped in cellophane leaned up against the marker.

"Maaa-um!" I heard my children calling in unison. Patsy's voice continued, solo. "We found the spot. Come on up."

I turned my back on the grave. From the top of the hill I could see the girls waving. Luck of the Irish, I thought. They'd picked the place where I'd found John Jensen.

Still, for anyone who hadn't known that, it was the best spot for a picnic. We emptied our backpacks, spread an old blanket on the grass, and set out a sumptuous feast of apples, potato chips, raisins, chocolate-chip cookies, and sandwiches of peanut butter and jelly, ham and cheese, and canned peaches. The peach sandwich was Linnea's idea, and she ate with as much gusto as she could, even though the peaches shot out of the bread every time she tried to take a bite.

I looked around at the rows of stones, at the girls, at the giant oak Patsy was innocently leaning against. John Jensen's tree. Nothing lasts forever, I told myself. If I was ever going to get my dreams off the ground, I'd better get started.

"I have a secret," I said. "And I'd like to talk it over with you." The girls were all attention. "But you can't tell Daddy just now—that's the secret part."

"But you said you and Daddy never keep secrets from each other." Patsy had a memory like an attic trunk.

"That's right, but I'm going to tell him soon. So it really isn't the same thing, is it?"

Linnea shook her head vehemently. Bless her little heart.

"I just wanted to talk it over with you. See how you felt about it." The girls were hooked.

"Remember how I told you I used to fly an airplane with Grampa, before you were born?"

They nodded.

"I told you Grampa and I had a business flying medical supplies to people far away who needed them real fast?"

They nodded again.

"Well, I'm going to start up a business like that on my own." The power of positive thinking. "But I'll have to be away from home a lot."

"But Mom—" Patsy looked worried.

"Mostly during the day, when you're in school."

Patsy relaxed a little.

"Linnea, you'll be in kindergarten at the elementary school next autumn, and you can stay for after-school care."

"Oh boy, Melanie gets to do that. Can I be with Melanie?"

"I guess you can. But once in a while I'll have to be gone overnight."

"But who—" Patsy's worry was back.

"Well, your dad will be home some of the time. And Phillip's old enough to be responsible for you."

"*Maaa-um!*" they both said at once.

"He's almost fifteen. In another year he'll be able to drive you around."

Patsy gave me a skeptical look.

"But for when he's not around, I've been thinking about getting Fran—Mrs. Kublik—to come stay with you during the day and see that you get wherever you need to go."

"Yay!" said Linnea. "Can Kelly come with her?"

"I imagine she could."

Fran's reaction to my plan had been unexpectedly enthusiastic: "The nice thing about knitting is, you can do it anywhere. And you can do it faster when you're away from your own phone."

"What about Dad?" Little Miss Reality.

"Well, that is a problem. But I think he'll understand how important it is to me, when I find the right way to explain it to him." I got up and started pacing around the clearing. "I'm just telling you this now because I want to know how you feel about it. I can't do it without your help."

"Our help?" Patsy cocked her head to one side.

"Well, yes. I'll need you to help plan the meals and do some of the cooking. And you'll be in charge of seeing that all homework gets done."

A gleam of potential power flickered in Patsy's eyes.

"What about me?" Linnea tugged at my shirttail.

"You, Linnea, you'd be in charge of keeping the house neat. You'll have to make sure everyone puts away their stuff, and see that the windows get closed when it rains. And you'll be in charge of Bacall—feeding her and walking her and everything."

Linnea swelled with importance.

"So, are you with me?" I asked. "Will you help me with my business?" I looked from one child to the other.

"I'll help you, Mommy. See, I can start right now." Linnea got up and began stowing the picnic remains, right on the paper plates, in the backpacks.

"And you?" I turned to Patsy.

"Why can't things just stay the way they are?" She half turned away.

"Because I really want to fly." I reached down and touched Patsy's hair. "You'll understand better when you're older. Anyway"—out of the corner of my eye I saw Linnea stooped over, picking a fistful of violets—"nothing ever stays the same. Even if we want it to." In my mind I could see a procession of orange zoning signs, stretching out across Clark County into infinity.

"Mommy, Mommy, look!" Linnea was pointing to something on the ground at her feet. "This plant has a little hat."

An oak seedling, less than two inches tall, had pushed itself up through the soil. But it hadn't traveled alone. One leaf had threaded itself through the open fretwork of a metal button and firmly held it in place. I gently freed the button and rubbed it on my jeans. It was silvery, probably rather expensive, a clever design of an anchor—it looked almost Celtic.

I wondered how long it had lain in the ground, dropped, perhaps, by some mourner who wouldn't even notice, in his grief, that it was missing.

"Maybe it's been buried for a hundred years," Patsy said. She took it from me and held it in her palm.

"I don't think so. It doesn't look very weathered."

"How'd it get stuck on that baby tree?" Linnea took it and polished it some more on her shorts.

"I can't imagine." I put the button in my pocket and finished filling up the packs. "Well, let's get going, troops, before it gets late."

As we started back across Cumberland Road, a swarm of patrol cars sped past. "Look at that," Patsy said. "Five—no six—*seven* police cars in a row!"

I looked around uneasily. "Must be something going on." Just then the deafening *wap wap wap* of a low-flying helicopter drowned out my voice. Before it had passed, another one joined it on the right—then another one on the left. It was like a squadron of giant punker dragonflies.

"What's going on?" The girls were starting to look frightened.

"I don't know, but let's get on home." I hurried them across the road and we jogged along, with police cars and helicopters racing about as if someone had sprayed Raid in a nest of law-enforcement hornets.

When we got home, we found a policeman knocking on our door.

"What is it?" I shooed the girls inside.

"A bear, ma'am."

I laughed. "I thought you said a *bear*."

"That's what I said." He looked behind him as if he were expecting to see Godzilla. "There's a bear loose around here somewheres. We're trying to catch it. Until we do, y'all stay in the house." He gave a quick nod and started down the steps, but stopped and turned again. "And keep your pets inside, too." He crossed the lawn to the Winstons' house, looking behind him every few steps.

"A bear! I don't believe it." Still, I closed the door and locked it—then laughed at myself. Who ever heard of a lock-picking bear? Bacall, asleep in a corner of the kitchen, shifted noisily, her feet twitching in hot pursuit of some dream beast.

"Listen to this!" Patsy squealed from the kitchen. The girls had tuned the tiny TV to the Clark County cable station.

"A sex-crazed black bear has wandered into central Clark County this afternoon." A pimply-faced reporter was standing next to the Shell station on Route 40, the wind riffling the notes he clutched nervously in his hands. He kept blinking his eyes as if he hadn't been outside the studio in two or three years.

"Experts speculate that the bear, most probably from the mountains sixty miles west of here, got turned around and came too far east in search of a mate." There was some videotape footage—evidently taken from one of the helicopters—of police armed with rifles and handguns, trying to close in on a pigeon-toed bear galloping across a swath of grass beneath some high-tension lines.

"Look, Mom. Those are the power lines over by the underpass." Patsy was pink with excitement.

"Go, bear, go!" Linnea chanted. The bear, looking over his shoulder as he ran, crashed into some undergrowth and disappeared into a stand of trees.

"Yahoo!" all three of us shouted. Overhead the helicopters sounded as if they were going to land on the roof. Bacall slept on.

"Although some residents have joined in the search," the reporter continued, "state troopers have strongly advised civilians to remain inside until the bear can be subdued."

Linnea put a little hand on my hip. "Will they kill the bear?"

"I think they're just going to shoot it with a tranquilizer gun, honey." But I could think of a number of men in the neighborhood who would shoot the poor thing for the pure "thrill" of it. I thought of the bear in the window of the Fur and Fin taxidermy shop.

Poor bear. I hoped the tranquilizer guns got it first. Or that the Great White Hunters accidentally shot one another.

We looked out a front window. There were no signs of life except for a rabbit nibbling on the salvia plants Berlie had just set out—and a squirrel scampering up the telephone pole across the street.

Probably the one that ate all our birdseed, I thought.

We watched the squirrel leap onto the phone line and then dance across to the next pole.

Kabaam! An explosion, louder than a fifty-millimeter mortar shell, ripped through the air, rattling the windows and making Linnea burst into tears.

"They shot the bear. They shot the bear." She burrowed her head into my belly.

The rabbit could be seen racing up the hill like a streak of lightning, but the squirrel was nowhere. On a hunch, I opened the front door and sniffed.

"I think the squirrel blew the transformer." Our nostrils filled with the smell of burnt fur and roasted meat.

"How could he do that?" Linnea was too amazed to be sorry for the squirrel.

"He must have made a connection between the wire and the transformer." I flicked the switch for the porch lights, but they didn't come on.

"Look over there." I pointed out in the court to something the size of a piece of charcoal, as an orange flame flared for a moment and then went out. We could see nine or ten more chunks lying about.

"Oh Mom, that's gro—" Patsy clapped her hand to her mouth and pointed to the edge of the woods. The bear, the one we had just seen on TV, took a cautious step into the Winstons' yard. He stopped and sniffed, then took a few more steps, looking all about him. Then he reared up on his hind legs. Standing, he was more than six feet tall.

"He doesn't look sex-crazed to me," Patsy whispered.

"How would you know?" I whispered back. I stole a quick look at my daughter. "Never mind."

When he came back down on all fours, the bear ambled slowly over to one of the chunks in the street. He sniffed. He roared. Then he scooped it up and sat back on his haunches and stuffed it in his mouth.

"He looks just like Uncle Bert," Linnea whispered.

Patsy poked her with her elbow. "Look, he's eating squirrel McNuggets."

I would have laughed, but I had just spied a man in chinos and an ammo vest sidling around from the back of the Harveys' garage. "Oh, no," I breathed. "Girls, go back to the kitchen."

But none of us moved. The man raised the rifle.

"NO!" Patsy shouted, but the gun went off at the same moment. The bear jerked backwards.

"Oh, no!" Both girls grabbed me. All three of us were crying.

But the bear got up. Policemen swarmed down over the hillside, pistols drawn. Three patrol cars screeched to a halt a few yards away.

The man in chinos motioned them away. "It's OK," he called. "I got 'em." The bear took a few steps forward, swaying from side to side, and then he crashed nose-first onto the street.

"The hunter killed him, Mommy." Linnea was holding me so tight it hurt. "Son of a bitch."

Just then the man pulled out a walkie-talkie and held it to his mouth. In a few seconds a white truck with ANIMAL CONTROL printed on its side came screeching around the corner and raced downhill into the court. Men jumped out and threw a net over the bear.

"No, honey. I think it's going to be all right. I think that man's one of the policemen with the tranquilizers. A plainclothesman, maybe."

We watched as a dozen men struggled to lift the inert behemoth into the truck. Someone pulled out a hypodermic needle stuck in its furry neck.

"Whew! Bear breath!" we heard one of them exclaim, along with some other words that were less suitable for tender ears.

When the truck, with the bear safely inside, finally pulled away, I closed the door.

"I'm sorry I said a bad word," Linnea began. "It doesn't sound very nice, does it?"

"No." I smiled. "But, I guess, considering what was going on, you had to."

It wasn't until bedtime, as I emptied my pockets to throw my jeans into the hamper, that I remembered the button. I sat on the edge of the bed and turned it over and over in the light, and then placed it on the nightstand. After a while I turned off the lamp and tried to drift off to sleep.

But the day's events paraded inside my mind, keeping my thoughts in high gear. I could see the helicopters, the bear, the police, and the tombstone with the little teddy bears beside it; the plainclothesman with the rifle, the curious button, and Patsy leaning up against the tree that had held John Jensen.

"Aahh!" I sat bolt upright, as if I'd been pinched. I turned on the light and fished around in my purse for a card. When I found it, I dialed the after-hours number. There was no answer. I dialed the police department.

"Is Sergeant Cloud on duty tonight?"

"Cloud? No, ma'am. He's not on." The voice sounded about sixteen years old.

"I need to reach him. It's very important. He's not home."

"Is this about a case?"

"Yes." What did he think—that I wanted him to install a home-security system at midnight?

"I'll check." There was a long wait and then the voice continued. "He has the weekend off. Musta gone somewhere. Can someone else help you?"

"No."

"Well, he's due back to work tomorrow. You could try then."

I hung up. Of course. I'd forgotten: He'd gone camping.

I lay in bed trying not to think about anything. But sleep never came.

Chapter Twenty-six

Monday, May 25

WHEN TOM BLACK CLOUD finally returned my calls at ten Monday morning, he was at some bar in Ulyssia. Rather early in the day for a bar, I thought.

"A button?" He seemed to be having a hard time understanding.

"A fancy button," I repeated, "under that tree in the graveyard."

He didn't have to be told twice. Within fifteen minutes he was on my doorstep. He dropped the button into his wallet and slipped it inside his jacket. I could see the gun against his chest.

"Will you let me know if it means anything?" I asked. He wouldn't do that, would he—make a breakthrough in the case and not tell me?

He looked at me for a long time before he nodded. "You're entitled."

I watched him drive away. Did he think of me as a friend, I wondered? Or was I just some woman who'd found a body? Maybe, when this case was closed, I'd find out.

The girls had already been picked up for school; I put on a hat to keep the sun out of my eyes and marched off in the direction of the Shell station. Today I'd get my car back.

· · ·

It seemed funny to Holly that her sister had waited all this time to hear what Detective Cloud had in his report on Frazier. Kay said she just hadn't been ready to deal with it until now. Holly wondered how a person would know when they were "ready." If she had waited a thousand years, Holly never would have been ready for the news she had gotten about John. The policeman knocking at her door last autumn—she hadn't been ready for that at all.

Holly could tell what Cloud had said by the way Kay came down the stone steps outside of Hagerty's, by the way she got in the car. It took some time before the traffic light changed, and Kay didn't say anything until Holly had pulled out into the stream of cars and headed west on Carter Road. The traffic, for ten in the morning, seemed awfully heavy. Memorial Day, she remembered. That explained it.

"I had it right." Kay stared straight ahead at the windshield.

"Ah." There it was, then. What could Holly say that would be of any use? The fact of the thing hung between them like a third passenger demanding to be acknowledged.

"They meet at a place not too far from your house, Holly. And at the fairgrounds. And other places." Kay's voice was flat.

Holly recognized the tone. It had been her own for months and months now. It bothered her to think of Frazier and some other woman screwing around so close to her home. "Where near my house?"

"In a tower in some woods."

Holly knew the place, up by the Country School. What a bastard. She felt anger slowly welling up, an anger stronger than anything she had felt since John had died. She didn't trust herself to speak.

"He was very polite, Detective Cloud," Kay went on. "As if there were some kind of protocol for telling a woman her husband is having an *affair*." She said the word a little too loudly, as if to keep it from circling back on her. "Do you think there is? A chapter in Emily Post, perhaps: 'How to Let the Cat out of the Bag'?

"Cloud started to tell me who she is"—the words kept rushing out, filling the car with pain and tension—"but I told him I didn't want to know."

I would, Holly nearly screamed out loud. I'd want to know.

Her anger had swelled to such an intensity that she could hardly focus her eyes on the rush-hour traffic. She stepped on the accelerator and passed a plodding cement mixer.

I'd want to know who she was and what she was thinking about when she slept with my husband. I'd want to know why he was doing this to me. But then, why does anyone do anything? Why did John do what he did? Why didn't he tell me something was wrong? Why wasn't I enough to keep him?

Kay was still speaking, but Holly could only hear the outrageous questions throbbing over and over in her head: *Why? Why? Why did you do it, John? Why wasn't my love enough to hold you? Why did you have to leave me?*

The right front wheel slipped onto the gravel shoulder for a second before Holly jerked it back on course.

"Holly, pull over." Kay's hand was on Holly's shoulder. "We're almost home."

Holly shook her head and strained to see the road in front of her. When she finally turned into Kay's driveway, she cut the engine and hugged the steering wheel. This time the crying wouldn't stop.

"Holly, come on inside. I'll fix us a drink." Her sister looked worried. "Come inside. I'm sorry to get you mixed up in this." She tugged at Holly's sleeve.

"No. No, it wasn't you." She turned on the ignition.

"Please, Holly. Stay here awhile."

"No, I have to go home."

But when she got to the farm, Sergeant Cloud was sitting on her front porch. Even though it had been less than an hour since he had met with Kay, he looked as if he had been waiting for a long, long time.

Kay watched her sister drive away. She pushed open her front door and went inside. The house was cold and dark; a good place, she thought, to keep secrets. She looked around as if she were seeing it for the first time. This is the chair he sat in, thinking about *her*. This is the fireplace he stared into, seeing her face in the flames. This is the phone he probably called her on when I wasn't around. This is the bed—no—Cloud said they hadn't come here. Honor among SOBs.

She went up to Frazier's study and stood in the doorway, staring at his desk. Would there be notes? Would some of them be in *her* hand?

His "ready bag" was stowed under the desk, filled with everything he needed if he were suddenly called away, as he often was—an annoying but routine occurrence in his job. She ran her finger over the brass zipper and hooked it in the ring at the end. She'd never gone through his things before. Did she really want to now?

There was nothing in the bag but the expected toiletries, a change of clothes, and his passport. She stood up and went to his desk. Everything was orderly, the contents routine. She looked in the closet: On the shelf were shoe boxes labeled by year in black Magic Marker. She pulled down this year's box. Behind it was an accordion file neatly tied with brown ribbon. She strained to reach it, and then sat down on the edge of his desk and untied the ribbon.

Bank statements and tax forms. And a thick manila envelope. She pinched open the clasp and took out the contents. "Operation Red-Det-Op" read the type on the top sheet of paper. A large *TS* was stamped at the top and bottom of the page. Tough shit, she thought, but then her mind quickly snapped to attention.

Top Secret. She rapidly leafed through the Xeroxed pages. They seemed to contain the details of the project he had been working on all these months. What would this be doing in with the bank statements?

She looked at a statement for April. It wasn't their account: It wasn't in Frazier's name, and it was addressed to a post-office-box number. There was a balance of $750,000 in the savings account; $2,500 in the checking. She took out the January statement. It was heavier than the rest, bulging out of its envelope.

Inside was a checkbook, a passbook, a passport in the same unfamiliar name, and a slip of pink paper—half of a receipt of some sort. She unfolded it, and froze at the sight of the words:

I helped him. I'm as guilty as he is.

It was her brother-in-law's handwriting. There was no mistaking it, with its neatly formed letters and the fine, old-fashioned curlicues at the beginning and end of each word. The bottom edge of the paper had been carefully creased and torn. Slowly, as the blood drained from her head, she realized what must have been written on the other half.

She sank to the floor, the room starting to grow black around her. Forcing herself to lower her head and take deep breaths, she brought back the light.

She rose carefully and put everything back as she had found it. Everything except the note.

She could feel the note burning in her pocket as she got in the car and backed out of the driveway. She checked the gas gauge. Three-quarters full. How much driving would it take to clear her head? She turned onto the main road and headed east towards the Chesapeake Bay Bridge.

Claiborne came home to an empty house. He wasn't surprised, but he wasn't pleased, either. It had been convenient when Kay had taken Holly off to Florida in the winter. But now that she was back, she was spending too much time with her sister. True, he hadn't told her he'd be home for lunch today—although she could have figured it out, with this being a federal holiday. And it wasn't convenient to come home to no supper two or three nights a week, even if the table conversation had become unaccountably strained.

"Rebecca?" he said into the upstairs phone. She was breathless: She must have run in from outside. "I've been trying to get you all morning. I've been thinking about your call. . . . No, it's always OK to call me at work. I know how upset you are about the farm."

That morning she had called him, almost incoherent with despair, to tell him she had awakened to find a FOR SALE sign in the field out front. Right next to the mailbox. "Don't worry," he had said, even though he knew it was wasted breath. "We'll figure out something before it's too late."

"Could you meet me for lunch?" he said. "The Red Lion? I'll see you at noon."

He opened the closet door. The contents of the accordion file fit easily into his ready bag.

He got a garbage bag from the kitchen, filled it with wadded-up newspapers, put the manila envelope on top, tied it with twine, and stowed it next to the ready bag in the trunk of his 450 SL. Glancing at his watch, he got in the car and drove off.

Chapter Twenty-seven

Monday, May 25

"HOW MUCH LONGER do you think it will be before Sergeant Cloud comes in?" The clock on the far wall read two o'clock.

"I don't know, ma'am, he's out in the field somewhere, and he hasn't checked in lately. We've tried to raise him for you." The officer in the blue shirt looked as if he had been up all night. Probably having an affair, Kay thought.

The glass partition between the entrance hall and the clerk's desk didn't permit much sound to pass. She sat back down on the black enamel bench and waited, rehearsing what it was she was going to tell Detective Cloud:

"I found this note. My sister has the other half. Her dead husband wrote it." No, no. She sounded like something out of *Dick and Jane*.

"I was looking for a note from Frazier's lover, and I found top-secret papers and a bank account I didn't know he had." That sounded pretty stupid too.

What did all of this mean? The implications of the papers and the bank account were terribly clear. But the note—every time her mind began to focus on it, she drew back, as if it were a black hole she might fall into and her life would cease to exist.

She thought about Holly. But Holly and the note and John and Frazier were inextricably interwoven, and she couldn't follow through. She'd wait and let the detective take the lead.

She looked at the clock again. Two-thirty. Around and around her finger she twisted her necklace—a rope of prehistoric amber that Frazier had given her for Christmas. Surely Sergeant Cloud would be here soon.

Frazier hurried along the back roads of Clark County. His timing, as usual, was impeccable, everything proceeding according to plan. But he didn't want Rebecca to be anywhere near when he went by her farm, so he had left her at the Red Lion to finish both of their desserts. He drove past the monastery, down to the dehydrator, where there were no signs of unusual activity, and past Rebecca's field of sorghum. He went down to the intersection and made a U-turn. When he was even with the pile of rubbish in the ditch, he tossed the garbage bag from the car and then drove off. It was a clear day, a perfect day. There wasn't another car on the road. He switched on the radio. Vivaldi. What could be more delightful than that?

Elena Popliteal felt like a new woman, a radiant woman, a woman who could do anything. She had slept through the night every night for a whole month. She had gone for a part-time-job interview at the Magic Carpet Travel Agency in Ulyssia, and they had offered her the job on the spot. And she had finally called her lawyer and told her to go ahead with the divorce. With the trees in full green splendor and the smell of new grass in the air, today, she decided, was a good day to finally see what the Elk Glen dehydrator was really all about. A good way to spend her lunch hour.

The trees lining the narrow private road didn't look so ominous now that they were covered with the adolescent plumpness of their leaves. Even the signs—NO TRESSPASSING and BEWAR OF DOG seemed less like stern admonishments than exercises in a child's workbook—"Can You Spot These Spelling Mistakes?"

But when she got to the clearing and saw all the patrol cars and the ambulance, her heart gave a little skip and then began marching double time.

"An agricultural accident. That's what he called it." Elena shuddered at the remembrance of the scene. Her lunch break had been converted into an afternoon of emergency leave. She looked toward the door. "Where's Jenny?"

"I couldn't get her on the phone," Fran said. "I don't know where she could be without a car."

"Elena, accidents like this happen all the time around farms." Jif took a bite from her Double R Burger. "What's the story on this one?"

Elena sipped her Coke, hoping it would settle her stomach.

"Oh. Well." Elena winced and laid her hand on her throat. "The dehydrator's a place that makes feed pellets from silage. You're not supposed to operate the machinery when you're by yourself. But there was only this one guy there today, and there wasn't much to process, so he must have decided to go ahead and run it through. Evidently he did that all the time.

"Only this time, they figure, the alfalfa must have got stuck in the chopping cylinder, and when he reached in to free it, the horrible thing grabbed him and mashed him down under a huge auger."

Her hands finished their delicately gruesome story with a final spiral motion.

"Ooooo." Jif put down her bacon burger.

"Yeah." Elena nodded. "It got him all the way up to his waist before his body jammed the machine."

"Oh, God." Jif wished she hadn't eaten hamburger. "You mean the rest of him went on through?"

"That's what they said. Mashed into feed pellets and conveyed up into the silo with all the rest of the feed. There was no way to tell which of it was him and which was just fescue or something. They'll have to bury the top half without the bottom."

"Was he dead when they found him?"

"Oh, yeah. The lady who owns the place went out to tell him he had a phone call, and there he was—or half of him, anyway—holding on to the sides of the trough. But he was so dead, the blood wasn't even running out of him."

"Oh, gross," Jif said. Nobody was eating by now. "Too bad we never asked 'What would you do if you drove down a road and found a man ground into pig feed?' "

Fran wrinkled her nose. "Stop it," she said.

"Did they tell you who it was?"

"Nobody you'd know," Elena said. "Guy name of Barton Stott."

"Detective Cloud." Holly climbed the porch steps and stood looking at him, trying to read his reason for being there in the movement of his hands, the angle of his head, the way that he was standing. Not a clue.

"Have you been waiting long?" she said, finally.

"No. I have something to show you. I want you to tell me if you've ever seen it before."

"Maybe we'd better sit down." The rockers were out, but the swings were still in the barn, where she and Cloud had lugged them last year.

She was feeling bad enough about Kay. The detective's sudden presence here made her feel even more uneasy. She stared at his hand as it went inside his jacket. He pulled out a wallet.

"Oh, no, I've never—"

"Not this, Mrs. Jensen." He opened up the wallet and fished out something shiny. "This is what I want you to look at." He held out a button: It was an anchor within a ring.

This didn't make sense. It was just like a button Kay had sewn on Frazier's jacket—why would Detective Cloud have Frazier's button? She shook her head as if to clear it and get her brain going again.

"Where did you get that?"

He put it in her hand. "You've seen it before, then?"

It felt almost hot in her palm. She quickly handed it back to him. "My brother-in-law has some buttons like that. On a blazer. I don't understand. Where did you get it?"

"It was found near the tree your husband was hanging from. Can you think of any reason why your brother-in-law might have been there at any time? Does he have relatives buried there? Does he belong to the church?"

Holly looked down at her hands, folded in her lap. She shook her head. All of the warmth, even down to her bones, seemed to be leaving her body.

"Could he have gone there after we took your husband away— to see where it happened, maybe?"

A shiver went through her, but she shook her head no.

"He was out of the country when John was . . . found," she said. "He had left early that morning, and he couldn't get back until late the night before the funeral. But that was seven months ago. He might have gone there later. I don't know." She didn't want to think about that time. It was in another life. Finished. But Detective Cloud's next question yanked her back into it.

"Can you think of any reason why your brother-in-law would want your husband dead?"

She was beginning to feel very strange, as if Sergeant Cloud were speaking to some other person sitting there on her porch, and she was merely listening to them talk on and on. She forced herself to think about his question—would Frazier want John dead?

What a dumb idea. Frazier and John. They were in-laws. They saw each other on holidays. If they'd been women, they'd call themselves acquaintances; but since they were men, they were friends—they engaged in brief, agreeable exchanges of grunts and nods when they happened to be together, and didn't give the other a thought when they were apart.

She shook her head again, but this time an ugly notion let itself in. What if John had found out about Frazier's affair, and Frazier was afraid he'd tell Kay?

Would John have told Kay? She swallowed hard. He probably would have, if he didn't think Frazier would break it off on his own. Poor John. He saw everything in black and white. But what about Frazier? Her sister's husband couldn't possibly be capable of killing someone.

But then, he was capable of having an affair, and the effect of that upon Kay was almost—

"Mrs. Jensen?" Detective Cloud seemed to have been saying something.

"I'm sorry," she said.

The phone rang. It was for Detective Cloud. Listening to the low drone of his voice, she felt herself growing colder and colder as she rocked back and forth, back and forth, in the rocker on her porch in the beautiful May sunlight.

"I have to go," he said, looking almost excited. "There's been an accident down the road."

When he had left, she brought the last piece of firewood into the house and lit the stove. But even though it burned with a flame that was almost too bright, there was no warmth in it.

Chapter Twenty-eight

Monday, May 25

I HAD MY CAR BACK; I'd had the whole day to myself, and now I was driving through a gorgeous spring afternoon—fake Memorial Day—to pick up my lovely daughter at school. I reached up and patted the wet muzzle that was resting on my shoulder.

"I'm glad you came along today, too, Bacall. But remember, when we get to the school, the seat goes back up and you'll have to ride in the cargo area."

Bacall harrumphed in my ear.

"Cut that out. That was our deal—hold on—I'm going to stop!" Almost simultaneously I pulled over and hit the brakes. In the ditch by the Flower Lady's field was a bright yellow piece of nylon rope. Brand new. Phillip would love it. Bacall stuck her head out the window.

I made sure no cars were coming my way and got out. As I stood there coiling the rope, I noticed the trash bags, still there after all this time. Crows were picking at one of the newer-looking bags. They stood watching me from a few yards away.

"Go away!" I flung my arms up and down, but the crows didn't move. They had ripped into the side of the bag, and wadded-up balls of newspaper were poking through. A long piece of twine held the bag closed. Well, I thought, at least we can keep the rest of this junk from blowing all over the county. Setting aside Phillip's rope, I grabbed the bag and started to stuff trash back inside the hole.

The corner of a manila envelope jutted out of the rent in the bag. It looked so clean; it didn't look like garbage. I set down the bag, pulled out the envelope, and opened its clasp. "TS," it said at the top. "Red-Det-Op"—sounded like the words to a song my parents used to sing. "TS" again at the bottom.

I looked at the text. ". . . Fleet proceeds to the Blue Sector to join USS *Tybalt* at lat 42"—was this some sort of government stuff? Somebody must have thrown it out by mistake. Or else—I wished Fenton and his warped little mind were here.

I heard a car approaching. From the corner of my eye I saw a black pickup driving by. A shiny black pickup with two men in it. It slowed down and then continued on. I looked down at the page in my hand. *TS. Top Secret.*

Clean truck, no gimme caps. A memory flashed through my mind: The night Phillip got sick. A farmer in shiny shoes, his black Ford parked beside the ditch. Fenton nearly blowing his cool when I'd told him.

The truck was down at the corner now, making a screeching U-turn. I got the distinct feeling they were headed for me and they weren't planning to discuss corn futures. I scrambled up the bank to the car, flung the envelope onto the passenger seat, and sparked the engine.

"Hold on, Bacall." In the rearview mirror I could see the truck gaining on me fast. The road was level, and in a flash I was up to fifth. But when I rounded the next curve, the truck was a lot closer.

This doesn't happen in real life, I thought. This is Clint Eastwood stuff. What am I supposed to do? Who should I call? *What would you do if . . . ?* The phrase ricocheted around in my head like a bullet in a tank. I wished I were safe back at McDonald's, playing that silly game with Jif and Fran and Elena. *What would you do if . . . ?*

Sweat ran down my sides and my back.

As the Honda zipped up a long hill, the truck jumped out into the other lane and careened up beside me on the narrow road. Before I could do anything, the Ford slammed into the side of my car and rebounded onto the far shoulder for a moment. I dropped into third and stomped the accelerator into the floor. I gained a few seconds' lead.

The car door was bulging inward, pushing against my left arm. Bacall was barking at the truck, which closed the distance in an instant. It was so close I could see the driver's blue eyes.

"Oh, God." I could also see the black stump of a pistol in the hand of the man in the passenger seat.

The nearest police station was at least five miles away—in the other direction. I could call for help at the school, but if the man was going to fire that gun, I didn't want it to happen there—not near the children.

As the Honda flew over the next hill, I spotted a white car up ahead. From the back, the driver looked like Fran, but it wasn't the Renault. Could she be driving Bob's Jetta? I was almost sure it was Fran. "Oh, let it be Fran." I was almost to the turnoff for Elk Glen.

I blasted my horn and tried to close the distance, but the Jetta speeded up too. I tried switching the headlights on and off, on and off. The woman looked in her mirror and then took a quick look over her shoulder. It was Fran. I flashed the headlights some more.

The truck was almost up my tailpipe. Every time I hit a bump, the car leaped up in the air and I expected to be sitting on the truck's hood when I came back down.

"Sorry, Bacall," I said, but Bacall was wedged in the well between the front and back seats, panting with excitement. Up ahead, Fran was doing seventy. The truck filled the rearview mirror. All three vehicles slowed to make a sharp curve.

Bud is waiting for me out at Ganton's Farm, I thought. If I can just get to the airfield . . .

As I neared the turn for Rainey Branch Road I could see a convoy of three Zephyr buses thundering towards me. "Please, God, let me make it." I clipped left just before the first bus reached the intersection. The sound of its horn lifted the hair on my head.

But there was no crash. I was still on the road.

I hunched my shoulders and jammed the car into third again.

"*Aaaaah!*" A blinding pain shot through my hand and up my arm. I could barely see straight, but I tromped on the accelerator and shot down the road, holding on to the steering wheel with my left hand and just the fingertips of my right one. The pain was excruciating.

I had to shift again. I could see the truck waiting for the last bus to pass. There was a blue Volvo right behind it, and a colorless old Cutlass behind that, but Fran had raced straight on through the intersection and was turning around farther up the road.

Only a little farther to go, I promised myself, and forced my hand to shove the gearshift into fourth.

The road into Ganton's Farm was one car wide and lined with silver beech trees. I swerved into the lane and was almost to the far end of it when the truck showed up in the mirror, raising a plume of dust as it churned closer and closer.

Off to the side came a flash of red, a little sports car blindly pulling out from a thicket of bushes into the path of the truck. Like an elephant swatting a gnat, the Ford smacked the sports car's front fender and spun it around. Coming up behind the truck, the blue car smacked the little car's rear fender and stalled out.

At the end of the road I wrenched the Honda to the right and skidded to a halt in front of the trailer. "Stay here, Bacall." I grabbed the envelope and leaped out of the car.

Bud, I moaned to myself as I raced towards the Cherokee, you'd better be here. You've got to be here.

I could see the truck as it stopped three quarters of the way up the drive. A heavyset man jumped out and was making for the woods beyond the far side of the road, and a tall, thin man, thrashing through the hay field beside the flight line, was headed my way. The man who'd been holding a gun.

I could see Bud's feet sticking out the door of the Cherokee as I ran around the plane kicking out chocks and ripping loose the lines. I leaped up onto the wing.

"Get up!" I yelled, and dove over his body into the other seat. I shot the envelope into the back. "We've got to get this thing going!"

"Jesus! What the—" Bud looked at me as if I'd come from outer space.

"Close the door and help me get this thing going! It'll go, won't it?"

Before he could answer, I yelled, "Clear!" and turned the key. The engine roared to life.

"What's going on?" He was buckling his harness and scowling at the instrument panel. I pointed to the man running through the field and reached down to shove the throttle forward.

"*Aaaah!*" I yelled.

"What is it?" He was fiddling with the radio.

"My hand. Something's wrong with it. Man the throttle for me."

He reached down and took hold.

"The wind," I shouted, "which direction?"

He twisted around to check the wind sock. "Take off from here."

"Right." I released the brake and taxied onto the field.

"But what the h—"

"Just do it. We've got to get out of here *now*—right now!"

Bud increased the power, I released the brake, and the plane started down the runway. I could hear the long, wet clippings of the new-mown grass slapping up beneath the plane, the clank of Bud's tools rolling around in the back, and the sweet sound of the engine as it powered us up into the welcoming sky. We lifted above the trailer, above the last stand of trees, climbing swiftly higher and banking to the right until we came about and passed the airfield at enough distance, I hoped, that a bullet couldn't reach.

The field was full of cars, some with red lights flashing, but the Cherokee was too far away for me to distinguish the people.

"For God's sake, Bud, what are you doing?"

He had unbuckled and was somewhere in the back of the plane. It sounded as if he were moving furniture.

"I'm trying to fix it so we can land, maybe. If I don't shift all this crap, we're going to be too tail-heavy." I could barely hear him above the engine. In a moment he returned to his seat, slapped on a set of headphones, and switched on the radios.

I pulled on my own headset. "Tell BWI we're on our way." Baltimore-Washington International airport was only fifteen minutes away—even with a head wind.

"Baltimore Approach, this is Cherokee November Four Zero Eight Hotel Whiskey. I'm at twenty-five hundred feet, twelve miles west on heading Zero Nine Zero. Permission to land, over."

"Four Zero Eight Hotel Whiskey, contact Baltimore Approach on One Two Eight point Seven Zero, over."

Bud and the voice on the radio went back and forth as I adjusted my altitude and course as directed. We were over the massive Social Security complex in Woodlawn. I wondered if I'd live to collect old-age benefits.

"Is the flight phone working?" I nodded towards the handset between the seats.

"Yep."

"Get the State Department. Ask for Gary Fenton. Don't let 'em give you the runaround. Tell him to have someone at BWI to meet us. Tell him I'm not coming down until they get someone there."

Bud never took his eye off the instruments. "You looking for something to tell your grandchildren, or what?"

"Tell Fenton I have some top-secret papers—I think I stumbled onto a spy drop."

He picked up the phone, and for a second his mouth twitched into a smile. "Is flying with you always going to be like this?"

He got through right away, but Fenton wasn't there. He tried someone else in Fenton's office.

"This is Bud Grimes of Ganton Farm airfield, Clark County, Maryland. I'm calling for Jenny Meade. I'm in a Cherokee Six, ten minutes out from Baltimore International Airport, and I need to have an agent—No! I can't hold!"

He looked as if he might throw the handset through the windshield.

"Look, I'm in an *airplane*. My partner found some papers, top-secret papers. She was pursued by men with guns. We—NO! I WON'T HOLD!"

He shoved the phone into my good hand. "Here," he said, "when they get back, tell them they can hold their asses 'til *I* get back." He got out of the seat and hunched aft. In a moment he returned, holding the manila envelope.

He grabbed the phone.

"You there? Tell Gary Fenton it says '*TS* Red-Det-Op . . .' " He only had to read two sentences before his credibility seemed to change. "Right. Have your man call and ask for QM 2298-4059 as soon as he gets to the airport. And hurry. We're flying under emergency conditions." He put his headset back on.

"What do you mean, emergency conditions?" We were over the big tower on Television Hill.

"Last two times I had Ganton take me up, she went real smooth for about ten minutes, and then she started missing." Baltimore Approach handed us off to another sector, and Bud busied himself retuning the radio and giving our altitude.

We were over the water, blue water with white sails wrinkling the surface. I could just make out the tower at BWI.

The phone rang and the engine quit.

"Bud!"

"I'm on the phone. Start the engine."

I adjusted the mixture and the engine started up. It sounded like a bean-fed lawn mower.

After a moment Bud hung up the phone. "Fenton's 'man' is a woman, but she's down there. Must've had somebody at the terminal. Guess we don't have to wait around up here." The engine was coughing and farting like an old drunk. Bud looked so calm I wanted to hit him.

"Tell 'em we're coming in." My shirt was soaked with sweat and clung to my body.

First fly the plane, I told myself. First fly the plane.

"Eight Hotel Whiskey, you're following a Cessna and I can't read him. Turn left Zero Five degrees."

We could hear the garbled static of the Cessna and the tower's efforts to make sense of it. The Cherokee bumped and bumbled around as if we were running over a pack of flying armadillos.

"I want to pack it in! Tell 'em we're in trouble." I kept one eye on the instruments and the other out the window. I could see the idiot Cessna at three o'clock.

"If we do an emergency approach," Bud said, "we'll have incident reports up the wazoo. You don't have your biennial; I don't have anything. Just cool it. We're doing fine."

Splutt-putt-pah-tut, the Cherokee responded. Bud and the plane were beginning to sound like a Smothers Brothers routine, with Bud playing Dickie to the Cherokee's Tom.

"Four Zero Eight Hotel Whiskey cleared to land on runway three-three . . . right. Over."

I felt my heart expand to a more reasonable size. Within moments the wheels touched down, and we taxied over to the Butler hangers, across the field from the main terminals. We were about forty yards out when the engine quit for good.

Chapter Twenty-nine

THE BUSINESS AT THE AIRPORT had taken hours, even though the only thing I could tell the woman from Fenton's office was how I had picked up the sack and found the papers and—well, it wasn't such a long story, after all.

But then Fenton showed up out of nowhere, sent the woman off on some errand, and ran me through the same course again. Bud spent the whole time out tinkering with the plane.

"How'd you get here so fast?" I asked Fenton.

He grinned—possibly for the first time in history.

"I was in the area, you might say."

I raised my eyebrows.

"Ever since your tip on the Seven-UPs, we've had the area under surveillance."

"Then you got the guy who planted the papers?"

Fenton rolled his eyes—a spectacular show of emotion for him.

"We didn't. Somehow the guy on the third shift got his times mixed up and didn't show. The man on the second shift kept waiting for his replacement, but before a backup could get there, he had to take a wizz. He must've been in the bushes when the drop was made."

"But you got the guys in the Ford, at least."

Fenton's shoulders slumped. He actually sighed. A full-fledged nervous breakdown.

"Not yet." He looked around. "This information can't leave this room."

I nodded.

"They're still searching the area for the one who took off on foot. But the other one took two women hostage, and we're still in a pursuit mode."

"Fran?" I felt sick. This had never been part of our "what would you do if" scenarios. "He's got Fran?"

"We haven't yet determined the women's identities. But the situation is under control . . ."

Under control! "You say *two* women?"

"One in a white Jetta and one in a blue Volvo."

Not Jif! Jif must have seen my flashing headlights too. Shit! Shit! Triple shit!

"Don't worry," he said. "We'll secure the hostages soon. Just a matter of time."

The rest of the interview went down the tubes: I could only think about getting home, making sure my family was all right— that Fran and Jif were unharmed. I was even worried about the dog, she must have been in the car for hours. At least the window had been open.

I'd had enough flying for one day, and Bud had made arrangements to tie the plane down at BWI overnight and return the next day to fix her up.

"Now I know what the problem is," he said as we were leaving. Mechanics: They all say that.

Fenton drove us back to Ganton's Farm; Bacall was definitely glad to see me.

"You OK, Bacall?"

She didn't say anything—just danced around after a two-minute pee. But I could tell she was glad. She let me scratch her ears for a moment, then jumped back in the car and immediately went to sleep. Still guarding my hand, I drove the poor banged-up Honda back home.

I found the girls waiting for me, safe and sound next door at the Winstons', but Berlie and Phillip weren't there; they were three hours overdue. I called Guy and Jerry, Berlie's caving buddies. They weren't back either.

Fran answered the phone when I called, but she sounded like I'd caught her on her way out the door.

"Are you OK?" I asked.

"I am now. So's Jif. How are *you*?"

"I'm all right, but—"

"I can't talk now. You sure you're OK?"

"Sure, but wait a minute—"

"I've got to run. Don't miss the eleven o'clock news. Channel Thirteen. Watch it and call me." She hung up.

There was no answer at Jif's.

I put the girls to bed in spite of world-class protests. It was late, and I couldn't deal with their questions right then.

I stood in the shower for a long, long time. Could enchantment of the deep strike in a shower stall? I wondered. Finally the hot water started to fade, and I gave it up and toweled myself off. The girls were in bed, listening to the radio, halfway asleep. I started downstairs to fix myself a drink. Maybe some brandy.

I was relieved to hear someone running the shower in the kids' bathroom. The guys must have just gotten home. A trail of nasty clothes littered the hallway.

But something didn't feel right.

In the kitchen, Berlie was sitting at the table, staring at the floor. His sweat suit was clean, but the rest of him was covered with filth. Cave filth. It was in his hair, on his face, under his fingernails. The smell, though familiar after eighteen years of knowing the man, was still indescribable.

"Phil's OK," he said, reluctantly looking up from the floor. "It could have been a lot worse."

My heart went cold. "What do you mean?" I said very quietly. "What's happened?" I was afraid to breathe.

"Jesus!" Phillip's voice roared down the stairwell and across the kitchen to my grateful ears. I breathed again. A moment later he thundered down the stairs, sounding like a herd of buffalo. "Who used all the hot water?!"

I turned to explain, but all my words abandoned me.

My son, my only son, looked like a large piece of raw liver. His feet, standing in the puddle of water that was forming beneath his towel-wrapped body, looked normal. But his legs, his torso, his arms, and neck looked like he'd had a fight with an oversized cheese grater. What damage the towel around his waist was concealing, God only knew.

"Phillip!" I rushed to him and reached out to touch his hair with my fingers. "What happened to you?" He had a huge black eye.

I swung around to face Berlie, my wounded cub behind me. "What happened to him?" I snarled.

"It could have been worse." He spoke so softly that I could barely hear him. He looked as if he might crumple in on himself. The sight of him like that made me hold back. I pulled up a chair and sat down opposite him.

"Phillip, honey," I said, longing to put my arms around the kid but knowing it would hurt him more, "go get on a robe or something, and I'll fix you some hot chocolate. That'll make you feel better." What a stupid suggestion. It would take a lot more than hot chocolate before he'd start feeling good again.

I watched my son limp out of the room before I turned to Berlie. "What happened?"

This wasn't Berlie's fault, I told myself. But if he hadn't taken the boy with him . . . I made the thoughts stop and forced my attention back to what he was saying.

"It was a freak thing. There was no way anyone could have predicted it." He wouldn't look up from the floor. Couldn't, maybe.

I got up and started the hot chocolate, guarding my right hand as best I could, waiting until Berlie found more words.

"We were on our way out, maybe a thousand feet from the entrance." The hollow sound of his voice told me that he was seeing it all in his mind. "Guy was already through the opening, but Phil was only halfway up the rope when he yelled 'rock.' "

Berlie, still looking down at the floor, shook his head slightly. *"Rock."* He was silent for a few moments.

"The whole ceiling broke loose."

I felt sick.

"Like someone had poured boiling water on a frozen windshield. It just shattered into a million pieces and came down on him. For no reason—no loud noises, no banging around. No reason." He shrugged his shoulders. "But the kid just hung on. He hung on for all he was worth."

For all he was worth. I shuddered, considering the true value of what we had nearly lost. I allowed myself to see Phillip clinging there with the ceiling coming down around him, shards and chunks of limestone, slabs of it, enormous swords of it, beating him on his helmet and piercing his clothes and scraping at his skin until he looked like a victim of a motorcycle accident. And then, when it was all over—probably within seconds—the terrible silence. And then I imagined one more thing.

"Where were you?" I scanned the exposed parts of Berlie's body for marks. It was hard to tell through the filth.

"I was under a ledge. It happened so quick—by the time I realized what was happening, it was all over. The ceiling was on the floor, and Phillip was still hanging on to that rope."

Berlie finally looked up. "You know what he said?"

"What?"

For the first time since he'd walked in the door, Berlie smiled . . . barely.

"He said, 'Dad, I didn't do it.' "

The phone rang.

Phil had limped back into the room and he picked up the receiver.

"Mrs. Ludloff says to turn on the set. Channel Thirteen."

The little kitchen TV slowly warmed into a picture of Ganton's Farm, a jumble of police cars and other vehicles scattered across it like the aftermath of a tornado.

"Look at that—" Phil said. "That's out where the air—"

"Shhh!" Berlie waved his hand at him.

"—a bizarre chase that began near Elk Glen Country School in Clark County this afternoon. A citizen using a car phone notified police that two men in a pickup truck were apparently in pursuit of an unidentified woman in a small foreign car. The first leg of the chase ended at a private airfield in the western part of the county."

"Look!" Phillip pointed to the set. "There's Dr. Masseter!" The screen showed a crumpled red Porsche hemmed in by a white Jetta and a blue Volvo station wagon. Dr. Masseter and some woman were scrunched way down in the seats, with their collars pulled up around their faces like felons entering a courthouse.

The reporter turned to the camera. "Several cars, their drivers on their way to pick up children at the private school, became involved in the race."

"Wow!" Phillip exclaimed. "That's—"

"Shhhh!" Berlie and I hissed.

"—the caravan of gutsy suburban housewives on a high-speed chase through western Clark County. One assailant fled the scene on foot, but two of the women, Mrs. Jif Ludloff and Mrs. Fran Kublik, both of Endicott Mills, were taken hostage by a second man as they attempted to hamper his pursuit of the unidentified woman.

"This woman took off from the field moments later in a single-engine airplane. Police allowed the man and his hostages to leave the scene, but later apprehended him as he was releasing the women, unhurt, at a McDonald's on Wisconsin and Western avenues, in Bethesda."

Jif and Fran, with a statue of Ronald McDonald waving jovially behind them, told the reporter they were fine, but that they needed to get home to fix dinner. It was obvious they had been told not to discuss any details about their ordeal.

Fenton, Jenny thought, would be pleased.

"Authorities have not yet released the name of the kidnapper or of the woman he was chasing." The news anchor turned to the other reporters on the set, shaking his head and chuckling. "All I can say is, when you're in Clark County, watch out for those caravans of gutsy suburban housewives." A mouthwash commercial came on.

Berlie looked at me with ice-cube eyes. "Elk Glen," he said. He continued to stare. "Fran and Jif."

I shifted a little in my seat.

"Jenny"—he got up and opened the door to the garage—"what do you know about this?" Beyond him I could see the silver Honda with streaks of black paint and gleaming naked metal trailing parallel lines across its concave door.

"Dad," I said with a lame smile, wondering how I was ever going to explain this one, "I didn't do it."

It took me until 3 A.M. to tell the whole story. Or most of it, anyway.

Tuesday, May 26

"You can't drive for a while, Mrs. Meade."

I had been staring at a macabre poster on the examining-room wall: a human being, half man and half woman, with successive layers of skin and muscle stripped away here and there to reveal points of interest for the orthopedically aroused observer. I struggled to shift my attention to the roly-poly man who had just skidded into the room as if he had been launched from a giant slingshot.

"Can't drive? Why not?"

"You've injured your median nerve. All the symptoms you've been experiencing—the pain in the palm of your hand, the numbness and tingling—that's all part of carpal tunnel syndrome."

I winced. *Carpal tunnel syndrome.* Old ladies got that.

"I want you to rest that hand completely. That means no writing, no typing, no wiping, and no driving." He gave me a wink and a nod. Cute.

"But—"

"No buts. Tie your arm to your side if you have to. If the hand doesn't get better in three weeks, we might have to operate."

"Operate!"

"It's a simple procedure. Nothing to worry about. But try resting it first. Maybe we won't have to do anything. Excuse me a minute." He pulled a tiny tape recorder from his pocket and began mumbling into it at high speed.

"The patient, Jenny *mfflfl*, age *mffmff*, suffered trauma to her *blffufuf* on May *mmmuhuhufuf*." Outside, a steady rain was pouring down.

I strained to make sense of what he was saying, but it was impossible.

"*Muffufufuf*," he continued in a low voice. Finally he switched the thing off and shoved it back into his pocket. He smiled at me. "Great invention. For the charts. Now my secretaries don't have to decipher my handwriting."

I wondered how long it took them to go crazy in that office.

Berlie opened the door of the Caprice for me and I dashed through pouring rain and jumped inside. "Well? What did he say?"

It was hard to speak the words out loud. Hard to comprehend the concept. "I can't drive," I said. Driving was what I did, how I spent almost every waking hour of my day. What would my life be like without it—for three whole weeks? I stared at him in bewilderment.

"Ever?" He looked at my hand as if it were a dead hamster.

"Just 'til the end of school. What on earth will I do? How will I get the kids—"

"Don't worry. Your friends will help."

I shook my head. "I know they will. But three weeks of driving— that's a lot to ask. And I'm not supposed to use my hand at all."

We pulled up to a red light.

"How did it happen? Your hand, I mean."

"I just banged it the wrong way." I knew him too well. All he needed was the slightest excuse to replace the little Honda with some dinosaur with an automatic shift.

"Banged it? On what? Something in the airplane?"

I willed the light to change. It did. "No, not on the airplane. It was already hurt when I got to the airplane."

"Well, when, then?"

"After I picked up the bag." We turned the corner into Tragus Court.

"You hurt it picking up a garbage bag?" He flicked the garage-door opener.

I reached over and opened the passenger door with my left hand and hopped out of the car. "Well, not exactly." I smiled lamely and darted into the kitchen.

"Phillip." I was surprised to see him standing there, eating a banana. "Shouldn't you be resting?"

"Aw, Mom, I rested all morning. I wanted to find out what the doctor said about your hand."

Carefully, I gave him a one-armed hug.

"What a nice guy."

I got some hamburger out of the refrigerator and started to form it into patties, but only got as far as gouging out a small lump of ground beef with my left hand. I felt stupid holding it.

"Would you make this into patties for me, sweetie?"

"Maa-um," he lapsed into a whine, "I'm too old to be called sweetie." He took the meat.

Berlie opened the door. "So how did you hurt your hand, Jenny?" He laid a big pile of mail on the table.

"Oh, I don't know. Maybe getting out of the—"

"How about the gearshift?" Phillip said. "I bet you hurt it on the gearshift."

"No, sweetie, I don't think—"

"Sure, Mom. Just like that time when you let me shift for you—remember? All the way from school to Dr. Masseter's. You remember. You hurt it shifting gears."

I thought about taking the hamburger I still held in my hand and cramming it down Phillip's throat. Instead, I handed it to him and tried to wash my left hand without using my right. It didn't work too well.

Out in the driveway, Fran was honking her horn for me to come out.

I could see a funny look on Berlie's face. There was an unpleasant hint of triumph in it.

Chapter Thirty

Thursday, May 28

"I'M NOT SURE we should gather this many heroes at one table." Jif beamed at the rest of us. She looked around at the crystal stemware and the white linen tablecloth and burgundy napkins. Heavy rain beat against the hand-blown glass in the windows. "This is a far cry from McDonald's."

She was right about that. The Red Lion was about as far from fast food as you could get in Clark County. That's why I had chosen it. My treat.

"My phone hasn't stopped ringing," Fran said. "I can't get any knitting done."

"It's been less than a day; things will quiet down." Jif carefully unfolded her napkin, evidently trying to remember the steps so she could restore it to its original bishop's-miter shape. A sudden clap of thunder made the lights flicker.

I tapped the crystal water glass with my fork. "Listen. I want to tell you why I made you come here today."

"Twisted our arms," Elena giggled.

"I did it out of guilt," I said. They all looked at me, trying to see if I was serious.

I turned to Fran and Jif. "I feel terrible about the danger I put you in. Thinking about it makes me feel sick."

"It was OK." Jif took a sip of her wine.

"You didn't put *me* in any danger," Elena said softly.

"I know. But I encouraged you to go down the dehydrator road. To find out what was down there. If I'd known what you'd find, I never would have—"

"Tell Jenny about it, Elena," Jif interrupted.

As Elena spoke, her beautiful hands danced about, belying the gruesome story she was telling.

That morning I had seen the obituary in the county paper. "Barton Stott, 62," it had read, "suddenly, at work." The old snapshot, blurry from being enlarged, showed a lean, weasel-eyed man in a panama hat.

> Mr. Stott, a lifelong resident of Clark County, is survived by his wife, the former Rebecca Winston, of Hilltop Farm.

With no children, I wondered, how would she run that farm by herself?

As Elena spoke, I balanced the facts as I knew them. On the one hand, Rebecca Stott was having an affair—why else would she be going to that tower? On the other hand, she had been married to a mean-spirited old man—if pictures and gossip meant anything at all—one that she might want to get rid of. On the other other hand, the woman seemed to care too much about living things to do anything like that. But what about the man she was having the affair with? Would *he* care? And did I really know who he was, after all?

"What if it wasn't an accident?" I said.

"Here we go again," said Fran.

I carefully presented my case in hypothetical terms. The consensus was, it wouldn't hold much water.

"I don't think she'd bump anyone off, either," I said, "or hire anyone else to do it. No, I just don't think she's the type."

I wondered if there'd be any bouquets for sale this year.

"So that's how you spent *your* Memorial Day, Elena," I said. "Let's continue with the debriefing."

I settled back in my chair, watching Jif fold and unfold her napkin. "Even today I'm still wondering if some of this stuff is real—I feel like I might be a little nuts, you know? Like when the man in the sheet jumped out to tell me that The End Is Near. Remember?"

They nodded.

Then, during two rounds of strawberry daiquiris and a quartet of shrimp cocktails, I told them what had happened from the moment I had stood in the ditch and pulled the manila envelope from the garbage bag up to when I saw Fran tooling along in front of me in Bob's car.

"The Renault was in the shop," Fran took over. "So I had Bob's Jetta. When I saw Jenny flashing her lights, I knew something was up, so I put the metal to the pedal and called the police on the car phone."

"Pedal to the metal," Jif said.

"That's what I said. You can't imagine how hard it is to go seventy on Benson Mill Road and make a phone call. I kept wondering what I would do if those steers were loose on the road. Remember, Jenny, that time—"

"I remember." Maybe this hadn't been such a good idea. Maybe I should have waited more than a day before going over it all again. I wasn't feeling so hot.

"Anyway," Fran continued, "it wasn't until I'd overshot the turn onto Rainey Branch Road that I saw Jif."

Jif took her cue.

"Well, it was like this," Jif said. "When you and Fran blasted past Elk Glen, I was just turning in at the drive. I figured something fishy was up. So I took off after you. When we all finally made the turn onto Rainey Branch, that's when the guy in that old Cutlass started crowding me. Your detective." She smiled. "Sergeant Cloud."

"Sergeant Cloud?"

"How was I supposed to know whose side he was on? I didn't

really meet him until later—when all those people started asking us questions." Jif snorted. "I'd never seen him before. I thought he might be with the guys in the truck. That's why I ran him off the road."

The waiter came with our orders. He kept staring at Jif as he set down the plates. Finally, he pointed at her and said, "Channel Thirteen. Weren't you on the news last night?" He re-aimed his finger at Fran. "And you, too?" Miss Manners would have been quite displeased.

They nodded as he stood there pointing and grinning.

"Gutsy suburban housewives," he said as he turned and left.

"Wait a minute, Jif," I said. "You ran Tom Black Cloud off the road?"

"Only into a little ditch," she said defensively. "I turned on my headlights to make him think I was slamming on my brakes. We were on that curve—you know—where the black Angus always stands? And his car swerved into a ditch. Just a little ditch."

"Was he hurt?"

"Nah. He showed up at the airfield, but it was too late. By then, I was sorry I'd ditched him. Anyway, when the truck and Fran and I were about to catch up with you, that's when Dr. Masseter and friend chose to come up for air."

Oh, yes.

"Most unfortunate timing," Elena laughed.

"You should have seen it, Elena." Jif wiped tears from her eyes. "That little red car got whipped around just like a hockey puck."

"But how did you and Fran wind up with that man—?" The last I had seen of him, he had been running towards the planes.

"Gavno." Fran looked reproachfully at Jif. "Really, Jif, he wasn't such an awful man. He was just a little scared."

"Scared, hell," Jif replied. "He was going to blow our brains out, wasn't he?"

Fran ignored the question.

"By the time we all got through playing hockey with Masseter's Porsche," Jif said, "you were running down the field to the plane, and both creeps had jumped out of the truck, and one looked like he was going to cut you off—and then he—"

"Gavno," Fran corrected her. "His name was Gavno."

Jif continued. "The jerk was gaining on you, Jenny, blazing a trail through that hay field, and, well, Jif and I, we scooted along in his wake and we sort of jumped him."

"Jumped him?" I would have given anything to have seen that. Well, almost anything.

"We de-pantsed him, was what it was," Jif said bluntly.

"We didn't mean to—we just grabbed what we could reach." Fran looked profoundly embarrassed. "They must not wear underwear where he comes from," she observed. Elena rolled her eyes.

"Anyway, by the time he got his pants back up, the cops were tearing up the drive, sirens wailing. He grabbed Jif, pulled a gun from inside his jacket, and put it to her head. He made us both get in his truck. I guess the police only pretended not to follow us, because when he finally stopped talking to himself—that's what he did the whole time we were with him—"

"Maybe he was talking to us," Jif suggested.

"How could he be talking to us? We couldn't understand a word he was saying."

"Except his name."

"You don't know if that was his name—he just kept saying it, over and over."

"Must have been his name."

"Anyway," Jif barreled on, "when he slowed down and motioned for us to get out, cop cars came out of everywhere."

"Well," I said, "thank God you're safe." It took me a long time for it all to sink in. Finally, I had to laugh. "You de-pantsed him?"

The waiter arrived with four of the most enormous strawberry shortcakes I had ever seen. We ate for a moment in delicious silence, until a clap of thunder shook the glass in the windows.

"What would you do," Jif said to nobody in particular, "if a man you knew came up to you in the Safeway, and he had his fly open and didn't know it?"

"Is this a joke?" I asked. I wiped whipped cream off the tip of my nose.

"No. It's a 'What would you do if—' "

"Forget it," I said. "I've had all of those I'll ever need."

Friday, May 29

For the three weeks that I couldn't drive, I discovered what my children had been born knowing: If you can't drive, people will drive you. They will alter their routines just to take you places. They will even come to you when you can't get to them.

Bud showed up the day after the lunch at the Red Lion. Linnea and Matty Kohlrausch let him in as I was bringing up a load of clothes from the basement.

"Linnea," I exclaimed, "this is OK, because you know Mr. Stilson. But you shouldn't let people in like that."

"Can I call you Uncle Bud?" Linnea's question came out of nowhere. She patted him on the arm.

His eyes crinkled up in a smile. "Uncle Bud? You bet."

"I have to go watch *Sesame Street* now," Linnea announced. "See you later, Uncle Bud."

I got us some crullers and coffee, and we sat down at the kitchen table.

"She's airworthy, Jenny."

For a moment I thought he meant Linnea. Then I realized he was talking about the Cherokee.

He pulled a certificate out of a leather zipper bag to show me.

"That's great, Bud. When's the owner going to pick it up?"

"He came out Saturday to inspect it and pay me off."

My heart sank. I wished I could have flown her one last time before he handed her over.

Bud picked up a cruller and dunked it in his coffee. "The thing is, he couldn't get on board. Lost his nerve, he said." He shook his head. "Damnedest thing I ever saw."

"He couldn't get in the plane? What'll he do?"

"It's been done." Bud slapped his hand down on the leather bag and then extracted another piece of paper. It was the title to the plane.

"He sold her to me for the cost of the parts. That's what I was calling you about Saturday—what I wanted to talk to you about when you came out Monday. Only"—he smiled a wrinkly smile—

"you never gave me much time to talk business when you got there."

I poured him some more coffee.

"Anyway, now I've got me a plane and no one to fly it."

I caught my breath.

"I need me a partner." He looked me steadily in the eye.

"Partner for what?" I didn't want to get my hopes up.

"A business I'm thinking about starting up. Medical transport service. Ever hear of such a thing?" He looked at me sideways, grinning.

"Bud!" I jumped up and threw my arms around him just as Matty walked back into the kitchen.

"Mrs. Meade!" he said. I pulled my arms away and stood there like an idiot.

Linnea came in, too, and looked at Matty with mild curiosity. "What's the matter?" Linnea asked.

"Your mother was hugging *'im*," he said, jerking his head in Bud's direction.

"That's OK. That's Uncle Bud."

Matty gave him the once-over before he turned back towards the living room. "Is he a *real* uncle?" we heard him ask Linnea. "Or is he one of those fake uncles—the kind that comes around when your dad's not around?"

Linnea gave him a poke in the back. "He's a real uncle, Matty. As real as real can be." Bud was nearly busting a gut.

I turned to him. "This partnership you're offering—you're serious about this—you want to do this, for real?"

"As real as real can be."

I was sitting on the front steps, thinking about all the possibilities Bud had just presented to me when a black Ford Ranger pulled into the driveway. It was Tom Black Cloud. He came up the curved brick walk smiling.

"I was just going to call you," I said.

"Great minds. I thought you might want an update." He sat down beside me on the steps.

"Update?" Too many things had been happening the past few days.

"Here." He handed me a Polaroid snapshot of the Elk Glen sculpture. "The work-in-progress." The figures of the child and the adult were clearly discernible, but without the fine detail that I knew would soon follow. Only the book the child was holding remained to be shaped.

"How much longer 'til it's done?"

He shook his head. "Hard to tell. What with the break in the Jensen case and all."

I jumped up from the step and planted myself on the sidewalk in front of him.

"What? What? Do you know what happened?"

He laughed at my reaction. If he'd been Berlie, I'd have kicked his shins. Gently.

He held up his hand as if to ward off a blow and motioned me to sit back down.

"Yes, we know what happened. That's why I'm here—to tell you it was the button that turned the tide."

I looked at him a moment before I spoke. "Then, it was murder?" I supposed that if I had been someone like Cloud or Fenton, I would have already figured out who killed John Jensen.

He nodded. "The button belonged to Holly Jensen's brother-in-law." My mouth must have dropped open so wide a Cessna 210 could have flown in.

"Frazier Claiborne? You're saying Frazier Claiborne murdered John Jensen?" What would Holly be feeling right now? And her sister—how could they begin to comfort each other? I began to play out in my mind the confrontation between the two sisters and the husband. I wouldn't want to be around for that one. Or maybe I would.

"Where is he? Is he in jail?"

"Not yet." Tom made a clicking sound with his tongue. "He skipped the country Monday. He's in some other trouble—I'm not at liberty to tell you about it—but I feel fairly confident he'll be apprehended very soon." He made that clicking sound again.

"What makes you think so?"

"Overconfidence."

I cocked my head.

"He doesn't think anyone knows. He thinks he's in the catbird seat."

Two squirrels dashed past us on the lawn, like furry little cops and robbers.

"I understand you were run off the road by a woman driver."

He smiled. "One of your friends. A menace."

"What were you doing out there, anyway?"

He rubbed his hands together and started pacing back and forth in front of me as I sat on the steps.

"I'd been checking out the scene of an accident at the Elk Glen dehydrator."

Elena's grisly description shuddered into my mind. I shook my head to clear out the image.

"I was on my way back to the office when I saw the truck take off after you."

"How'd you know it was me?" There are lots of silver Hondas on the road.

He smiled a strange smile. "I know your car. And you were talking to that dog of yours—the one that talks back."

How'd he know about that? I wondered. Besides, Bacall didn't seem to have much to say these days.

"So I followed suit. Quite a little parade by the end of it. I didn't make it to the airfield in time."

I looked into his obsidian eyes a moment, trying to think of an opener for what I wanted to say. "That was Mr. Stott at the dehydrator. I read about it in the paper." No use mentioning Elena. "Have you thought that maybe what happened to him might not have been an accident?"

Tom's look was noncommittal.

"Rebecca Stott was having an affair."

He looked at me sideways before turning to face me.

"Do you know who with?"

"No, but I wouldn't be surprised if it were Frazier Claiborne."

To my surprise, he laughed.

"What's so funny?"

"Kay Claiborne paid me a thousand bucks to find out what you just told me for free. What tipped you off?"

I told him about the look in Claiborne's eye when he met Rebecca after the funeral. I told him about Rebecca and the tower and about Holly's worries about her sister. It all added up.

"But now Stott's dead—" I didn't want to put any ideas in his head, but then, he'd probably run through all the possibilities already. "I don't think Rebecca Stott—his wife—could ever do anything like that—kill him, I mean. Do you?"

He shrugged. "You never know. She's a little strange, I hear. But Claiborne's prime. The motive for killing Jensen isn't clear in my mind yet, but for bumping off Stott—that one would be pretty straightforward: pest control. I spent yesterday sifting through stuff at the dehydrator, but I couldn't find anything to place Claiborne there on Monday. He'd been there before—when I was tailing him. I'm going back now to try again."

He gave me a sweet grin. "Want to come along?"

"I can't. The kids—"

"OK." He held up his hand as if he already knew what I was going to say. "Some other time, then. Some other case."

Another case? According to Phillip, this was the place where nothing ever happened.

Tom hadn't been gone long before Yupplettes on Wheels dropped Patsy off at the end of the drive.

"Hi, sweetie. Did you have a good day?"

"*Did* I? Guess what? Miss Jackson is going to marry Mr. Hargrave, and Mrs. Fenwick is pregnant!" She banged the screen door and clattered up the stairs to her room.

Well, it certainly gave one pause. As Patsy went in the front door, Bacall came out and sat down beside me. I put my arm around her neck and spoke in her ear. "Did you hear that, Bacall? Miss Jackson is going to marry Mr. Hargrave and Mrs. Fenwick is pregnant. Or is Mrs. Fenwick marrying Mr. Hargrave, and Miss Jackson is pregnant?"

I waited for a response. Nothing.

"Not funny?"

Nothing.

"Bacall, answer me."

She grinned and stuck her nose in my armpit, but she didn't say a word.

"You haven't said anything since . . ." I wasn't quite sure. Was it the day the car broke down? Or the day of the Big Chase? I couldn't remember.

"Come on, Bacall. Say something." I pulled her close and scratched under her chin.

"I just love it when you do that." It wasn't Bacall's voice at all, it was one of those funny little voices people use when they're putting words into animals' mouths.

I looked up. Gary Fenton stood in front of us on the sidewalk. I hadn't even heard his car in the drive. If one more person comes here today, I thought, I'm going to feel like the oracle at Delphi.

"Does she talk to you often?" he said.

I wasn't going to answer that one. "Come on in," I said, getting to my feet. "Would you like some lemonade?"

Sweat trickled down the sides of our glasses on the kitchen table. Upstairs I could hear Linnea and Patsy fussing over whose towel had been left on the bedroom floor.

"We found the man, Mrs. Meade."

"What man?" There was too much information rolling around in my head today: planes, buttons, pedagogical pregnancies. I didn't think anything else would fit in.

"The person who dropped off the information on Benson Mill. The man who sold out his country."

"The spy?"

Fenton's face twitched almost imperceptibly.

"How'd you get him?" I asked.

"We haven't apprehended him yet, Mrs. Meade. But it's just a matter of time. We have reason to believe you might know him."

"Me?" I looked at him as if he had a rabbit on his head. "I don't know any spies. Who is this person?" I folded my arms across my chest and waited for his reply.

"A man named Frazier Claiborne."

Chapter Thirty-one

Friday, May 29

CLAIBORNE HADN'T EXPECTED to be in Vienna, but waiting the few hours for the connecting flight to Berlin proved to be curiously relaxing. He had done all his speculating about what was going on at work and at home as he crossed the Atlantic in the 747.

He had gone to BWI as soon as he'd received the call from Karski. "Go," was all he'd said. Obviously the drop had gone bad. He wouldn't know how bad until someone contacted him. Until then, he'd concentrate on everything that had gone right.

If the wrong people got hold of his documents, it would take a while to trace them to him. His absence at work, of course, would eventually do the trick, although he had called Clary at ASA to tell him he'd need two weeks off—family crisis.

No need to worry if they caught the agents doing the pickup. They were just glorified garbage collectors—he smiled at the comparison. Peons. All they knew was that something had to be picked up at a certain place at a certain time. What it was and where it came from was not considered necessary for them to know.

How long would it take Kay to figure out he was not coming back? He'd left a note saying he'd be gone two weeks. Nothing there to make her suspicious. But after the two weeks, what would she do? A call to his office—but, then, they'd be calling her by that time. No matter, she'd do all right. You could trust Kay to follow the rules, observe the conventions. That would get her through.

And there was nothing that would connect him to Jensen's death. Everything had gone so smoothly. It was a mistake, of course, to have used his property for a drop last summer. But it was such a nice wooded corner of his land—who would have thought Jensen would be out hunting rabbits and would find him stuffing the documents inside a log? Bad luck, that was all.

But when his brother-in-law met him the first time at St. Obturator's to discuss it, Claiborne thought he had convinced him to go along with the deal—forty thousand dollars just to keep quiet and let him use the log one more time. Later, when Jensen had called and said he couldn't go through with it, he'd had to do some quick thinking to get him out to the cemetery one more time. But it had worked.

And Jensen had done a good job of covering his own tracks, too. Told Holly he was going to pick up farm equipment at 4 A.M.—farmers are always doing things at god-awful hours of the morning. Made perfect sense. And Claiborne himself hadn't had any trouble accounting for his whereabouts—he'd told Kay he had to fly to Stuttgart, which he did, only he'd left the house a half hour earlier than he needed to. That's all it took—less than that, really, except the fog slowed him down a little.

It had been just long enough to meet Jensen in the graveyard, pull the gun on him, and force him to write the note—"I helped him. I'm as guilty as he is"—so Jensen couldn't change his mind and turn him in. At least, that was the reason Claiborne had given him.

Then the trick he learned in commando school, pinching the

nerves in his neck. Jensen had dropped like a brick. All he'd had to do was to take the rope from his briefcase, string him up, and get a milk crate from the back of the school and kick it to one side under the body.

Then he had taken the top half of the note and left Jensen with the other—the part that said, "Please forgive me. I love you Holly." That evening he'd received a phone call telling him to come home from Germany—there was going to be a funeral.

Claiborne had always liked the Berlin airport. It smelled of Cosmoline and wet fur. He checked his watch: everything according to schedule. He'd wait here by the gate. If no one had shown by 16:50 Z, he'd go to the Hotel Berlin and wait for another contact.

Too bad the boys at the drop had screwed up so spectacularly. Even here it was all over the papers—but no mention of him, of course. How could there be? The jerks just hadn't followed the plan—hadn't paid attention to details. That's what keeps your ass out of the soup.

He couldn't help laughing. Done in by some lousy hausfraus. How stupid could you get?

Four men walking through security caught his attention. This must be it. But no, they looked too much like Americans trying to look like Germans.

Well, OK, he thought, the door to my left leads out to the—

Something hard rammed into Claiborne's back. He turned his head to see who was there. A man with jolly blue eyes—a man who had come off the same plane he had—stood behind him, smiling and puffing his moist breath on Claiborne's neck.

The four men approached. This couldn't be happening. He'd made no mistakes, no bad judgments—how could he?

"Herr Claiborne?" The accent was pure Alabama.

Claiborne said nothing.

"Let's go, *bitte*." East Alabama.

"Who are you?" He wasn't lost yet. They couldn't have anything on him.

Alabama reached in his pocket. "A little birdie sent us."

Claiborne remained silent.

The man held up a photo. "Poor little bird. Somebody done her wrong."

It was a picture of Kay, standing beside him at the spring ASA awards ceremony.

Chapter Thirty-two

Monday, June 8

BERLIE WAS OUT AT THE MAILBOX when Bud dropped me off at the house. The two men nodded at each other, not blinking or saying anything—the way men do when each one of them wants to convey the ridiculous idea that he knows better than the other what's best for some perfectly capable female third party. It always made me think of bighorn rams on *Zoo Parade*.

"She just passed her biennial flight review." Bud dropped that little bomb on Berlie as he pulled out of the driveway. I didn't wait to see the reaction—I dashed inside and flung a frozen pizza into the oven before Berlie stomped in.

"I want to talk to you about flying," he said, closing the kitchen door behind him and folding his arms across his chest.

"Good," I said. "I want to talk to you about caving." I'd given this some thought on the way home, and I was ready for him. We hadn't begun to explore the ramifications of Phillip's caving accident last week, and bringing it up was a good offense—or defense, depending on who got the kickoff.

Berlie, immediately recognizing the game plan, looked at me with a curious mix of exasperation and guilt. "Now, look here, it was an—"

"Jesus Christ!" Phillip shouted from the bathroom. "What asshole used all the hot water?" He burst into the kitchen, wrapped in a towel and righteous indignation. His scrapes and bruises were beginning to fade now, but right after the accident he had started taking at least three showers a day to soothe the soreness, and now he was addicted.

"Phillip, you can*not* use language like that in this house." I looked to Berlie for backup.

Phillip marched to the front door and flung it open. "OK, I won't use it in the house." He went outside and boomed across the lawn, "WHAT ASSHOLE USED ALL THE HOT WATER?"

Berlie grabbed him by the scruff of the neck and yanked him back inside. "Go to your room! And don't come back out until you're a civilized human being!"

Patsy passed him as he stomped up the stairs.

" 'Bye, Phil. I guess we'll never see you again."

She dodged her brother's right jab and sashayed into the kitchen. She had on jeans she had outgrown last autumn and a black T-shirt that said "Born to Die."

"What's for dinner?" she demanded.

"Your mother and I are having a discussion." Berlie looked at me.

"Shouldn't you be studying, Patsy? Don't you have a test tomorrow?" I said.

"Aw, Mom, there's only a week of school left. And besides, it's too hot to study."

Berlie went to the thermostat. "I can fix that. It's time we put the air conditioning on anyway."

I sighed. The annual Battle of the Air Conditioner was beginning early. I liked the feel of the warm breeze coming in the window, the sound of the birds; Berlie, on the other hand, would be deliriously happy if the house stayed a steady 63 degrees all year long, like some cave in West Virginia.

"I can't find Barbaloot," Linnea called from the basement. Her teddy bear, already strange-looking when she got him, had been rendered more bizarre by years of being slept on. To save herself embarrassment, Patsy had developed a habit of hiding him before her friends came over.

"Patsy?" I looked at my middle child with suspicion.

"I didn't do anything, Mom. Honest, I—"

A blast of rock music exploded from Phillip's room.

Bamm! Berlie brought his fist down hard on the table.

"Enough!" He looked around the room wildly, as if tigers might leap from the corners. Grabbing me by the arm, he pulled me out to the garage.

It looked so empty there, with the Honda gone to the body shop.

He held open the back door of the Caprice.

"Get in," he ordered, climbing in after me. The back seat smelled of cave mud and brand new sales manuals, annual reports, and something I couldn't quite place. I raised up and peered over the front seat.

"Phil's track shoes?"

"Fran couldn't make it last Friday, so I picked him up."

I settled back onto the seat and looked at Berlie, who looked like smoke might come out of his ears any minute.

"Well?" I said.

"Well." He reached over and touched my shoulder. "I have been listening, Jenny, when you've talked about flying."

I turned slightly, to face him better.

"I think I can understand how you must feel," he said. "Almost. But you've got to understand how worried I am about your—"

"Worried? What about—?"

"Whoa, whoa." He leaned forward and made a placating gesture. "I said I think I understand. Me asking you to give up flying would be like you asking me to never go in a cave again."

Clever bastard, I thought. That's what fifteen years—no, sixteen, by the end of this month—that's what sixteen years of marriage does for you. I wanted to follow through on the caving remark, but I decided to see where he was going. I raised an eyebrow and waited.

"I know how you must have felt when Phil and I didn't get home on time."

I raised the other eyebrow.

"And I know how you felt when you saw him all banged up."

That did it. I opened my mouth to speak.

"I felt the same way," he said.

I closed my mouth.

"But I figure some of the best things in life have risks attached. Even when you take all the precautions you can, sometimes the unexpected happens. But if you don't accept the risk, you can wind up spending your whole life not doing the things you most want to do."

He scratched his head. "I'm not explaining this very well. What I'm trying to say is, I'm not happy about you being up in the air like that, but I know you worry about me being down beneath the ground. So I guess we just have to trust each other to handle the risks the best way we can and go ahead."

I was quiet for a minute. "I don't want Phillip down in your caves."

"I don't want him up in your planes."

We looked at each other.

"We can't protect him forever, Jenny."

I sighed. "No, I don't suppose so."

Berlie opened the car door, got out, and offered me his hand. "Well, no use worrying about him right now. Like Patsy says, at the rate he's going, he'll be thirty before he gets to come out of his room."

It turned out to be a good night for many things.

Later, we went over the plans Bud and I were developing for our company. He was surprised, sure. But he handles surprises a lot better than I do, and it went OK. Berlie's a good guy, really, once you get his attention.

Tuesday, June 16

My three weeks of nondriving ended on the last day of the year—
the last day of the school year, I should say. Tom Black Cloud
had stopped by just as I was getting ready to leave to meet my
friends for lunch.

"Why do you think he did it?" he said as he got out of his car.
I knew who he meant.

"Claiborne? You mean, to sell out like that?"

Cloud nodded.

"I couldn't figure, until Holly said something. She told me Kay
kept saying the same thing over and over—how could he have
done such a thing, and how could she not have known? Holly has
this theory, and she set her straight.

"She told Kay that until lately Frazier was part of her. But not
when he started doing awful things. That's when he became sep-
arate. Kay wasn't part of that—even by association.

"Holly told her—the way she saw it—Frazier had always been
good at everything he'd done. When he was in the Navy, he was
the best sailor they had; and when he went to Applied Science
Associates, he rose right up to the top levels—best submarine-
weapons analyst in the field. Even the little things—like when he
took up squash, hammering away at it 'til he'd taken every trophy
in the Eastern amateur divisions.

"Whatever Frazier set out to do, everyone knew he was going
to be the best at it there was. So if he decided to be a spy, *nothing*
could stop him from being the best spy in the world. And a really
good spy would be the last person to arouse suspicion. That's why
Kay never could have known."

"Until Kay checked out the affair," Tom said.

"If it weren't for the affair, I guess nobody ever would have
known. It's all so crazy."

"I kept thinking it was taking the shop an awful long time to
fix my door." With a plastic spoon I made a swirl in my Frosty.
"The whole time Berlie was just waiting for the next shipment to

come in. He'd already traded my little Honda in on the Incredible Hulk."

We all turned to look out the window into the parking lot. A shiny red Bronco, complete with skid plates, brush guard, and an ugly winch on the front, gleamed in the sunlight.

"Isn't it awful?" A rhetorical question, but I felt good asking it.

"But how could he turn in *your* car?" Sleek, self-confident Elena was very conscious of marital rights. The settlement agreement had been signed: In less than a year, the divorce would be final.

"It was in his name, and his company just came through with a big raise for him. And besides, he said—just listen to this—he said he got it *for me*!" We all sniggered. "It has an automatic transmission, see, and he and the doctor say I shouldn't drive a car with a stick shift."

Jif put everyone's trash on her tray. "That *is* how you hurt your hand, isn't it?"

"Well . . ."

"Well, I say to hell with it, then. Drive an automatic." Jif gestured towards the Bronco. "Drive the Incredible Hulk. Who cares? You're not going to be down here on the ground much longer, anyway."

That was true. By next October, Bud and I would be in business together, and Berlie had agreed to let me borrow against the house for my share of the start-up money.

"I think the setup's going to work out really well," I said. "Bud can't fly the plane because of his eye. But he can sure keep it going, and he's a great navigator. And there'll be times when I'll really need his help when it comes to loading and unloading. And I guess the Hulk"—I gestured towards the monster in the parking lot— "will come in handy doing business.

"Except—guess what Bud wants to call the business?" I waited a beat. " 'Great Escapes Flying Service'! Sounds like an airline for illicit lovers."

"Magic Carpet Travel would book you in a minute." Elena looked perfectly serious.

"No, we're sticking with the medical supplies, thank you. Next he suggested 'Parts R Us,' but that sounded too gruesome. And he didn't like my idea—'Nightingale Transport.' Said people would say we were for the birds."

Fran looked up from a vest she was knitting of grey, mauve, rose, and green mohair. "How about 'Air-Med'?"

"Air-Med." I had to smile. I could see it on the side of the plane, with wisps of clouds scudding past the shiny red and blue lettering.

"I've got the three-forty radial of the Roanoke VOR. What do you think?"

"I see that little lake, and there's the armory. There's the field at two o'clock. Take her on down." Bud puts the chart back in the rack.

"Did I tell you I bought my Honda back from the dealer?" I smile, my eyes still scanning the area beyond the windshield.

"No kidding?" Bud chuckles. "What did Berlie say?"

"What could he say? I told him we'd need a backup when he's off caving. And besides, Phillip will be driving next year. He can help with the carpooling." What a thought.

"We made great time, Bud. We can get back home before school lets out."

"Aw, hell. Let's get a big lunch and catch our breath. You called Yuppies Anonymous, didn't you?"

"That's 'Yupplettes on Wheels.' Yes, they'll pick up the kids, but—oh, Jesus!—what's that noise? Sounds like the cowling's—"

I pulled the Bronco over to the side of the road and looked into the back. A duffel bag had come untied, and twenty or thirty aluminum carabiners—the odd D rings Berlie used on his cave gear—had clattered all over the bare metal floor. I got out and secured them. Climbing back into the cab, I had to smile at the magazine rack Berlie had mounted inside the door. It was stuffed with copies of *Flying*. Not bad for a peace offering.

The visor held the snapshot of Tom Black Cloud's work-in-progress. Next to the picture was the old wooden clothespin clamped down on the day's schedule. There was just one item on it: My first day back behind the wheel, and I only had to get some peanut butter.

Linnea was over at Matty's, helping him make mud pies—who said people don't change? With extra time on my hands, what did I do—I decided to drive around a little and enjoy the countryside. I headed towards Elk Glen.

The field in front of Holly Jensen's was planted with something I didn't recognize: not corn, not soybeans, not hay. But across the road was a familiar sight. The old wooden table had been pulled out in front of the maple, and two bright bouquets of tiger lilies and oxeye daisies glistened in their Mason jars.

When I got to Patsy's school, I pulled in behind the "caravan of gutsy housewives." Within minutes, children exploded from the building, each step taking them closer to two months of exquisite freedom.

"Mom! Mom! Look at my award!" Patsy shoved an official-looking paper in front of my face. Crista Galli and Pontine Kohler hoisted themselves up into the back seat of the Bronco.

"Patsy and Crista and me got citizenship awards for saving the tree." Pontine rolled down the window and waved to a buddy.

" 'Crista and I.' That's great." I smiled at them in the rearview mirror and started down the drive. Being in the truck gave me a different perspective, it was so high up. It would take some getting used to—I couldn't quite tell where the first speed bump was. I hit it at full speed.

"Good takeoff, Jenny. Short runways like that give me the creeps."

"Thanks, Bud. Look over there—the cows are running. I thought they only ran like that in old John Wayne movies."

"Maybe they didn't think you'd make it, either."

Green pastures stretch in odd geometric shapes for as far as I can see. The beginnings of rounded mountains mark the horizon to the west, and beyond that the sky surrounds everything—the mountains, the fields, and the sturdy aircraft—with a solid, everlasting blue.

"Earth to Mom. Earth to Mom," Patsy's NASA-control voice

droned from the back seat. The sound of giggles continued for a moment more. Patsy was pointing to the Flower Lady's bouquets.

"Can we stop and get some? Please? For Linnea?"

I pulled the car over and stopped in Holly's drive. While Patsy scampered across the road, I looked more closely at the Jensen field. Purple loosestrife and sweet everlasting. I had never seen so much of it in one place.

I looked at my giggling daughter, at the flowers she held in her hand as she strained to get back up in Berlie's beloved red truck. Across the field I heard a voice singing a song I had heard somewhere before:

> *I wish I were a tiny sparrow*
> *And I had wings and I could fly*

I smiled to myself and revved the engine.

"Runway Six Zero cleared for takeoff. Proceed when ready."

About the Author

MARY CAHILL lives in Ellicott City, Maryland, with her husband, two children, and a huge, slobbery dog. She was born in 1944 next door to the orange grove that later became Disneyland; this set a surreal tone for most of the years that followed. She is a recipient of a Maryland State Arts Council Fellowship Grant and has been named "Baltimore's Best Humorist." A graduate of Dickinson College and Towson State University, she either has been or still is a teacher, farmer, quilter, weaver, pastry chef, free-lance writer, and carpool driver.